FALL OF THE
BROWN RECLUSE

FALL OF THE BROWN RECLUSE
Copyright © 2019 by Randy McKay

Paperback ISBN: 978-1-948543-74-3
Digital ISBN: 978-1-948543-75-0

FALL OF THE BROWN RECLUSE

RANDY MCKAY

TABLE OF CONTENTS

PROLOGUE

"So I have this client," said Ron Poe.

"You don't represent clients—you represent insurance companies. You occupy the frontline in the fight for corporate greed. You may have a lot of things, but a client is not one of them," said Miki Martin.

Ron started looking around and stared at the base of Miki's barstool. "Where is it?"

"Huh? Where is what?"

"Your soap box. I don't remember you dragging it in," Ron replied.

"Whatever," Miki retorted, "sellout."

"By sellout, do you mean I get what is called a paycheck? You know—one of those things that you get every two weeks or every other week. You use it to buy things like electricity, food...perhaps even a house. How is apartment living treating you, Mik?" Ron asked.

"Ah, kicking a man when he is down, "Miki chuckled. "Impressive."

"Please Miki. It ain't that bad for you."

"Really? Its 3:30 in the afternoon and I am here at a bar for my fourth happy hour of the week, and its only Thursday. And now, you suddenly have clients versus corporate bean counters."

"Listen, if you don't want to talk business, then I understand. Besides, you're just on a bad streak," Ron responded.

"A bad streak is a football team losing three games in a row."

"You are a good lawyer who is going through a rough patch. It happens to all of us."

"An eight-year rough patch? It hasn't happened to anyone else I know," Miki fired back.

"You just need to lay off the booze and the women," Ron observed.

"You asked me to happy hour!" Miki smirked.

"Didn't mean you had to come."

"What else do I have to do?" Miki grumbled. "Why did you pick this place? It's a dump."

"So I don't have to worry about running into any of my 'insurance companies'," Ron said, using air quotes, "catching me slipping out early for a drink."

"Guess you gave up freedom in exchange for the almighty billable hour," Miki replied.

"If your life exemplifies the benefits of freedom, then I will continue to live in the gilded cage built on the billable hour," Ron responded. "But you're right—this place reeks."

The bar smelled like cigarettes and bad grease from fryers that hadn't been changed since a Bush was in office—and there is no telling which Bush. The owner saddled his wife with the floundering enterprise as he served time for manufacturing crystal meth. The bar was more of an alcoholic's row where a messy collection of human misery ravaged by years of drinking converged to begin its daily 10-hour benders.

For Miki, it was refreshing to be around people who made his life resemble some measure of success.

"Well, seeing how I don't have any clients of my own, let me live vicariously through you. Tell me about this client. Is it a human being or an entity that poses as a human through a pitch person on television?"

"She is a person and not a corporation," Ron responded.

"And how did you encounter such a thing?" Miki acted aghast.

"I met her through an employee of one of my larger corporate clients. She is his daughter's best friend," Ron mumbled. "But that's not important."

"So, a big wig insurance adjuster needs a favor," Miki grinned, "and you, of course, obliged. I love it. So, let me hear your facts."

"Ok," Ron said, taking a swig of his beer, "there are two couples—a husband and wife and a girlfriend and boyfriend. The girlfriend works for the wife."

"Is the girlfriend your human client?" Miki asked.

"Yes, Miki, she is the human being I represent. May I continue?"

"But of course." Miki finished his first beer and ordered a second. Ron was barely a third though his first.

"So, the couples go out and have a nice dinner," Poe continued.

"Where did they eat?" Miki interrupted.

"Really?" Ron questioned.

"I need details." Ron was wound tight with a short-fused temper. Miki perfected lighting it since they first met in law school. He continued to derive joy watching his friend lose his cool over the smallest infractions.

"I know what you're doing and it won't work."

"Why are you getting so upset?"

"I'm not," Ron stated.

"It seems like you are," Miki jabbed.

"Well, you're mistaken." Ron took another swig of his beer.

"Then why is your face turning red?"

"It's not."

"Yes, it is. Ma'am, is his face turning red?" Miki asked the bartender.

She glanced at Ron and responded, "Like a beet."

"See, told you." Miki smiled.

"That's it. I am outta here." Ron slammed down his beer and pushed away from the bar.

"C'mon, I'm kidding." Miki grabbed him by the shoulder and gently nudged him back against his stool. "I was just having a little fun. I really want to hear about your case. Look, this is my focused face." Miki squinted and looked at Ron intently.

Ron reluctantly sat back down and continued. "So my 'human client'," Ron threw in another pair of air quotes, "her boyfriend, her boss and the boss's husband all go to dinner. They have a couple of bottles of red and then they hit a bar. They have some shots."

"What kind of shots?" Miki smiled.

"Miki," Ron hissed.

"Last time, I promise." Miki showed his hands as if surrendering. "Okay, they are drunk, I assume. What's next?" Miki asked.

"They come up with the brilliant idea of swapping. It was actually the wife's idea because she had seen my client's boyfriend when he visited the office several times. So, she suggested the swap."

"Gifts?" Miki couldn't help it.

"No asshole...swap partners," Ron snorted.

"Oh, *that* kinda swap."

"But they come up with rules," Ron replied.

"Rules. There are rules to swapping?" Miki asked.

Ron glared at him. "Miki, can I finish?"

"Sorry. I'll behave. Promise." Miki was already half way through his second beer and flagged the bartender for another.

"So the rules are that the couples must be together in the same room at the same time and they cannot leave until everyone is done."

"So no one leaves until everyone is done."

"Correct. My human is with her boss's husband and the boss is with my client's boyfriend. You got it?" Poe asked.

"Following you," Miki replied.

"Well...the boyfriend and my client's boss are the first to finish...a very quick finish."

"And the boss's husband and your client?"

"That horse wasn't as fast." Ron smiled. "It takes him a while. A long while."

Miki scratched his face. "And his wife...your client's boss...was in the room?"

"Yes sir." Poe smirked and thought, "Now the smart ass is listening."

"Am I to assume that his performance was different from when he was with his wife?"

"That is correct, counselor. And here is the complicating issue."

"Wait a second, you mean the other stuff was not complicated. Now, you have my full attention."

"I am so excited about that development." Ron's tone was dripping in sarcasm. "The husband and wife have been married for a while. Their kids are grown. She hit menopause a few years ago."

"Okay," Miki said.

"So he kinda lost his bearings and finished as he normally does."

"Finished?"

"You know, completed the task."

"I am not following," Miki said with a look of confusion.

"Shocking," Ron replied. "He finished sex as he normally would with his wife. Inside. He had unprotected sex with my client, the employee of his wife, in his wife's presence. And now that poor girl is pregnant."

Ron took a final swig of his first beer and smiled in satisfaction at Miki's obvious bewilderment over the scenario.

Miki paused and reloaded with his third beer. "Is she going to keep the child?"

"She didn't find out until she was too far into her first trimester. She doesn't want a surgical abortion. So, yes," Ron replied.

"So who hired you to do what?" Miki asked.

"Well, the girlfriend got fired and she retained me to sue someone...anyone. But who? It's a right to hire and fire state. The wife could fire her for bad breath."

"No federal laws?" Miki asked.

"Wife owns small, high-end clothing boutique downtown, so no federal guidelines as to firing because of pregnancy. She doesn't have any insurance or real assets." Ron paused and ordered a second beer. "I can get child support from the husband but in this state, that is nothing."

"What does the husband do, or rather the baby's daddy?"

"Oh, he's a retired doctor but all the assets are in his name. He's loaded."

"And your client's boyfriend? What's that status?"

"They were engaged, set to be married next month. That of course is off." Ron shook his head. "And here's the real kicker."

"There is more?" Miki asked with a raised eyebrow.

"Yep. My client's boyfriend is loaded. Family money. He was an only child. She said their wedding gift would have been a beach house on Sullivan's Island near Charleston."

"Oh, I know all about Sullivan's Island," Miki drifted to thoughts of his past.

Ron grimaced. "Sorry about that, of course you do," Ron said as he patted Miki's shoulder. He was embarrassed over mentioning the location.

"All good. Can't change the past, right?" Miki took a hard gulp of his third beer. Shots would be next. "So what about this house?"

"Well, it's paid in full. A joint gift to both of them until now."

"It was a marital gift to both of them which means she would have received one-half regardless of who gave it to them?" Miki asked.

"Yes," Ron said.

Miki ran his hands through his thick head of brown hair as he contemplated the situation. Ron stared with jealously. He hadn't seen a full head of hair since college. Ron relented five years ago and went for the Lex Luther look—Miki called him Mr. Clean without the physique.

"And the doctor, the employer's husband, is rich?" Miki asked.

"Oh yeah...he retired a few years ago when he sold his orthopedic practice," Ron replied. "So, Mr. Champion of the Downtrodden, how can you help my human client out?"

After another gulp of beer and a few seconds of thinking, Miki replied. "Well, this may be a little creative and aggressive."

"That is what a good lawyer does."

"A proposal to marriage is like a contract. You follow?" Miki continued.

"Okay."

"Do you agree with that concept?"

"Sure, there was a contract to marry between my client and her boyfriend...well, fiancé," Ron replied.

"And if the contract was fulfilled and they married then she would have received one half of what...a three-million-dollar house. It's a house on the beach. God's not making any more beaches."

"Right," Ron said. "Where are you headed with all this?"

"And except for our doctor's decision not to pull out so to speak..."

"Don't forget my client had a hand in this. She went along with it," Ron interrupted.

"At the bequest of her employer," Miki replied, "and except for this request, your client would have completed the marital contract. And in return, she would have received at least one-half of the home. Correct?"

"Yeah, I guess so," Poe answered.

"So he interfered with her contractual relationship with her fiancé, which equates to tortious interference..."

Ron interrupted. "With contractual relations. Someone interferes with your contractual relationship then you can sue that person for the damage relating to the breach." Ron nodded in approval. "But who is to say that they would have actually married. People get cold feet all the time."

"And the law also allows for tortious interference with prospective contractual relationships. Which means that…"

"If there was a potential for contract, a potential for marriage, and the doctor interferes, then he has to pay for damages." Ron smiled. "Mick, this is good. I think this will fly."

"Sure it will. You just need to get to a jury. They'll pay."

"I want to associate you in this case. I have it on a 40 percent contingency. What do you say?" Ron asked.

"Well, that would make my third case this year. Yay me!!" Miki pumped his fists in the air. "Perhaps my rough patch is over?" Miki then shook his head and ordered from the bartender. "Let me get a shot of Patron, chilled, no training wheels."

Ron knew Miki was a shell of the person that he used to be. And while he jabbed at his friend, men typically use humor to diffuse a serious situation. Ron knew this was not the time for more humor. His friend needed help even if he would not ask. "Mick, you know I can get you onboard my firm. It's not great pay but you could at least get a fresh start."

"I do appreciate that, but I am not in a spiritual place for a professional intervention. So let me get about 10 more shots and stumble my way home."

"Okay." Ron paused. "And sorry about bringing up Sullivan's Island. Big old brain fart," Ron said with an empathetic tone.

"Like I said, you can't change the past. You just learn to live with its consequences."

CHAPTER ONE:
GRAFTON HOOD

For most of his life, he was known as Grafton Hood. At six feet tall, Grafton's looks alone made him a formidable political opponent. He had caramel-colored skin, a square jaw and cunning brown eyes. Grafton bragged that his silky low voice put people at ease, but his adversaries claimed it was more akin to luring his prey. Grafton's political success was an amazing feat. But it wasn't a rags-to-riches story—no, Grafton came from money.

His grandparents owned and operated a bed and breakfast in Ocho Rios, Jamaica. It was a ten-bedroom white Victorian with a breath taking view of the Atlantic. They had one child, Grafton's mother. When she was 23, his grandparents died in an airline crash while vacationing in Europe. The crash resulted in a large settlement for Grafton's mother. After their death, she tried to run the B&B alone but it proved too much. Then she met Grafton's father, a guest. Their summer romance blossomed into an engagement. He abandoned his life in the United States to be with her. Their plan was to run the B&B and raise a family. That changed when they received a ridiculously obscene offer for the B&B from a corporation developing an all-inclusive resort in Ocho Rios.

Grafton's parents relocated to his father's hometown of Atlanta. He was their only child. Raised in the Buckhead area, Grafton attended West Paces Ferry Academy. His childhood friends' parents included members of President Carter's administration, professional sports stars, and top executives of major corporations headquartered in the city.

As far as the racial composition of his school, he was a black dot in a sea of white. But he did not experience sheer racism. His family was one of the richest amongst his friends. And Grafton knew his wealth was a powerful weapon against racism. He also knew there were certain lines he could not cross. He could not date a white girl, which made it difficult to find a girl that met his parents' approval. They simply did not exist in his social circle. Thus, Grafton did not have the sexual experiences of most high school males. He had to listen to the amateur sexual conquests of his friends and play along as if he had shared the same experiences. It led to a sexual frustration that would plague him into adulthood.

He was immensely popular in school. In his junior year, he was elected student body vice president followed by student body president in his senior year. He was accepted by the most popular athlete (who owned the world in high school) but could connect with the nerd who was simply trying to endure the high school experience—that same nerd would later in life employ the athlete.

But as Grafton glad-handed his way through the school hallways, his sexual frustration was replaced by an inner rage as he watched acts of public affection between girlfriends and boyfriends. While they were on dates, he was home masturbating. But he learned to hide his rage. In his world, perception was reality and the perception was that he had the world by the tail.

And that perception caused him to catch the attention of his peers' parents. They were Atlanta's elite and they were concerned about the growth of minorities in their city. Money allowed them a world where they did not have to adjust their personal beliefs about racial segregation. However, they feared losing their utopia. They were convinced that their city would become a target for all up-and-coming black politicians. The city's elite needed politicians that could court the minority vote but still maintain the status quo once in office. It needed puppets. Grafton was the perfect choice.

Grafton was courted. At first, he was invited to play golf every week with men whose wealth rivaled his parents. Each round ended with another round or two of high-end Scotch. They practically owned the club so no one raised an eye as 17-year-old Grafton drank a glass of Macallan 12. Then the regular meetings took place. There were conversations about his future in politics. The teenager's head was filled with thoughts of being mayor and perhaps even governor. His rage was quelled with the excitement of his future as predicted by men nearly four times his age. The men even influenced the school to ensure that Grafton graduated with honors.

It was all going to plan. Grafton graduated *cum laude* and gave the commencement speech at graduation. He would attend the University of Georgia in the fall after working as a page in the U.S. Senate, courtesy of a West Paces Ferry alum. But then life happened.

Grafton's father operated a non-profit organization called Stay on Track (SOT) designed to help homeless teens. It was a 10,000-square-foot home housing as many as 25 kids. But Grafton's father made sure that it flew under the radar. SOT did not accept donations or applications of potentially eligible teens. SOT sought teens for the home.

A week after telling his fellow classmates not to allow their quest for success drown their moral soul, SOT was in the headlines. It was being investigated on charges that Grafton's father used it as a front for a teenage brothel. The headlines read, "STD not SOT. Homeless Teens Were Sex Slaves!" The clientele were mainly wealthy Asians. While everyone questioned his father's motive to concoct this operation, Grafton later learned that his mother maintained control over all of the money. She received it before marrying his father and wanted to ensure that it remained non-marital. This enraged his father. He was a proud man who grew up in an era when the husband made the money and the wife stayed home. He was emasculated by his wife's control over the finances so he resorted to the oldest profession.

Grafton's mother never got a chance to read the article. As soon as his father saw the headlines, he calmly went in his bedroom, retrieved the nine-millimeter Berretta from the nightstand drawer, and put a bullet in her head just before turning the gun on himself. Grafton surmised that he blamed her for all of it.

The very same men that predicted such a bright future for Grafton now scurried from him like rats on a sinking ship. He was alone and the avalanche of litigation against his family was beginning to roll. He knew he was finished in Atlanta, branded with SOT across his forehead. He also knew that if he attempted to raid his family's fortune the lawyers would track him down. He simply needed to escape.

He took a modest sum from his parent's estate and in the dark of night, left his life of privilege. He relocated to Charleston and began life anew as Grafton Hood. He attended technical college for the first two years and then transferred to the College of Charleston, where he graduated with honors. Grafton existed on a steady diet of Raman noodles, student loans, and tip money from various jobs as a waiter. But between school and work, Grafton had no time for a social life and his inner rage from high school reemerged and began to grow into a quick temper. It was a demon that he struggled to control.

It was during this time that Grafton met the single most important influence of his life—Allen Pontet.

Allen Pontet was a tall, thin product of the late 60s, hitting high school just after Nixon was impeached. His proclivity for long hair and an unshaven look gained him the nickname Shaggy from Scooby Doo. This made it difficult to enjoy the high school experience while being compared to a character that played second fiddle to a talking dog. He wasn't particularly athletic unless smoking pot is recognized as a sport. And when it came to grades, his motto was do as little possible to achieve the bare-minimum of what was required. He took full advantage of 60 being considered a passing grade.

Pontet was a Charleston native, but far from blue blood. His ancestors were more likely to have drowned in the bowels of Provost Dungeon than to have signed the Declaration of Independence. His father worked on a shrimp boat (but never owned it) and his mother was the butcher's assistant at a local grocery store.

Between them, Pontet's home smelled of a unique mixture of raw meat and dead shrimp. He didn't have many "spend the night" parties as a kid, and when caught with pot in his room, he would blame his parents. He claimed he was trying to mask the rancid smell of the house. His parents chuckled at the excuse and ignored his drug use. They simply didn't care—they had been beaten into submission by life.

As he grew older, Pontet replaced his use of marijuana with alcohol. His long blonde locks turned grey. His unshaven look transformed into a goatee. He believed the facial hair coupled with his tortoise-shelled glasses made him look more intelligent—truth be known, he had 20-20 vision. His morning scent was a mixture of Ralph Lauren and last night's alcohol seeping through his pores.

Pontet subsided on the occasional real estate deal or "multi-level" marketing scheme. He spent the majority of his free time (which was most of his time) frequenting local bars from the barrier islands to North Charleston. His array of friends spanned the social gamut. On any given weekend, he could spend a Friday night at a bachelor party of a mid-shipman stationed at the Charleston Naval Base. On Saturday, he was a guest at a wedding of family that inhabited the Holy city since the Revolution. He used Sunday to relax at the beach home of one of Charleston's new rich.

It was through his countless hours at the bar that Pontet was able to learn every piece of seedy gossip that existed in Charleston. He could outdrink anyone and learned that people would reveal the most amazing things given the right amount of alcohol. He parlayed that endless source of knowledge into his latest revenue venture— political consultant.

The two met while Grafton was volunteering for a county council campaign. Pontet's job on the campaign was to disseminate the vile unfounded gossip about the opposition. Grafton was the only volunteer who was neither a relative of the candidate nor a rising high school senior.

Grafton was the unofficial campaign manager, which he relished. He scouted events of more prominent officials. He sent his candidate to events for a perfect photo bomb opportunity. He cropped those photos on signs to create the illusion that the candidacy received endorsements from the mayor, local statehouse representative, and even the district's congressional representative.

Grafton took it one step further. Since many of his volunteers were using the experience as part of their social studies class, Grafton convinced the school to allow extra credit based on outstanding service as a volunteer. He created an unofficial policy that gave extra school credit based on the number of opposition campaign signs that were stolen.

Pontet studied Grafton for a month before asking him to lunch. Grafton was reluctant. He knew of Pontet and considered him nothing more than a gossip-happy drunk, which was actually fairly accurate. But he had not eaten a real meal in months and decided to accept the invitation. While it was lunch for Grafton, it was noon-time happy hour for Pontet. He desperately needed a hair of the dog that bit him last night.

Grafton soaked in the sights and sounds of the upper class dining in the linen tablecloth restaurant located off East Bay. He hadn't been this close to real wealth since leaving Atlanta. Normally, he would have relished the lunch and allowed himself to pretend that he was part of the rich once again. But the stale stench of booze dripping from Pontet's pores reminded him that this was more about getting fed than indulging in fantasy.

He ordered as soon as the waiter greeted him. Pontet's lunch would be poured. Grafton slammed down his meal while Pontet slammed down his first Gin and Tonic.

"I have never seen anyone devour an oyster Po Boy and fries so quickly," Pontet smiled. "Either you don't eat much or you eat so much that you really don't care about the taste, just the consumption. Based on your body type, I am guessing the former."

"I budget $200 per month for food so that fried oyster sandwich represents a high end meal for me," Grafton replied.

"Spoken like someone who has enjoyed a fine meal before," Pontet said.

"Perhaps," Grafton drank his sweet tea and wiped the remnants of his sandwich from his mouth.

"Would you like another? I have a hard and fast rule that I don't leave lunch until I have had at least three drinks. That was my first."

"No. No, I am good." Grafton gave a polite smile. He attempted to make small talk, hoping to bore his lunch date into leaving early. "How do you think the campaign is going?"

"It's in the bag," Pontet said.

"How so? From what I hear it is fairly close."

"Not for long, not when they find out about the mother-in-law of our opponent."

"What about her?" Grafton asked with a raised eyebrow and curious smile.

"She was a den mother for some Girl Scouts and used money from the cookie sale to fund her coke addiction. Folks don't like that kinda stuff."

"Is that true?" Grafton asked.

"I really don't think so. He's never been married." Pontet motioned to the waiter for another drink.

"That seems very underhanded," Grafton replied.

"So is your photo bombing trick or campaign signs for school credit. It's the same thing, just differing degrees of effectiveness."

"You're talking about permanently damaging a man's reputation. I am simply cropping some photos and stealing a few signs."

"Well, why are you doing that?" Pontet asked.

"To win the campaign," Grafton answered.

"Me, too. The only difference is that my tactics are far more effective than your sophomoric antics."

"No, the difference is that your methods destroy the opposition rather than run a successful campaign. It is more of a win-at-all costs attitude."

"How do you think these things are won?"

"There have to be some boundaries," Grafton stated.

"I am sure there are and I am sure that the losers can tell you the exact limits of those boundaries." Pontet chuckled. "Winners don't know those boundaries; they only know victory."

Grafton dismissed Pontet's statements as the mutterings of a drunk. "This is my first campaign. I guess I didn't think that kind of stuff went on at a local level. Maybe I am just a little naïve."

"Mr. Hood, the last thing you are is naïve."

The remark and use of his last name caught Grafton off guard. "What the hell does that mean?"

"Nothing. Forget I said it." Pontet grabbed his second drink from the waiter before it could hit the table. There was a painfully uncomfortable silence, painful in the sense of passing a kidney stone the size of a marble. It was now official. Grafton was ready to leave.

Pontet broke the silence. "Why are you part of this campaign?"

"Because I believe in your—rather, *our*—candidate and think he has a real potential to..."

"To what?" Potent interrupted. "Rename a little league baseball field, dedicate an overpass to a deceased town clerk. That's about all they fucking do." He paused and started into his second drink. "Why are you here? Really?"

Grafton began to feel uneasy as if he was being interrogated. He was also still trying to digest the naïve comment. "Does it matter if I am helping? Do you normally question a volunteer?"

"I mean, I guess not, but you just don't seem to fit. Kinda outta place," Pontet replied.

"I don't know how to take that."

"Oh, it's a compliment. You just don't carry yourself as someone befitting a county race. You seem more, um, what's the word...polished."

"Well, I appreciate that. It may not be glamorous so to speak, but at least I am doing more than digging holes for campaign signs."

"So", Pontet paused. "Is that to say that you considered other campaigns but opted out of those in favor of being a bigger fish in a small pond?"

"I guess so. Post-hole digging for a national campaign never really appealed to me." Grafton smiled.

"Nice pearly whites, Mr. Hood." Pontet smiled back. "Still, you act almost like you've done this before—not your first rodeo. What did you say you did before coming to our fair city?"

"I didn't," Grafton thought to himself. "Who is this guy and why the hell has he invited me to lunch?" And then he regurgitated his same story to cover his real background.

"I grew up in Portland, Oregon." It was far enough away that Grafton thought no one would or could check. "Parents died and I wanted to get a fresh start. I wanted something on the east coast, but not a big city. I also don't like cold weather. So, I found Charleston and she fit the bill."

"How did they die?" Pontet asked the obvious inappropriate question but he knew the answer.

Grafton was taken aback. Most people heard "parents died" and felt uncomfortable to the point that they didn't ask him anymore. Grafton knew this wasn't a social blunder. He was definitely being interrogated. "I really don't like to talk about that."

"I am sorry. That was rude." Pontet didn't even attempt to pretend that the apology was real. "I don't enjoy much of a relationship with my parents. I guess I have an overdeveloped degree of insensitivity for folks who are lucky enough to be without their parents," Pontet replied.

"Lucky enough?" Grafton replied in disbelief over the statement.

"I know. That is a horrible thing to say. I would blame the booze but I am not even buzzed yet." Pontet laughed.

"I am going to have to take your word for that." Grafton pointed to the drink.

Pontet stayed on topic. "I mean, when your parents bring you into this world and do nothing to help you conquer the hurdles of life, you kinda have a jaded view of them. Right?"

Grafton was uneasy. He always was when discussing his parents. "I guess."

"I mean it's tough when your parents join the parade of hard knocks that march over you."

Grafton just nodded as Pontet continued.

"I mean it really takes a toll on you. You know what I mean?"

Grafton wasn't touching that comment. The conversation was hitting too close to home. Grafton would have raced from the table but was concerned that would raise suspicions.

"I don't mean to be rude, but I really need to get back to the…" Grafton tried to get up.

"I got one more drink, remember?" Pontet interrupted. "So, Grafton? Family name?"

"Um…yes." Grafton nervously straightened his dirty plate and arranged his used silverware. His name was the least of his lies.

"You know they have busboys for that," Pontet said. He used his eyes to point to Grafton's hands mindlessly cleaning the table.

"Yeah, right." Grafton let out a nervous laugh. "Old habits die hard. Put myself through college waiting tables."

"Right." Pontet smiled. "So, father's side or mother's side? Grafton?"

"Huh?" And Pontet was back to Grafton's least favorite subject in this world. "Um, my mother's side." Grafton nervously scratched the back of his neck.

Pontet had grown tired of toying with this ball of string. He decided to test Grafton. He wanted to see if what they had told him was really true. "Mother's side, you say?"

"Yeah. Yeah, that's right."

"Her name was Celion Brown? Right?"

The only thing that kept Grafton from hitting the floor was the chair he was seated in. That was indeed her name. He hadn't spoken it aloud in years, and to hear it come from the gin-soaked breath of Pontet was proof positive that you really have no control in predicting life.

Grafton's temper started to overtake him like a cancer. If unchecked, he would explode on Pontet in a physical fit of rage that would reduce Pontet's face to a tenderized slab of meat. Grafton visualized his first, second, and third punch. He could feel Pontet's cheekbones cracking against his knuckles. He felt the warmth of Pontet's blood from a broken nose splattering across his hands. He had to remain calm.

"Grafton, you there?" Pontet dug in. He wasn't impressed. One name and he drew in like a turtle.

Grafton again thought about darting out of the restaurant but decided against it. He wanted to learn the proverbial who, what, and how as to Pontet's knowledge. But his mind was in a battle—his desire to obtain an orgasmic release of physical violence versus the rational side to maintain the calm necessary to learn what Pontet knew.

The best he could muster was a gruff, "What do you want?"

"Excuse me." Pontet finished his second drink. "I just asked a simple ques…"

Grafton's temper interrupted. "Why the fuck would you mention her name?" Grafton hissed.

Pontet just stared at his lunch partner. He was enjoying the show at first but was now getting nervous. "Will this guy really hit me? The cats in Atlanta got this guy wrong," he thought to himself. There not even an attempt to playfully dismiss the name. He had expected Grafton to quip, "I don't know who you're talking about." Pontet was confused…this was their handpicked politico?

"You must want something." Grafton held out his right hand and extended his index finger. "Either, I leave town." Next, his middle finger was raised. "Or two, I pay you to shut up."

Pontet shifted back in his chair.

"We both know I don't have any money so why do you want me to leave town?" Grafton pressed.

Pontet didn't want to waste any more time until he talked with someone from Atlanta. "You know, never mind. Just forget it. Let's get this bill and go."

"But your third drink." Grafton grabbed Pontet's hand and slammed it to the table. The other patrons noticed. A waiter approached the table to render some assistance. Pontet shook his head to waive him off.

Grafton was oblivious to the scene he created. He did not loosen his grip. "Listen, you don't just mention that name and then decide to drop it."

"Okay," Pontet mumbled.

"If you know that name, then you know of me and my past. Correct?" Grafton pressed.

Pontet just nodded as he divided his glances between Grafton and the firm grip on his hand.

"And for some reason you asked questions just to watch me lie. Why would you do that?" Grafton started to cool down. The overboiling pot was off the stove and his political acuity was running the kitchen.

"Why don't you ask yourself that? How did I come by that information and why would I want to see your reaction?"

Pontet looked at Grafton's hand and then around the restaurant. "As much apathy as I harbor for others' opinion of me, I really don't want all these folks thinking that I am in a lover's quarrel. Can you let go?"

Grafton released his grip.

"Thank you. Last thing I need is some of Charleston's proper thinking I am the bitch in this relationship."

Grafton smirked. "Sorry." His temper now contained, Grafton remembered why he remained at the table. He need answers. "Okay, so how do you know about me? And why confront me with it?"

"To gauge your reaction, which left much to be desired and," Pontet paused, "to let you know that folks in Atlanta still want to help you."

"Atlanta?" Grafton was shocked to have learned the source. "Why would those folks profess any knowledge or connection with me?" Grafton thought to himself.

"Yes. And your former backers have become more organized since you left. They have even started a corporation known as Practical Solutions."

"Practical Solutions?"

"Yep. And the first order of business is getting you back on track. Making you a candidate rather than a posthole digger."

"Who exactly is part of all this? I had quite a few folks in my camp."

"That isn't important; those sources may or may not be revealed in time."

"Okay." Grafton was intrigued. He never thought the folks from Atlanta would help in his planned resurrection.

"What is of paramount concern is your temper... rather... rage."

"Yes, I know. It is my Achilles's heel."

"I wouldn't be that diplomatic. Having a weakness is one thing; a demon is another. The former will hurt you," Pontet said.

"And the latter?"

"Will actively destroy you," Pontet said as he waved down the waiter. He ordered one more drink.

"So where do we begin?" Grafton asked.

"Yes," Pontet replied.

"Huh?" Grafton asked.

"We begin at the beginning. Need to start you as a newbie. Someone without money or real backing."

"Make me earn my stripes, so to speak," Grafton replied.

"No. It's not that simple. We need more time to pass and let your history continue to be just that," Pontet paused and sipped his third drink, "history."

"Right." Grafton nodded.

"Not many good demographics for sons of teenage pimps," Pontet said.

CHAPTER TWO:
MIKI MARTIN

At 6'2, Justin "Miki" Martin was an athletic-looking 39-year-old. With his thick dark hair and olive skin, he never had a problem attracting glances from the opposite sex and sometimes the same sex.

He was born in Hendersonville, North Carolina. Like Grafton, he was an only and somewhat lonely child. His father was the manager of an IHOP and his mother was a tour guide at Biltmore Estates. Miki did not have a good childhood. His parents never married and neither relished their roles as parents. His father chose to spend spare time hunting and drinking with his childhood friends. He never thought to bring his son along. His father still didn't want Miki's existence to interfere with his simple life of beer, guns and dead animals.

Miki's mother was a woman trapped in the 1960s. She was too busy with self-discovery than to be bothered with a child. "How can I be a good mother to you until I learn who I am?" she would often say to him. She was on a constant journey to "discover" herself. She became Catholic and then converted to Judaism. Last Miki heard, she was a Buddhist. And through all of this self-discovery, it never dawned on her that she could learn about herself through raising a child.

Until 9th grade, Miki's life was the definition of loneliness. There were no friends nor sleepovers. His meals were eaten alone. And there were a few missed birthdays. He was the kid in class that everyone considered weird but without a discernable reason as to why. His entire 5th grade class proclaimed that no one should have any contact with Miki for an entire school year. And they followed through on the edict.

In his alone time, Miki found companionship among books and movies. He was a regular at the local library and video rental store. Both fed his insatiable intellect. Miki never had a problem with grades. He also learned that movies and books are not as complicated as relationships with people.

He was accustomed to having a dialogue with himself. Every day was like a play he wrote in his head. He wasn't crazy—he simply learned to overcome his loneliness. Miki was good at adapting, a skill that would ensure his survival.

Then one summer, Miki sprouted. He grew five inches and his pale, acne-covered skin was replaced with a beautiful olive coating. Miki discovered that he was a naturally athletic person, especially with football. He made varsity as a high school freshman. He was the star wide receiver. He routinely beat the junior and senior defensive backs in practice. And when he caught the game-winning touchdown in the opening game, the entire 9th grade class proclaimed that everyone would have contact with Miki.

Miki attended all four proms. He was dating juniors and seniors as a freshman. He was proud of the fact that his dates had to drive him around. There were the occasional verbal and physical assaults by others jealous of his recently found success. Some still saw him as the main suspect of the fictitious question "Who bombed the school?"

When he was verbally challenged, Miki replied with a barrage of one-liners and wit garnered from years of reading and watching movies. When challenged physically, Miki beat his opponent by a brute force borne from years of frustrated isolation.

Instant popularity can either be worn like a hand-tailored suit or like an undersized pair of jeans—they don't fit right, everyone can tell, and no one wants to see you in them. For Miki, he wore it like a suit. He enjoyed his new life but wasn't afraid to go back to being alone. He wasn't afraid to be himself. That gave him an unwavering confidence that attracted everyone to him.

Miki was offered a full ride to play football at Vanderbilt University. He spurned offers at bigger schools because he knew he would never play at the next level. He needed a great education.

Miki started all four years at Vanderbilt. He was named to the third team All-SEC in his senior year. He had almost 900 hundred yards receiving that year and caught the game-winning touchdown against instate rival Tennessee. He was a minor celebrity and, more importantly, he caught the attention of a fellow alumnus, who was a partner in a prominent plaintiff's law firm in Charleston. It was a combination of coaxing and drunken promises of long-term employment that lured Miki to attend law school in South Carolina.

Miki's law school experience was like his high school and college years. It was a joy to wake up every morning. Grades and girls were his primary goals and not necessarily in that order. As promised, he landed a job as an associate in a Charleston law firm after graduation. As an associate, he garnered a reputation for being smart, aggressive, and tenacious. He was confident in his abilities. He didn't need to bully witnesses or opposing parties. He oozed Southern charm as he fired questions and executed tactics that brought opposing attorneys to their knees. And then came the Liberty Trucking case. People hate to use clichés but sometimes they just say it best. Liberty was the case that put Miki on the map.

Liberty Trucking was a regional trucking company servicing states across the Southeast. For the owner, business was war and he was absolutely ruthless.

One afternoon, a Liberty truck driver was making a delivery to a local supermarket when he veered from the road, jumped over the curb, and crushed a nine-year-old girl riding her bike on the sidewalk. Her parents witnessed the entire event. It was her first ride without training wheels. And thanks to Liberty, it was a closed casket funeral.

Miki was assigned the case. While he was second chair in the case, the first chair lawyer was preoccupied with his 19-year-old son's heroin addiction. Mike was in charge.

From the outset, the case had issues. There were several eyewitnesses that stated the Liberty driver was drunk—they said he was swerving. The parents of course could not recall anything except the sight of their firstborn child being grinded under the front wheel of a Liberty 18-wheeler.

The investigating highway patrol officer literally whisked the driver from the scene before other law enforcement agencies could arrive. When they showed up, the officer had the driver in the back seat of the squad car claiming that he was driving with a suspended license. The driver was quietly booked and released. A blood-alcohol test was not given.

The criminal charges of vehicular manslaughter were dropped when the Liberty driver claimed that another car cut him off and the accident was caused by his overcorrection to avoid the car. All of the witnesses admitted to seeing another car, but no one could definitively say whether the car interfered with the truck. It was enough reasonable doubt to cause the district attorney to drop the case.

Miki did some digging. While the driver was charged with Driving Under Suspension, his actual driver's record reflected that his license was active. With a simple judgment search, Miki learned that the highway patrol officer was recently divorced. Miki knew that if he wanted to learn about the skeletons in the officer's closet, then he needed to talk to his ex-wife.

The ex felt that she had been screwed in the divorce. She couldn't afford a lawyer but somehow her ex-husband (the highway patrol officer) had a $500-an-hour lawyer. She was living off reduced child support for three kids and an hourly wage from Target.

Her impoverished state fueled her diligence to prove that her husband had extra income. She had bank statements for the entire ten-year marriage showing regular deposits on a monthly basis for $1250. And while most of the deposits were in cash, Miki found a check deposited in his account—the remitter was Liberty Trucking.

Miki sent a notice of deposition to the author of the Liberty check, but he no longer worked for the company, supposedly due to corporate downsizing. In reality, his wife's Type II Diabetes diagnosis made insurance premiums too expensive for Liberty.

The ex-employee was happy to talk. He had supporting documents for his sworn testimony that hundreds of trucking wrecks were investigated by officers paid by Liberty to ignore obvious traffic infractions. The case settled soon after that deposition for over eight figures. The law firm also contacted the families of other accident victims caused by Liberty drivers (which were covered up) and each of those cases settled in the seven-to- eight figure range. Miki wasn't a partner, so he didn't receive a direct cut from those settlements. But he received a healthy bonus from each settlement. Liberty had indeed set him free.

Miki bought a 6,000 square foot, waterfront house on Sullivan's Island with a three-car garage—one for each of his BMWs. He had a $120,000 26-foot Regulator housed on his dock. He had a different girl for each day of the week (including Sundays) and was able to cherry pick only the best cases in the office.

And then, eight years ago on Sullivan's Island, life happened to Miki and his world crumbled.

Miki was now far removed from a world where he only knew success and the pleasure of its rewards. He was no longer leading the wave of the next generation of high-powered plaintiff's lawyers. He was squirreled away in a drab one-bedroom apartment in the state's capital.

He was a solo practitioner with an office in a building shared by a palm reader and global marketing opportunity company (i.e., a pyramid scheme for selling weight loss shakes). He survived off the interest from the modest residual bonus money left in his account and whatever came in the door. His cases were either DUIs or the typical soft tissue injury wrecks. There was nothing complicated. His emotional fortitude couldn't handle anything more. Sullivan's Island wiped him clean. But he still had his intellect and ability to survive, given enough alcohol. While most people would have quit drinking after the incident,

Miki reluctantly discovered that his only measure of peace was through a good buzz.

It was during a courtroom battle that Miki would discover the most important person to enter his life. Miki was cross-examining while battling a nasty red wine hangover. He spent 15 minutes in the bathroom trying to brush the crimson red from his tongue. A cheap California Pinot Noir turned his head to lead and dehydrated every cell in his body. He guzzled three bottles of water and two cups of coffee but still could not piss an ounce. Unfortunately, his current pursuit of "justice" did little to invigorate him through the hangover.

He represented a client claiming personal injury due to an assault by a stripper at a local gentlemen's club. Gentlemen's club is an interesting term because there are no gentlemen and there is no club unless you consider a $5 cover as membership dues.

Miki's client brought a nine-inch purple dildo into the club and tried to insert it into the rectum of one of the club's employees. She grabbed it and hit his client, breaking his nose. Miki sued and the insurance company would not offer a dime.

The lawyer on the other side was an overprivileged kid who grew up on Hilton Head Island. He was greener than a Palmetto frond. He just graduated law school with a ridiculously high GPA and worked at the city's largest law firm that was built on insurance companies and the all mighty billable hour. This was his first trial and he showed up in the $2,500 Armani suit bought by his parents as a graduation gift.

Miki was beginning his scintillating cross-examination of the stripper. It was not exactly a hallmark moment of jurisprudence history.

Her name was Gabbie Street. She was a beautiful woman in her mid-20s. She was an unusual ethnicity— Black/Korean. She was 5'4 and weighed 110 pounds. She wore a knee-length black dress with long sleeves to cover tattoos on her arms and thighs. The club's lawyer—rather the insurance company's lawyer—directed her wardrobe for the day. Her hair was pulled into a bun and she removed the earrings from the corner of her nose and tongue.

With her high cheekbones and hypnotic brown eyes, Miki had a hard time focusing on the task at hand. Of course, the three bottles of red wine trying to escape his system didn't help either.

"Now, you're name is Gabbie." Miki began.

"Yes."

"Now is that a stage name or your real name?"

"I don't know what you mean by stage name."

"You know, a fake name. A name you use at the club so your 'client's' don't know who you really are." Miki used air quotes for clients.

"Why are you using air quotes on clients?" Gabbie responded as she mocked Miki's use of the air quotes. "I ain't no lawyer. I don't have clients. I have customers."

"Well, I know you're no lawyer."

"Yeah, are you? Representing that piece of shit," Gabbie said pointing to Miki's client. The jury laughed.

The judge interjected, "Now listen, ma'am. You will answer his questions without commentary and without profanity. If you don't, then I will lock you up for contempt of court."

"And then who knows how many customers will be disappointed?" Miki chimed eliciting a chuckle from the jury. He smiled at them as he delivered the line.

"Mr. Martin, I will do the same for you. Now get on with this exercise." It was Friday and the judge had plans. He had forgotten his last two wedding anniversaries and had plans for his wife for the weekend. They had dinner reservations in Asheville at 7 p.m. He needed to leave in two hours and didn't want this case to disrupt that. He was pissed at everyone involved that this shitty case had not settled.

Miki's third cup of coffee finally kicked in. He was getting a rare moment of sobriety. It was his first in three days. "Let me ask you this," he paused, "Miss. Gabbie." He used air quotes for her name.

"Sure, Mr. Martin." She returned the air quotes using only her middle fingers.

"These customers—they pay you for what?"

"Entertainment."

"What kind of entertainment? Balloon animals? Perhaps, juggling? What do you do? Be precise."

Gabbie coiled like a snake. She glared at him with her

arms crossed. She did not want to respond. Gabbie hated her profession and didn't want to disclose it to a courtroom of strangers. Gabbie's co-workers were there because poor choices forced them into the profession. For Gabbie, she had no choice. Life dictated this path without any input from her.

"Answer the question please," the judge instructed.

"I dance," she growled.

"Really!" Miki exclaimed. "Is it a river dance? Are you doing a disco? What kind of dancing are we talking about?" Miki paused. "Moonwalk involved?"

Her lips tightened. Her profession was a gaping wound on her soul and Miki was pouring a mixture of salt and lemon juice on it. "I dance on a stage," she hissed.

"Oh, you dance on a stage. Fred Astaire danced on a stage. Do you dance like Fred Astaire?" Miki retorted.

"No."

"Do you take your clothes off when you are on stage? Miss...Gabbie is it?"

"Your Honor, I object to the relevancy if this," the insurance defense drone spouted.

The judge seized on the objection. It was something that could shorten this spectacle of a trial.

"Sustained. Mr. Martin, we all know that she is a stripper and performs on stage. Let's move on down the road."

"Yes, your honor. Miss Gabbie, you take your clothes off for money correct?"

"Objection!" The drone shouted, buoyed by the confidence of having his earlier objection sustained.

"Your Honor, if I can have a little latitude and the witness answer honestly, then I can move us down the road," Miki commanded.

The judge liked that idea. Move down the road, done with this trial and on to Asheville. "Objection is overruled and Miss Gabbie, or whatever you call yourself, no more commentary. Answer his questions. Do you understand?"

"So you take your clothes off for money? Correct?"

"Yes," she answered begrudgingly.

"Do you get more for taking you clothes off in the VIP area or on stage?"

Gabbie was fidgeting in the witness stand. It was nervous anger. She wanted to hit Miki. He was tall, sexy and smelled of a mixture of cologne and red wine sweat. But all she wanted to do was break his nose. "I don't know what…"

"Your Honor, I really must object," the drone squawked.

"Overruled! You don't even know why you are objecting at this point!" The drone's confidence sank. "Now ma'am, please just answer the questions so we can move on with this case."

Gabbie relented. "You get more in the VIP area," she said in a low tone more befitting of a dog's growl.

"Why?"

Gabbie felt judgment being cast upon her by every juror in the box. The embarrassment fueled her anger. "Because it is closed away. The bouncers cannot see you."

"Which means what? You can do more in those areas? In terms of touching?"

"Yes," Gabbie responded.

"Objection!" the drone shouted.

"Overruled!! Now shut up and sit down!!" The jury flinched at the judge's reaction. A small stream of urine ran down the pant leg of the drone's Armani suit. It was his first taste of adversity in life.

The judge realized his reaction and tried to regain composure. "Mr. Martin, are we moving down the road?" the judge asked.

"Yes, sir. Yes, we are." Miki directed his attention to the witness. "So when you bring a customer to the VIP area, you expect more money? Correct?"

Gabbie paused.

"Answer the question!" The judge interjected. If he messed up this anniversary, then there would be hell to pay. It was close to 4 p.m. and Asheville was two hours away.

"Yes!" she yelled. Gabbie had lost complete composure and like the judge, she wanted this exercise to be over.

"So, you get up on that stage and you don't dance like Rogers and Astaire do you?!" Miki fired.

"No."

"You don't even dance like Michael Jackson or Justin

Timberlake?"

"No!"

"No! No, you don't." Miki walked over to the jury box as he asked the questions. "Instead, you bump and grind on that nasty, sweaty pole for what? A dollar? A two-dollar bill?"

Gabbie nodded.

"For a two-dollar bill, you contort your half naked body in sexual positions for men you don't even know. Married men, perhaps? Men with children and families. You do all this for a two-dollar bill?" Miki paused. "I find that hard to believe. I think you dance on that stage to lure these men into the VIP area where they can actually touch you and you charge them for that touch. Isn't that correct?"

Gabbie paused again. Her anger was overflowing. The drone summoned all of his courage and began to stand. He had to do something. The judge saw him rising.

"You're objection better be the best of your young life as a lawyer. If it isn't, then I will throw you in jail," the judge fired. The drone eased back into his wet seat. The judge then directed his focus to the witness.

Gabbie could feel the glare of the judge. She had been beaten down by men her entire life. The judge was no different. And her savior of a defense lawyer was trying to piece together his ego shattered like porcelain on the courtroom floor.

"Yes," she hissed.

"So when my client went to the VIP room with you and then told you he didn't want to spend any real money, you got pissed? Didn't you?"

Gabbie was silent.

"You got mad and you hit him! You assaulted him because he wouldn't spend more money on you! You broke his nose because he didn't pay you enough!" Miki continued to look at the jury. They were intently watching her reaction.

"No, I hit him because he brought a dildo to shove up my ass! So yes, I hit him. So if that is an assault, then yes," she paused, "I assaulted your fucking client!" Gabbie shouted.

"Your Honor, I have nothing else. She can be excused unless defense counsel has some questions."

"Um...no, Your Honor. I have no questions," the drone practically whispered. He couldn't spell his name at this point let alone attempt to question his client.

Miki sat down and looked at the judge. "I have some motions, your honor."

"The witness is excused. Bailiff, please take the jury to the back. I would like to talk with the attorneys in my chambers. Now!" The judge barked.

Back in the judge's chambers, Miki secured an award for his client.

"Your honor, she has admitted the..."

The judge interrupted. "Yes, I know. I will grant that motion when it is made. She assaulted him."

"But Your Honor, he came at my client with a dildo

to ram up her anus. She acted in self-defense. At the very least, he was negligent in bringing the apparatus into the club."

"Apparatus into the club? A club is Augusta National and I doubt that they openly invite that kind of apparatus," Miki quipped.

"She didn't invite that kind of perversion," the drone responded.

"Her very existence relies on that kind of perversion. I doubt anyone would believe that she's never had experience with that kind of 'apparatus.' I got dollars to donuts that she has a collection of them," Miki replied with more air quotes.

The drone was incensed and ready to respond but the judge stepped in. "Don't say a word. You're a new lawyer. You don't want to risk a sanction over defending a stripper."

Everyone in the room knew Miki's history. The drone was ready to throw personal aspersions that would have cost him his license. The judge was trying to help. The judge's brother-in-law was a partner at the drone's firm.

"This is what will happen. If Mr. Martin moves for a directed verdict as to liability, then I will grant it. This means that your client will be found legally liable for the damages. Do you understand?" The judge stared at the drone.

The drone nodded.

"At that point, it is a matter of damages. How much

does this guy deserve for a broken nose?"

"I think a broken nose is worth at least $35,000," Miki volunteered.

"I am sure you do, Mr. Martin. I am thinking about $20,000," the judge replied. "So, if this jury awards less then $20,000, then I am going to add to the verdict. I am going to make it $20,000." The judge pointed to the drone.

"I don't know if I can get that much. We may have to appeal," the drone responded.

"Your firm has a long history of complicated and important appellate cases. Some of these cases have changed the way we look at insurance law. I really don't think that your firm wants this case part as part of their appellate lineage," the judge huffed. "Get the fucking money."

An hour later, Miki's hangover was completely gone and he received a check for $20,000 as a settlement for his client's claim. He took the case on a 50 percent contingency and was $10,000 richer.

Miki went to his favorite restaurant to celebrate. After a bottle of 2001 Caymus Special Selection and three shots of Pappy Van Winkle, Miki made the brilliant move to get a cab and visit the workplace of his former adversary, Gabbie.

Dimly lit and smelling like a horrid combination of cigarettes, cheap perfume and sweat, a strip club is more suited for a serial killer than a mass of upper middle class men. The so-called dance stages are runways from hell with a pole that houses more germs than the CDC. Miki found Gabbie on Satellite Stage Number 1.

With a crisp two-dollar bill in his hand, he squirmed his way through the mob of men adoring her. She was the best-looking woman in this club—a rose amongst kudzu.

She took the bill with her teeth and smiled. "Counselor. Heard you had a big day in court today at my expense."

Miki smiled. "Well, not exactly. It was at the insurance company's expense. Besides, it looks like your employer will make up $20,000 in an hour."

"He might, but I won't."

"Any chance of you joining me at a table so I can buy you a real drink?" he asked.

Gabbie was in. She had at least three guys lined up for the VIP experience but she knew herself all too well. Once she got something in her head, it wasn't coming out. And Miki was in her head as soon as he started questioning her in court. "Oh, a real drink? What makes you think that I need a lawyer to buy me a real drink? I got a club full of guys wanting to do that."

"Mine has a cork and bubbles." Miki smirked. "Your other suitors will try to seduce you with a can and carbonation."

Gabbie paused. It was a challenge to play 'hard to get' in a G-string. "I like Moet White Star."

"Isn't that the stage name of the next entertainer?" Miki said as he pointed to the main stage.

Gabbie laughed as she took a $2 bill from the closest

sex-starved male. "That's funny," she sarcastically replied. "Why don't you find a bottle and a table, and I will find you."

About ten minutes later, Miki was seated at a two-top with a prime view of the main stage. Gabbie pulled out a chair and plopped down.

She was in nothing but a bra and G-string. She had a body of someone who hit the gym twice a day, but in fact, she had not seen a gym in her life. She figured life had not been generous to her except genetics. So she ate and drank whatever she wanted and still looked like a model.

She took a sip of the White Star. "That's nice. Normally I get this in the…"

"VIP area," Miki interrupted. "Well, as much as I would like to get exposed to that disease ridden couch in the VIP area, I thought we would have some out here." He noticed as Gabbie removed the half used ashtray from the table. "A stripper who doesn't…"

"Entertainer, counselor." Gabbie interrupted.

"Entertainer," Miki replied, "that doesn't smoke. That's like finding a unicorn or the tooth fairy."

"Or a way to make $20,000 from forcing a plastic device up someone's ass."

Miki shrugged.

"And please don't tell me to hate the game and not the player," Gabbie retorted. "Even you are above that." She took another sip of her champagne and studied the contours of his face. She despised being attracted to him.

Miki, however, was perfectly at peace with his attraction to her. He was buzzed from a small courtroom victory, loads of alcohol and confidence that he had the hottest woman in the club who wanted more than a typical VIP experience with him.

"You know," Miki paused and swigged on his full glass of Maker's and Coke, "I have had a great day. Just a really great day."

"That is wonderful and sad," Gabbie replied. "Great that you're happy but sad that happiness is defined by screwing a strip club out of $20,000."

"Entertainment club! Remember you're an entertainer, not a stripper. I have sworn testimony to that effect." Miki toasted and took another swig. Gabbie laughed out loud. She didn't do that much and Miki could tell it was a rare event. Even she was caught off guard by the laugh. He leaned over to her. "Listen, I am drunk and if you put a little effort into it, you could be drunk too."

Gabbie smiled and took another sip from the plastic champagne flute. "Yes, I probably could be."

Miki clapped his hands. "So, we've reached an accord."

"Which is?"

"An accord? Well it is…"

"I know asshole. It is an agreement. What is our agreement?" She laughed again as she interrupted him.

Miki paused. "Well, in the words of the great Jimmy Buffet, we need to get drunk and screw."

"I don't remember reaching that agreement," Gabbie

replied. She was still smiling.

"Of course, you will need to be a lot more drunk than you are now because let's face it," Miki took another swig of his drink, "I would definitely fuck you sober but I cannot say the same of you."

"Not necessarily," Gabbie whispered.

Miki looked at her in shock.

"Listen, I have made enough money this week and clearly, you have drank enough for the week. Why don't we cut to the chase? You close out and we get the hell outta here?" Gabbie said as she downed the rest of her champagne.

Gabbie insisted on his house. And he insisted on driving. His black BMW coupe was one of the only things that remained from his glory days as a lawyer. He did not want for her to wreck it—even if the chances of the car's survival were infinitely better with her behind the wheel than Miki.

His paranoid, drunken senses locked onto the headlights of the car that started following him from the parking lot. Miki had been with a lot of unhappily married women in his recent past. When he received a subpoena to testify as the paramour in a hotly contested divorce action, he raised his level of awareness as to who was following him.

On this night, there was definitely a pair of headlights following them. The headlights followed him from the interstate and through a pair of right hand turns. So he ducked into the closest, and probably dirtiest, hotel the city had to offer. Miki pulled into a spot near the entrance and watched the headlights drive by. Even in his drunken stupor, Miki was convinced that he saw the driver of the car, which was not a police car, turn his head and look in Miki's direction as he drove by.

CHAPTER THREE:
EIGHT YEARS AGO, PART I

On the same evening that Miki lost his life on Sullivan's Island eight years ago, Grafton started his path toward resurrection in Charleston, a scant 10 miles away.

Charleston and Grafton were very similar. The city now floods the senses with history and the smell of some of the best cooking on the Eastern seaboard. However, prior to 1989, Charleston and its barrier islands—Sullivan's Island and Isle of Palms—were not attractive to outsiders.

Charleston was known for its carriage tours and unmistakable stench of horse urine and feces. The smell improved when the Holy City made horses wear diapers as opposed to just dropping it in the streets—a little fun fact that you won't find at the Visitors Center on Meeting Street.

The Isle of Palms was a beautiful community refuge for the wealthy Northerners (Yankees, to the locals) who did not need a Ripley's Believe It or Not Museum or roughly 1,000 different gifts stores to enjoy the coast.

To them, Sullivan's Island was simply the place where Edgar Allan Poe wrote short stories in a bar that used to be a grocery store.

Then in 1989, God decided to change Charleston. Hurricane Hugo slammed the coast with its eye passing through McClellanville (a small town just to the north on Highway 17). The Category 4 storm wiped Charleston clean. The Holy City was reborn. It replaced the 1,500 square foot ranch style homes located a block from the Atlantic Ocean with 7,500 square foot homes with a pool on the roof and a weekly rental rate of $10,000.

Slowly but surely, the inhabitants of the small southern city rebuilt their town just as they had done after the Civil War and Hurricane Gracie. But now, they no were longer a hidden gem. Charleston became an international destination.

Its port became a central hub for the receipt of international cargo. Big city law firms expanded into the area, rewarding long-standing partners with the opportunity to replace the smell of carbon exhaust with fresh salt air. Manufacturers located to the area and its executives were placed in high-end neighborhoods in Mt. Pleasant (the town between Charleston and its barrier islands).

And then the doctors came. Charleston became renowned for being *the* city in South Carolina for the best medical care. Surgeons making seven figures divorced their wives and relocated to multi-million dollar homes on Sullivan's Island and Isle of Palms. Their new, younger wives wanted nothing more than to one-up each other with the latest fashion. All of this helped to boost the city's economy.

In 2011, the Holy City once again became an historical site when Grafton picked Charleston to host the party to celebrate his historical victory. He was South Carolina's first black governor. He hated the term African-American. He was from Atlanta and had never even visited Africa. He often thought to himself, "If Ernie Els (the PGA star from South Africa) decided to become an American citizen, then wouldn't that make him African-American"?

The victory was even more symbolic because he was a Republican.

Grafton and about 4,500 of his closest friends finished celebrating the occasion of his election. He was tired, a little drunk from alcohol and ego (although which was the more powerful intoxicant was debatable), and on his way to meet Pontet. He was frustrated about the meeting. This was his occasion for celebration. He didn't want to share it with anyone.

He didn't have the energy to indulge in a night-long celebration to honor Pontet's massive ego, with whom none of this would have occurred as claimed by Pontet. He knew that Pontet's hotel room would be filled with the aroma of gin and Pontet's bullshit.

As he entered his hotel room, Pontet was waiting, sprawled on a chase lounge next to the bed. He was admiring the view of the Holy City at night. To Grafton's amazement, there was no drink in hand.

"No drink? You feelin' okay? This November chill sneak up and give you a cold?" Grafton asked.

Pontet ignored the jab. "I would say congratulations but we said that when we rigged the results in the lesser known counties," Pontet replied.

"Lots of 'we' in that statement," Grafton observed.

"Well, we are a team. Right?" Pontet asked with a grin.

Grafton shuttered at the thought. He wanted to part ways with Pontet after the election. He had outgrown him. In the beginning, Pontet captured Grafton's attention with his sermons on the art of politics and human manipulation. But Grafton soon found that the once wise and sage advice was a by-product of a gin bottle. Grafton's confidence grew as he experienced success on both the campaign and legislative fronts. He was no longer a frightened pup hiding from his past. He was now reclaiming his life. He had made it so far without the support of a wife—why did he still need Pontet?

As for Pontet, he knew their relationship had deteriorated into a bad marriage. What started with promise and undying affection had become an endurance contest. He knew that Grafton endured him like a person swallowing stomach bile with a smile. He assumed Grafton was going to to fire him, but unfortunately for Grafton, Pontet was not going anywhere.

"I have been talking to some folks. Some folks who look at things on a national level," Pontet said.

"Let me guess, you had drinks with a former member of the White House staff to circulate my name as president? Or maybe talked to a retired UN Ambassador to some poor impoverished African nation?" Grafton wasn't in the mood for Pontet's pathetic grasps for reasons to keep him around.

"No, Governor-Elect. No, I have been talking with a representative of Practical Solutions." Pontet sat up. "Do I have your attention now?"

Grafton paused. It was a feeling of exhilaration and disgust. On the one hand, he was exhilarated over the potential of becoming a national player. On the other hand, it meant more bile to swallow.

"Are they looking at 4 or 8 years?" Grafton asked.

"Eight. And you're on the list."

Practical Solutions had become a political think tank. While most believe that meant an organization employing highly intelligent people to spend all day pontificating over the ideology of politics, P.S. was in the business of influencing elections rather than merely discussing them. It was built on the mission to find political and private sector candidates capable of influencing and enhancing the bottom line of its clients.

P.S. was the ultimate vetting company. In the private sector, it vetted potential candidates to head multi-million dollar corporations. Members of the board don't want a renegade. They want someone who will play ball. Some of the largest professional players' unions believe that Elite was responsible for vetting commissioners of each major professional sport to make sure that the owners' interests were protected.

In the political sector, P.S. solicited donations from its clients to vet potential candidates and create the list. While not the only company in the field, P.S.'s philosophy set it apart from the competition.

Members of P.S. didn't just check into the background of each candidate. P.S. essentially infiltrated the candidates' campaigns through placing well-trained operatives into key spots, allowing them to get a true understanding of the exact character makeup of each candidate.

P.S.'s clients want an electable candidate that it can control. That determination was not effectively made through a series of interviews with high school classmates or former mistresses. Even the best private investigative report will only provide a street view of the candidate. In order to get an inside view, you must place key people in circumstances where the candidate drops his political façade and shows his true colors.

Thus, P.S. placed individuals skilled in the art and science of reading people and gathering information that is protected. It was the largest privately run spy company in the world, regularly recruiting from the CIA, FBI, KGB, and even the famed MI6.

Through this political espionage, P.S. established a solid reputation as the most reliable source of inside information for any candidate, even the presidency. For each presidential race, it formulated a top-five list based primarily on the candidate's willingness to enforce a political agenda suggested by the biggest political supporters. P.S. only endorsed candidates that could be elected and were willing to sell the presidency in exchange for winning the election.

There was no dearth of candidates seeking P.S's approval. All viable candidacies needed the private money.

For the last presidential election, each candidate spent over one billion dollars. With the advent of political finance reform, candidates turned to the private sector rather than the public funding available to candidates. It was a choice. If you take public money, then you are limited in what you can raise and spend. If you decline the option, then you can spend as much as you want.

In the last election, the winner raised $700 million in private donations and the loser only $446 million in private donations, and the winner was at the top of the P.S. list, just as the previous three winners had been.

Grafton knew of P.S.'s growth. As a teenager, he played golf with the founding members. The men always saw him as the most viable candidate. They helped to suppress his background for all these years.

While Pontet infrequently made references to friends in Atlanta, Grafton never fathomed that Pontet was with P.S. It supposedly recruited employees from spy agencies or federal law enforcement—not the local bar. But Grafton placed his opinions of the stereotypical of P.S. mole aside and instead focused on his history with Pontet. Grafton examined how he met Pontet and the role he played in his life. It was clear that Pontet was with them and the perfect operative for the job.

"So did P.S. hire you to help me or just to spy on me?" Grafton asked.

"Well, in order to get to know you, I had to occupy the role of political advisor, which of course means I have to give advice to play the role," Pontet replied.

"So a little bit of both, I guess?" Grafton replied.

"Yes, but mainly I am hired to gather information and present it to others. From that point, they make the decisions. They control the chessboard. I am only the Knight or the Rook." Pontet had too much ego to consider himself a pawn. "And my instructions are to remain with you through your gubernatorial administration and continue to feed information to them. Assuming you want them to vet you?"

"Well, yes," Grafton quickly replied. "I know the stats. If they don't give you the nod, then the closest I will come to the White House is a tour. "

"This is true," Pontet said.

"But you were permitted to tell me that I was on the list. Why? If you want to know the real me, it seems that you would not share that information for fear that I would simply do and say what I think you and your company want to hear?"

"Also true. " Pontet paused and gazed out of the window at St. Phillip's Church. "Grafton, there are few things I know with certainty in this world. I know how much gin

I can drink before I am drunk. I know that I will always pay taxes. I know that I will die. And, I also know you."

"What does that mean? How do you know me? You only know what it is that I want you to know," Grafton quipped.

"You're not as complicated as you want to be. You are not a mystery wrapped in a riddle. You're a fucking billboard. Your actions are not tempered by notions of morality, or even basic human decency."

"And you've been right there with me," Grafton fired back even though he knew that the observation was accurate.

"Yes, I have. Even with our first victim. You remember him?" Pontet asked.

"Of course, I do. I remember them all."

"What was his name?" Pontet asked.

"Gallagher. Roger Gallagher." Grafton took a moment to reflect on his past and his first real political victim.

After graduating college and through Pontet's connections, Grafton secured a job as a loan officer in a local bank. It was here that Grafton honed his skills of manipulation and use of information to become president of the bank. He focused his efforts to discover and expose the acts of co-workers succumbing to human frailties and weaknesses. While most of his information was more embarrassing than actually harmful, his co-workers did not possess Grafton's tenacity to conquer the world. They were simply working in a local bank and enjoying the ease of Charleston life. If Grafton wanted a favor, then they would rather just give it to him than risk embarrassment.

However, as he rose to more prominence, the competition stiffened. He was faced with men and women who did not view this bank as a job—they wanted a career. Grafton tried for vice president twice but lost each time. His normal tactics did not faze the competition. They did not care about his gossip about their personal lives. They laughed him off.

He was up for vice president for the third time. The other candidate was a married father of a six-year old daughter. He was an honest and respectable man dealing with a hard life. About three years ago, he and his wife were driving home from a date night. He had a little too much to drink but wasn't drunk. On their way home, a deer darted in front of the car and he instinctively swerved to miss it rather than just hitting the damn thing. He overcorrected and lost control of the car, hitting an oak tree. The passenger side of the car took most of the impact and his wife was paralyzed from the waist down. She was 32 years old and confined to a wheelchair.

He was suffocated by the guilt of hurting her. They were high school sweethearts and enjoyed an almost euphoric life after the birth of their daughter. They were trying for a second child at the time of the accident. And now, he was simply enduring life knowing that his daughter would never see her mother walk again because of him.

While she never blamed him for the accident, she did not cope well. Before the wreck, she was a vivacious person who never met a stranger. He was the recluse and she the social butterfly. They meshed perfectly. But now, she was completely dependent upon him. She could not muster the strength to perform the most menial tasks for her daughter or herself.

She regularly talked about suicide, spending hours trying to convince him to let her end it. She told him that he should move on with another woman who could give their daughter the normal mother that she deserved. It was a daily emotional onslaught on his soul.

There were no guns or prescription drugs in the house. He would routinely have neighbors go into the home unannounced to check on her. Everyday at the office was unmitigated hell as he waited for the phone call that she had taken her own life.

The man needed this promotion. He was the sole breadwinner for the family and health insurance did not cover all of her medical costs. He also needed it for his sanity. He needed something to ward off the guilt. Everyone in the office knew his situation and they all rooted for him to get the promotion.

After being passed over the second time, Grafton made a list of potential co-workers who may compete for the position if it became vacant again. This poor man was at the top of his list and Grafton decided to befriend him months before the vacancy was announced.

He and Grafton became close, or at least that is what the man thought. They would regularly go to lunch or the occasional happy hour. He would tell the man that he needed to make sure he was doing things for himself and not just living to be a guilt-ridden father and husband.

It was at one such happy hour that the man confided in Grafton. He had succumbed to temptation. Grafton's ears perked up. He soaked up human frailty like a sponge. It was the ultimate weapon for him.

He told Grafton about his exchanges with a divorced mom whose daughter played on his daughter's soccer team. They saw each other about three times a week. She was recently divorced. Her ex-husband had cheated on her and moved to Key West with his new girlfriend. He left her with a nice alimony payment but no help to raise their daughter. She was heartbroken and alone.

Their innocent flirtations at soccer games morphed into brazen sexual advances. It was shameless and embarrassing. He would feel guilty about his conversations but he became dependent upon the interaction as his only means to deal with the pain. Then one day, he crossed the line. They bumped into each other at Wal-Mart. About 15 minutes after telling him that she had a baby sitter, they were at the closest Motel 6. At first, he hated himself and he was once again choking on guilt. But soon, he became dependent on the physical relationship. They met every Wednesday night at the Motel 6 to ease each other's pain. It wasn't love, just an escape. He did not know any other way to cope.

Then the announcement came. The position of vice president became vacant. Grafton and his "buddy" were the only candidates. They exchanged the obligatory "you should get it because you deserve it." But secretly, each man wanted the other to lose.

Grafton, however, had the upper hand. He had hired a private investigator over a month ago. He had full video of the Motel 6 meetings and showed his "buddy" the report. Grafton did not flinch or show any emotion as the man crumpled into a mess of human misery. Grafton never saw such pain and torment, yet he never entertained a single thought of sympathy for the poor man.

The man had no choice but to relent to Grafton's demands. Even though he knew his wife would never divorce him, this report would literally kill her. The next day, the man pulled his name from consideration. He said that it would take too much time from his family. The man later left for a different job. Grafton was promoted to vice president.

It is hard to define the exact moment when someone loses his or her moral compass, the part of the soul that tells right from wrong. It's that little voice that tells you to stop when your innermost demons yell for you to press on. This was Grafton's first real victim. And like any first, it educated him. He learned he had a limitless capacity to harm another if it served his own interests. He was impervious to human suffering as long as it was not his own. Pontet knew that.

"Grafton, I am just a hired gun. I can wear the white hat just as easy as the black hat, if the price is right. But you're different."

"Please enlighten me, Dr. Freud, as to my psyche."

"This world is a war to you, and in your war, all actions are justified. And in war, you want the upper ground. This is why you crave power and why you have pursued politics. Not only do you want to secure the ground you have, you also want to climb higher, no matter the cost. You're the only candidate I can imagine that would sell the presidency to the highest bidder. Hell, you've already sold your soul. The Oval Office is a no brainer with you."

"I am so glad to have your endorsement," Grafton replied sarcastically.

"You need to be because I have not been entirely forthcoming with my employer about you."

"Such as?" Grafton asked.

"Rumblings I have heard about mistakes of your youth. Not Atlanta-based but more local," Pontet said.

Grafton was silent.

"I never asked for details because I didn't want to be accused of withholding information. My employer is not very...um... forgiving, let's say. Plus, if these rumblings are true, then you're out," Pontet continued. "But like I said, I believe you're the right man for this job."

"What kind of rumblings and from who?" Grafton knew exactly what he was talking about.

Pontet raised his eyebrow and replied, "Grafton, let's not discuss those details. I prefer to remain as blissfully ignorant as I can. The only question I need answered is whether you have taken care of that issue or will it reappear?"

"That issue was just put to bed," Grafton replied coldly.

"So no loose ends or dangling strings we have to worry about?"

"None," Grafton said emphatically.

CHAPTER FOUR:
CHANDLER MURRAY

Chandler Murray was a well-respected lawyer until he unwittingly became Grafton's enemy. He was a 54-year-old widow raising a 15-year-old daughter. His wife had a horrific drinking habit. That, coupled with her bi-polar medication, made her incapable of making sane decisions. Her criminal record was more befitting of a cheap prostitute than a lawyer's wife. There were two DUIs, several drunk and disorderly charges filed by a handful of bars that she frequented, criminal domestic violence charges filed by three of her ex-boyfriends, along with three restraining orders. Chandler grew up in a rural county as a Southern Baptist. His father was the local sheriff and associate pastor at the family church. Chandler was raised to believe that divorce was not an option, no matter how dire the marriage.

One night it all came crashing down when his wife and a male companion took the family boat out for a midnight spin on the local lake. About 15 White Russians later, she and her boyfriend were sliced in half after the boat slammed into an island about a mile long. Lights on a boat are meant to be seen and not for actually seeing.

Chandler's law practice focused mainly on real estate closings. It was a small practice dedicated to closing the loans of a handful of builders and a few banks. It provided him a good living and allowed him the freedom to pursue his interest in politics. He started slowly with an election to city council, then county council, and then his home-builder contacts helped him land a seat in the state House of Representatives. His largest client was a homebuilder who decided that he wanted a friend on the House floor.

Chandler's tenure in the House of Representatives was uneventful. He only offered a few pieces of legislation that were certain to gain support (raising the legal limits for DUIs) or obscure land use statutes geared toward the needs of his real estate clients. The fake potted plants on the floor of the House of Representatives contributed as much to the legislature as did Chandler. But unlike Grafton, he was completely harmless.

One night at a fundraising event to celebrate his re-election, Chandler had a few too many glasses of wine. As the night wore on, conversations turned to the House Majority Leader seat vacated because of the elections. With the drunken support of his clients and constituents, Chandler reached a "God-Zone" drunk level. He announced his decision to run for House Majority Leader. He had no clue that Grafton was pursuing the same seat. Chandler had just entered a swimming contest with a Great White.

The next morning, Chandler vaguely remembered the moment and laughed it off when others, less inebriated at that time, reminded him of his announcement. Chandler's plate was full with a law practice, being a single father, and playing lawmaker six months a year. He didn't need any added headaches. But unbeknownst to him, the damage had been done.

Pontet immediately reported the development to Grafton. After a couple of hours and a few libations consumed by Pontet, they determined that Chandler was the only viable challenge to Grafton's election as Majority Leader. Whether Chandler wanted it or not, he was designated an obstacle in Grafton's quest.

"You see, Chandler is a real estate lawyer," Pontet mused. "Do you know the quickest way to lose your license to practice law in this state?"

"I know a bunch of lawyers. They're all dishonest but still practice. So clearly, I don't have a clue," Grafton replied.

"The trust account."

"A lawyer with a trust account. Now that is funny." Grafton laughed.

"Everyone hates a lawyer until they need one, Hood. Then they want the meanest, nastiest one they can find."

"True."

"Anyway, the trust account houses money that belongs to others," Pontet continued.

"Okay."

"When a real estate lawyer closes on a purchase of property, the loan, buyer's money, and seller's money all get deposited into the trust account." Pontet paused. "From there, the money is disbursed. It is a sacred thing for lawyers. You don't monkey with your trust account or you lose your license to earn a living."

"So we infiltrate his trust account?" Grafton asked.

"Yes!" Pontet exclaimed. "Chandler is a one-man practice. He probably handles about 50 to 60 real estate deals a month. This means between his time in the legislature and being a single dad, he must rely on someone in his office to handle all of the mundane tasks of a real estate closing."

"Closing?"

"Real estate deal. It means that the transaction is done."

"So what is involved with that?" Grafton asked.

"Writing the checks and making sure that the trust account is reconciled." Pontet noticed the puzzled look on Grafton's face. "You know, that the money goes where it needs to go. He relies on his paralegal to do all this."

"So Murray's real estate paralegal, you are saying, basically controls all of the money that flows through his trust account? And that if the flow of this money is mishandled, then it lands on Murray?" Grafton asked.

"Exactly. Even if she outright steals the money, Murray will lose his license because he is responsible for the oversight. It is the ultimate 'the buck stops here' mentality as espoused by the Bar. "

"So the paralegal is the key?"

"Yes! We replace his current paralegal with someone that we pick. We need someone willing to steal and destroy another person for the right price," Pontet continued.

"And I am sure that you have the exact person for that job," Grafton said with a laugh.

"Yes, Grafton. Of course I do. I have walked through enough pools of human filth to have met such an individual, present company excluded, of course."

"Oh, but of course, "Grafton said with a smirk. "How do we force Murray to have to hire someone else? How do we get rid of his current paralegal?" Grafton asked. "Get her arrested…an auto wreck that hospitalizes her?"

"No." Pontet took a three-second sip of his drink to clear his head. It was always easier to eliminate another person on a buzz rather than sober. "About five years ago, one of the managing partners of the state's largest law firms was going through a nasty divorce. It was bad. She thought her husband was cheating on her, but she also thought that he was gay. It's tough to prove a homosexual affair."

"I guess. I have never really given much thought to it." Grafton shook his head.

"Well, think about it."

"I'd rather not," Grafton replied.

"Good to know. Anyway, she was trying to figure out how to prove it, and I helped."

"Did you sleep with the guy?"

"No. I am not that much of a sellout. I just gave her advice," Pontet said as he shook his head.

"I bet you did."

"So, I met her at a bar that I frequented."

"Who haven't you met at a bar?"

Pontet ignored the comment. "Anyway, we have a couple of drinks and she tells me about her suspicions about her husband. She starts telling me that if she can catch him, then she doesn't have to pay him any alimony. He didn't work. He was one of those guys that started about 15 different businesses but never succeeded at one. And in this state, if you commit adultery, then you lose your right to alimony."

"Yes, this I know. I have been approached by several people to propose a change to that law," Grafton replied.

"Crazy law. I can beat the hell out of my wife but if she cheats once then I don't have to pay alimony." Pontet grinned as he shook his head. "Anyhow, I listened to her bitching about the husband and his best friend, who is also married. She says that they spend a ton of time together."

"How much time were these guys spending together?"

"Oh, all the time, but doing the normal guy stuff. Watching football, drinking beer, and making crude jokes about sex and bowel movements. They were putting on a show. But she said they were only alone when they worked out, which was about three times a week."

"Where were they working out?" Grafton asked.

"Exactly. She tells me that her husband had a personal fitness room in the house. And so I make the drunken suggestion that she hide cameras in the fitness room," Pontet said.

Grafton smiled.

"You see, she had never thought of that. She was the managing partner of this huge law firm but had zero street smarts. I told her about the television shows where parents hide cameras to catch nannies. I even gave her the name of a good PI that could install the equipment."

"And what happened?"

"She caught them. They were fucking like rabbits on Viagra, doing all sorts of things with those weights that had nothing to do with physical fitness. She got a divorce, paid no alimony, and somehow the fitness room caught fire. She said that the treadmill had a short," Pontet said with a grin.

"And her husband?"

"He wasn't in the fitness room, if that is what you're asking?"

"No, what happened to him?" Grafton asked.

"Oh, I will get to that. So about a year ago, a friend's son graduated law school and needed a job. Nice kid but just dumb as a bag of hammers. I told him to put me down as a reference and send the resume to her. Didn't think anything of it."

"And?"

"She calls me out of the blue. Tells me that they hired the kid even though they wouldn't have even looked at his resume. They only hire the top five percent of law school graduates. But because it was for me, then it got done and that if I ever needed any favor, I can call her," Pontet said with a defiant nod.

"So I am assuming that this huge law firm is going to offer a new place of employment to Chandler's real estate paralegal?" Grafton asked.

"Oh yeah, it will be twice as much as he can afford to pay. That's a phone call away."

"That's great," Grafton said.

"And so she represents the largest legal employment agency in the area. I will get her to call the agency and get them to highly endorse any candidate that I send to them," Pontet continued.

"And when Chandler calls seeking viable candidates to replace his paralegal, our person's name will be at the top of the list?" Grafton asked.

"Yes, sir." Pontet pointed to him.

"And our candidate? Our inside person?"

"Oh, yeah. That's the kicker. It will be the ex-husband of my lady lawyer friend."

"Her ex-husband? Mr. Physical Fitness?" Grafton was surprised. "You do wallow around in human filth. Present company excluded."

"But of course." Pontet lifted his glass in Grafton's direction. "You see, her ex-husband was destroyed by the PI report. He agreed to take nothing from the marriage. He assumed that his paramour, who was very rich, would leave his life and wife. They would wander into the sunset to lead a life of love, sex and gym equipment."

"I take it that didn't happen," Grafton replied.

"Oh, no. No way. He wasn't going to give up his life-style."

"Interesting decision to say the least," Grafton remarked.

"They're still married. I saw something on Facebook about them celebrating an anniversary."

"And our boy Friday? The ex of your lady lawyer friend?" Grafton asked.

"Ah, the only thing worse than being broke is being broke with a broken heart. He had it all. He was part of the upper one percent. He only knew high-end vacations, the latest foreign-made SUVs, and a 6,000 square foot home to host the quarterly dinner party. All of the trophies that showcased financial success. "

"And then all of a sudden? Gone," Grafton said with a snap of his fingers. "I know that emotion."

"Yes, yes you do. But our guy wasn't young like you. He had no work history and was pushing 60. He ends up working two jobs as a cashier at a gas station and stock boy at a CVS. He currently lives in a one bedroom apartment and bicycles to work."

"Hardly qualified to be a real estate paralegal for Murray?" Grafton questioned.

"It is going to take a month before he is in place. And being a real estate paralegal is really about the software and knowing enough to generate the documents. We just need to get him enrolled in a couple of classes to learn that shit."

"But is he really going to hire a 60-year-old male paralegal?"

"I admit that a broke, homosexual adulterer isn't the best candidate, so I don't know. But I know that his choices will be limited because this will be the only candidate from the employment agency, per the request of my lady lawyer friend," Pontet said with a sly grin.

"Can you think of anyone else?" Grafton asked.

"Nope. He is the best candidate that I have," Pontet answered.

"And I don't know anyone who has navigated more puddles of human filth than you," Grafton said.

Pontet smiled as he toasted to Grafton once again.

"If this plan works," Grafton started.

Pontet interrupted. "If this plan works, you will be the most powerful politician in the legislature."

And the plan worked.

About four weeks after hiring his new paralegal, Chandler's real estate account went into the red. It was reported to the Bar and to the Feds. Chandler was arrested and his law license suspended.

He spent two months in jail until he could secure a mortgage on his elderly mother's house. It had been in the family for over 100 years but was later lost to the bank in foreclosure.

The criminal charges were dropped after the Feds discovered the body of his former real estate paralegal. No glamorous death. There was a single shot from a store bought .38.

While Murray's real estate paralegal masterfully embezzled millions into his offshore account, his heart never healed from the loss of his ex-lover He couldn't bring himself to leave the country. He convinced himself that if he showed his former lover that he could take care of them, then they could be together.

The paralegal persisted in stalking his former lover using all of the normal stalker tools—texting, emails and social media. Eventually, the wife of his ex-lover discovered the contact and told the Feds. She also called the paralegal to inform him that the Feds would be knocking. That was the last voice he heard prior to putting a bullet in his head.

As for Chandler, even though the criminal charges were dropped, the Bar still took his license to practice for two years. Life is like entering the ocean. Sometimes the water is calm and you can walk right in. Sometimes the waves are rough and may knock you down. It is then that a person must decide whether to get off the ocean floor and press on against the waves to reach the calm, or just lie on the bottom and hope the waves will stop crashing. Chandler stayed at the bottom.

He never regained his law license back, electing to stay on the bottom waiting for the waves to stop crashing. He eked out a living as a cab driver. As he lay on the ocean floor of life, Chandler's cynicism grew into a firm belief that the world is cruel and evil is rewarded. He became convinced that someone other than his former employee had thrust this evil upon him. He knew of only one other person with the desire and ability.

CHAPTER FIVE:
THE GABBIE SITUATION

Over the next two weeks, Gabbie became a fixture at Miki's apartment, but it was nothing more than a superficial relationship grounded in sex and drinking. These were the only relationships that either could sustain.

Gabbie was a survivor. She never knew her biological parents, as she was put up for adoption as an infant. She bounced from foster home to foster home until age seven, when she was finally adopted. Her adoptive parents were lower middle class. While they could not clothe her in the latest name brands or afford the most expensive school supplies or toys, they provided something more valuable—a brief semblance of a normal life. She no longer had to wonder where she would spend Christmas or if her latest foster parents would remember her birthday.

Gabbie also felt for the first time in her life something that all children should feel—unconditional love. For her adoptive mother, Gabbie was a gift from heaven and she treated her as such. Her adoptive mother was unable to have children and her maternal instincts ran strong. She dedicated all her energy to raising foster children in hopes of adopting. She stopped working after she and her husband began to foster children. That was a mistake that would haunt her and Gabbie.

Gabbie's adoptive mother was the first face she saw in the morning and the last she saw at night. Other than school, they were tied at the hip. And even at school, Gabbie felt her presence—from the homemade lunches to being dropped off and picked up at the car rider line to attending every school event. Gabbie was overcome by the sheer gratitude her mother felt for every moment with her. Gabbie would often tap into the memories of her adoptive mother's hugs and warmth for strength to endure what would become her tortuous life.

Unfortunately, Gabbie's adoptive father was the opposite. He was apathetic. He was always polite and never raised his voice or hand at her. But this was his wife's child, not his. In his mind, they weren't able to have his child because of his wife, but he would play the bigger man and allow her to indulge in the fantasy that Gabbie was actually her child.

He married Gabbie's adoptive mother after a pregnancy scare that ended in a miscarriage shortly after the honeymoon. They tried for a few years to get pregnant but each pregnancy ended in a miscarriage. As his wife became more obsessed with having a child, he began to abhor the thought of continuing to try or even becoming a father. Eventually, her doctor warned her that the next miscarriage could be her last and they needed to stop trying.

Gabbie's adoptive father was overjoyed, thinking that he would stay with her a few months more to give her time to grieve, and then he would leave the marriage.

But that idea was quelled when he was guilted into fostering children. He figured it was a phase that would run its course and allow him to escape the marriage, but he didn't expect that they would be able to adopt so quickly. It of course didn't hurt that they were a young white couple willing to adopt an older ethic child.

And while he didn't mind the young girl, after three years he had his fill of being an adoptive parent. One afternoon, Gabbie's adoptive mother opened the front door to find an overnight delivery person with an unsigned letter from her husband.

I am not coming home. I am leaving you. Please don't try to find me. I have already called the police to let them know that I am fine and have given them my new phone number to verify my health. They will not share it with you.

I didn't want you to waste their time on the hopeless goal of looking for a person who is not missing but simply wants to go away.

You've wasted enough of my time on your hopeless goals; please, don't waste any of their time.

Gabbie's adoptive mother called the police under the guise that the letter wasn't written by him but by a third party who had harmed him. The police verified the authenticity of the letter and that her husband was very much alive and, to quote his words, "quite well indeed." After an hour of pleading, the police finally released his phone number to her. She quickly dialed it. It was no longer in service.

For the second time in her brief life, Gabbie had her world turned upside down by a man. But it would not be the last.

With no job skills, Gabbie's adoptive mother was suddenly thrust into the life of a single mother. Scared and alone, she clung to the first man with a job who paid her any attention. She divorced her husband for abandonment and married her new beau the next day. Gabbie now had a stepfather and he was a demented soul.

At six feet tall, he towered over Gabbie, outweighing her by at least 200 pounds. He had huge bug eyes and wore a beard to hide the massive acne scars on his face. He kept his shoulder length hair in a ponytail. It was always greasy as he only showered twice a week. He also wasn't a firm believer in the power of deodorant. He mandated that she call him "Daddy," but in private, she referred to him as *Ursula*, after the villain in the *Little Mermaid*.

She was barely 12 when the abuse began. Gabbie's adoptive mother worked late nights at a local fast food restaurant. Ursula worked the day shift as a Wal-Mart security officer. He and Gabbie spent practically every night together, alone.

It began with him interrupting her in the shower to hand her a clean towel or to put away toilet paper. She began to notice that he would linger around after completing his alleged task, supposedly straightening up the bathroom while she showered. The lingering then advanced to him sitting on the toilet waiting for her to finish. He said he was there to hand her a clean towel so she didn't slip getting out of the shower. Then he began to pull away the shower curtain to hand her an unneeded bar of soap or shampoo.

Ursula told her that he was going to be in her life forever and that they needed to bond. He said that part of the bounding was him tucking her in at night. That evening ritual soon evolved into him lying next to her until "she fell asleep." He would rub her head, as she would close her eyes pretending to sleep in the hopes that he would leave. She knew something was wrong but didn't know what to do.

The eventual caressing of her head developed into groping. When she asked him to stop, he replied that it was part of their bonding. He also said it was special bonding that only they could know about. She could never tell her adoptive mother about it. And she never did.

She was 13 when she had her first sexual encounter with Ursula. He no longer told her this was special bonding, but rather threatened to leave her adoptive mother if she told anyone. He told her that her mom would be "devastated beyond repair and probably end up killing herself. And that means you will go back to foster care."

At first, she tried to fight him off but she soon realized that she would never tell her adoptive mother and he would never stop. It was never going to end. She decided that it was quicker to just let him finish. While that decision lessened the physical damage, it only intensified the mental damage. Almost every night was an exercise in burying all emotions in order to endure the misery. She went from uncontrollably sobbing after every time to quietly crying. As she continued to harden her soul, the quiet crying became just a single tear. Eventually, she became numb enough that she gave a lifeless stare as she waited for him to climb off.

After two years of endoring Ursula's abuse, Gabbie ran away. But it wasn't a spontaneous decision. It was methodical and took a month of planning. Every evening her adoptive mother worked was the same ritual. Ursula would rape Gabbie and then retire to the master bedroom, or lair as Gabbie called it. He would then wash down half an Ambien with a glass of Jim Beam. He was fast asleep within a half an hour. Gabbie spent every available evening scouring his wallet for all identification information. Every night Ursula finished pillaging her, she began her pillage on his credit.

She used his information to apply for credit cards allowing cash advance checks. Gabbie timed it so all cash advance checks would arrive within a day of her escape. She forged his name to make the checks payable to her. She had perfected his signature after hours of imitating his driver's license signature. She deposited those checks into her personal account, presumably opened to save for a car. She then had the bank issue her a certified check for all of Ursula's cash advances deposited into her account; it totaled $15,000. That event occurred about an hour before he arrived home.

With Ursula fast asleep from his concoction of "Jim-Bien," as Gabbie called it, she grabbed his wallet as she raced out the door. She would say good-bye to her adoptive mother later, if at all. It was a cold response but one learned from countless hours of enduring Ursula's torture.

On her way out of town, Gabbie stopped at an ATM and maxed out Ursula's daily withdrawal amount of $500. She then arrived at a late-night gas station and waited for the arrival of her classmates. Using *Ursula's* newest gas card (which he never saw), Gabbie had a fire sale. She filled up each student's car using the card. In exchange, they paid her 50 cents for every dollar she filled. At the end of the sale, Ursula's gas card was maxed out and Gabbie had $1,500 in cash. Having fully exploited his wallet, Gabbie flushed it down the gas station bathroom. She knew there was nothing more annoying than having to replace your entire wallet.

Gabbie then focused her charm and blazing good looks on the nearest boy with a car and absolutely no chance of dating her. He was more than happy to take her to Charlotte, North Carolina. She repaid him with a pat on the back, a kiss on the cheek, and a full tank of gas. Once in the Queen City, she then bought a bus ticket to her actual destination, Savannah. Now that her adoptive mother was out of the picture, she had only one other person who could help.

Gabbie met Mary Madison while in foster care in the years prior to Gabbie's adoption. Even though she was only 6 and Mary was 12, they instantly bounded and stayed in touch through the years. Mary ended her servitude in foster care just as her aunt ended a five-year sentence for selling prescription narcotics. Rehabilitated by the power of prison and church, Mary's aunt provided her a stable home life and helped her flourish into a beautiful young woman.

After graduating high school, Mary was working her way through community college as a bartender in Savannah's River District. It was there that she met her fiancé, a young man training to become a U.S. Navy Seal. They moved in together after only three months and she continued to work in Savannah as he completed training in California. She was going to finish up her last semester of school and then move out west to join "the Seal," as she called him. After a few months of less frequent than normal emails, Gabbie showed up at her doorstep, unannounced, with a $15,000 check made payable to her.

Gabbie told her everything. It was the first time she talked about Ursula and what he had done. But Mary was more concerned about the manner in which Gabbie told it. There was no emotion on her face and no infliction in her voice. She described it as if it occurred to a third person.

"Gabbie, we really need to tell the authorities," Mary pleaded.

"Why? I am out," Gabbie casually replied.

"So he can be punished...so he won't do this again. For a lot of reasons."

"Listen, if I call the cops then they will make me go back up there. I will have to be a witness and I will have to relive all of this shit. On top of that, I will have to live in a small town where everyone will know my history. I don't want to wear some Scarlet fucking letter because this asshole abused me."

"Scarlet what?" Mary asked—literature not being her strong suit.

"It's a book." Gabbie shook her head. "Plus, why put my mom through the pain? For that poor woman, ignorance is bliss. She doesn't need another guy dumping her."

"So, you're gonna let her stay saddled up with that cretin?"

"Don't know Scarlet Letter but know cretin? Really?"

"Word of the month calendar." Mary smiled and pointed to her kitchen counter.

"Congratulations on your vocabulary wealth." Gabbie laughed aloud. Mary was beautiful enough to make her flakiness seem sexy. "But cretin or no cretin, I have to worry about me and not her. And right now, I am about $15,000 richer and will stay $15,000 richer as long as I let bygones be bygones.

"Speaking of which, why is this check made payable to me?"

"So they cannot trace where I am. Madison is your aunt's last name and not the one you were tagged with in foster care. I need you to cash that so I can set up an account."

"Aren't you afraid that this guy will try to track you down?"

"Not really; I left word for him that if he does try to find me, then I will get the authorities involved or perhaps, worse."

"Worse?"

Using Ursula's money, Gabbie paid a couple of high school seniors (who were dubbed by the classmates with the "most likely to fail in life" superlative) to beat Ursula with a pair of aluminum baseball bats. Two displaced orbital fractures later, the pair was assured that Gabbie would never hear from him again. And she didn't.

"That's not important." Gabbie ignored the question. "So when do you leave?"

"Well, last semester ends in the second week of December. I am hoping to be out there by Christmas to see the Seal." Mary frowned as she looked at Gabbie. "But now that you are here, I am sure I can get him out here for Christmas or maybe you can come with me for a bit?"

"Mary, we have had this discussion. He's a great guy for you but the Seal doesn't want me around." Gabbie stared at her emphatically. "He wants a life with you and you alone. He doesn't want his children being raised around a half-breed,"

"He never said 'half breed,'" Mary interrupted. "Those are your words."

Gabbie resumed her thought. "Crazy, aunt-like figure that you met through foster care. He's gonna have a very abnormal career and wants a normal family life. And honestly, I get that. Hell, if I were him I wouldn't even want to start a family with me around."

"Well, I will just change his mind. Now, that you're here, I will change his mind. I can be very persuasive," she said with a smile.

"Honey, I have no doubt about that. With your sick figure, stunning looks and sexual prowess of a porn star," Gabbie was interrupted again.

"Hey, what does that mean?"

"Foster care kid. You got all sorts of daddy-daughter issues. No telling what you have put on that poor boy." Gabbie laughed. Mary's face grew red from embarrassment as she giggled back. "But, you and I both deserve fresh starts. You deserve a new place and a new beginning. You don't need me around as a constant reminder of what you came from. I can take care of myself."

Mary simply nodded. Gabbie was right. Mary was secretly happy that the Seal balked at her emails asking if Gabbie could move to California with them. She loved Gabbie but she craved a normal life. She also knew Gabbie would do the same if in her position. "Well, it's only

October so we have plenty of time to figure it all out. I am sure my aunt would love for you to stay with her."

"I am done staying with others. I am ready to do it on my own."

"You're 15."

"Going on 25. I can take care of myself."

"Yeah, I have discerned that." Gabbie raised an eyebrow. Mary pointed in the direction of the word of the day calendar and smiled.

Gabbie returned the grin. "I just need a little help with the logistics. I need you to keep this apartment after you go. I will pay the lease. No one in the city would rent to a teenager."

"What about grade transcripts? Enrolling you in school? You are going to finish high school, aren't you?"

"I just embezzled $15,000 from the pedophile who sexually tormented me for about two years. Somehow, I think the whole high school experience will be somewhat wasted on me." Gabbie smirked. "Not exactly excited about prom and don't see me trying out for the cheerleading squad. I just need a driver's license that says I am 18 and a GED. I can take it from there."

"My aunt did some time. I am sure she knows some folks and she'll do anything for me. She says that the simple sound of my voice brightens her day."

"That's because your voice is mellifluous." Gabbie said with a nod. Mary was stumped by the word. "Don't worry, holiday season is just around the corner. We can get you a new calendar then."

Gabbie's experience with Ursula damaged her again. She became addicted to the fast, easy dollar. While studying for her GED, Gabbie worked as a bar back with Mary's former employer. She was too young to bartend, and she found it difficult to adjust to a minimum wage paycheck. It would take her a year working part time to match what she stole from Ursula.

Then late one night after a particularly long and slow shift, Gabbie started talking with some of the wait staff. They told her of a gentlemen's club where women earned $500 to $2,000 in cash in one night. They told her, "If you have a good body and can stomach strange men groping you, then you can make good money." Gabbie knew she was qualified.

It started as an occasional, once a week shift just to give her a boast in the money coffers. But within three months, she was hooked on the fast cash and stripping became her profession.

After Mary moved to California, they stayed in touch for about a year until Mary got pregnant with her first of three children. Gabbie never visited her and only saw pictures of Mary's children through social media. Mary represented Gabbie's last significant personal relationship. After they drifted apart, she kept all relationships, friendship or otherwise, completely superficial. If she was with anyone, it was to cure brief moments of feeling lonely or bored.

And for the time being, Miki was that cure, but what she didn't know was that he would become much more.

CHAPTER SIX:
A FUNERAL WITH RON POE

1 0 a.m. on Saturday, Miki and Gabbie were lying in bed after an evening of hard drinking and rough sex. They both retreated to the soft glow of their smartphones. Gabbie flipped through Facebook and Instagram. Miki flipped through the newspaper. Then he saw the article that would change his life.

Chandler Murray was dead. According to the article, he was a beloved lawyer and former legislator who lost his license when his paralegal embezzled over $5 million. But to Miki, he was a mentor and one of his only positive male role models. As a second year law student, Miki took Chandler's real estate class. At that time, Chandler was immensely successful and took a liking to Miki. Chandler saw Miki as an average student with above average potential. They spent countless hours together over lunch and the occasional happy hour. Miki even clerked for him.

The funeral was today; service began at 11:00 a.m. Miki smelled like a whiskey factory but had to go. Miki would not lose a wink of sleep if he missed the funeral of his mother or father. But he could not miss this. And he demanded that his only law school friend, Ron Poe, join him. Miki threw on his only pair of unwrinkled dress pants and clean button-down Oxford. After guzzling down two cups of coffee strong enough to melt barnacles from a ship, Miki met Ron at the funeral.

Ron was startled when Miki knocked on the window of his car. He had been there almost an hour waiting for his arrival. Ron didn't know Chandler, but It was yet another favor to his longtime friend. They missed the viewing and service, but made it in time to watch the coffin lowered into the ground. Ron was pissed to throw away a Saturday on this exercise.

But then again, Ron was always pissed. Never did a more successful, unhappy white male exist than Ron Poe. He met Miki in their first year of law school. Ron was 22 years old going on 42. He was 5'10 and completely bald. He shaved his head when he realized that he had more hair on his back than on his head. His parents were both lawyers. His father was the managing partner at a large insurance defense law firm. His mother was a cold-hearted person who specialized in intellectual property law. They had one child and were determined that he would not disappoint.

Ron once told his parents that he wanted to be a regular person and not a professional. He just wanted a normal, happy life, like a postman or restaurant manager. They told him if he got anything less than a graduate degree then he would never see them again. They told him that his genetics dictated that he would be a professional success even at the cost of personal happiness.

In college, Ron met Lillian Spring. She was the eldest daughter of Julius Spring. Since Reconstruction, the Spring family had inhabited (and essentially owned) a small county in western South Carolina. Lil's dad was a second-generation state senator. She and Ron went on three dates. She was pregnant by the third date and her freshman year in college.

Ron was aged by marriage, parenthood, and meeting his parents' expectations. His thick head of blonde hair was gone by his junior year of college. His size 28-waist jumped to a size 36. Meanwhile, Lil's beauty intensified with age. She would sometimes get drunk and introduce Ron as her father at parties. The sad part was that everyone believed it. Lil was seen as a young mother and Ron was a middle-aged dad. She did not indulge the adventurous spirit of her youth and that would come to haunt them. By the time Ron entered law school, he was living his parents' dream—professional success at personal sacrifice.

Ron met Miki as part of a study group for first year law students. Their topic was Property Law. It was Ron, Miki and three attractive female law students in the group. Miki had sex with all girls, including twice with all three at the same time. Ron loathed and envied Miki. He was a father, while Miki partied with college seniors and crammed his way to passing grades in law school.

Eventually, Ron and Miki comprised the entire study group. The girls found it very awkward to study with

Miki, given their shared experiences. But like everything in his life at that time, things worked out for Miki. Ron's lineage gave him access to outlines, the Holy Grail of law school. Older students took classes and created outlines that were passed along to a select few law students. They were Crib Notes for the hardest classes.

Slowly, the relationship between Miki and Ron transformed into something real. Law school is the equivalent to intellectual boot camp. It is a mass of Type-A personalities vying for success and survival at the cost of their colleagues. The key is to find someone that doesn't have a hidden agenda based on your failure—you need to find someone to trust. Miki and Ron trusted one another. Their study hall meetings became lunch meetings and then dinner at Ron's house. Lil's youthful, playful side enjoyed Miki, while her motherly side liked hearing her children call him "Uncle Mik." Miki enjoyed that as well.

Their graduation from law school epitomized the differences between the men. Miki's family celebration consisted of his parents taking him to Olive Garden. His father drank a few Bud Lights too many and regaled Miki with his feats of shooting defenseless prey. His mother lectured about the cruelties of killing animals. It was her Vegan phase. Miki experienced an epic lower class moment when his parents' fight over the value of an animal's life led them to being thrown out of Olive Garden before their undercooked pasta could hit the table.

Meanwhile, Ron's celebration was held at the city's most prestigious club. Between his in-laws and parents, the upper echelons of the state's political and legal communities were congratulating him. Miki joined the party after leaving the dynamic duo of dysfunction that he called his parents. Ron made sure that Miki was part of the celebration and not just a guest. Miki and Ron were more than just friends—they had become brothers.

After law school, they remained close even as their professional paths were headed in polar-opposite directions. Miki took his job at the plaintiff's firm and Ron started his professional career as an insurance drone with his father's law firm.

Before Miki faltered, Ron leaned on Miki as he would a brother. The life of privilege with Lil did not quell his depression over living a life for his parents. They shared nights when Miki talked Ron from divorcing to start his life anew.

"Don't worry about your parents or peers. Don't let them make you feel like you have sacrificed life in order to be successful. You have not sacrificed anything. Your life with Lil is good…no…it is great." Miki would proclaim at the end of a bourbon-laced evening. "You just think it sucks because it is what your parents wanted."

But after Sullivan's Island, Miki needed help. He turned to alcohol and happy hours to ease his own pain, and Ron's issues had not been a focus of conversation for almost eight years.

So when Miki asked him to attend the service for Chandler Murray, he obliged.

Miki insisted on I-Hop after the funeral. His mind was in a haze and his body was famished. He had not eaten in nearly three days. Miki was on a steady diet of sex and liquor.

"Why are we eating here?" Ron asked.

"Carbs my friend. Carbs," Miki replied as he scanned the laminated menu. "And judging from your waist line, that isn't a term foreign to your diet." Miki smiled. "Your wife looks like a model and you...her older, perverted agent."

"Ah, fat jokes. How original," Ron said. "Should I resort to career jokes?"

The male psyche between close friends is a tricky beast. The key is to cut deep enough without scraping the bone. The line between good-natured ribbing and outright venom is fine and blurred. If the cut is not too deep, then the friendship is superficial. If the cut is too deep, then someone is going to get punched. It was a miracle that a punch had never been thrown between either of them.

"If that is your tool of choice," Miki continued to study the menu.

"Tell you what, I will bet you $1,000 that I can lose 30 pounds quicker than you can gain 30 new...paying clients," Ron grinned back, "which I estimate gives me between 3 to 5 years to lose 30 pounds.

Miki closed his menu with his decision made. "Well I have news for you, my obese friend," he replied.

"The strip club case." Ron nodded and also closed his menu. "Yes, I heard. You have created the sentinel legal case about sex toys as weaponry in a public establishment built on exploiting women. Well done, Justice Holmes."

"Didn't your firm defend that?" Miki asked as he pointed to Ron. "Why did you send one of your drones? Why didn't *you* do it?"

"I am busy with bigger cases. We leave the turds to the associates."

"You mean drones?"

"They're associates. They are associates who make a lot more than you," Ron fired back.

The waitress provided a distraction to the sparring match.

"Y'all decide?" she asked.

"Yes ma'am!" Miki exclaimed. "I will have a sweet tea with extra lemons and a Fresh and Fruitie, Tootie-Fruitie breakfast." He paused and looked at Ron. "And my well-nourished colleague will have the yogurt and fresh fruit cup with a side of hot tea." He paused. "Hold the cream."

Ron glared at him.

"Our 30 days starts today, Chubs." Miki grinned.

The waitress looked at Ron to confirm the order. He begrudgingly nodded.

"You don't even have $1,000," Ron gritted.

"No, I have $10,000 because of your worthless drone," Miki got distracted. "What is that?" Miki nodded to the door.

Ron turned his head like a rubbernecker on the highway. He saw a 5'7 slender, green-eyed blonde whose taste for fashion exhibited her figure and success. She was dressed in a handmade Rubinacci suit and wore a pair Manolo Blahniks.

"What is that doing in here?" Ron asked. It was a question that was shared by everyone in the restaurant. Ron became nervous, as she appeared to be making a beeline to their table. He reverted to his law school days when he deferred to Miki when it came to the company of attractive women. "Um, Miki. She is coming this way. What do we do?" he whispered.

"We pray for low standards," Miki said as he smiled toward the beautiful goddess.

"Which one of you is Miki Martin?" It was cold voice not befitting of such a warm and inviting-looking creature.

"That's me." Miki raised his hand with a smile.

"That's him," Ron, the skilled construction litigator, fumbled for words in her presence. He pointed at Miki.

"Yeah, judging from your dining choice, that sounds exactly correct," she replied. She pulled a chair from the table next to them and sat down. She didn't bother asking the patrons at the table if anyone was using it.

"I don't have much time," she huffed.

"What are you, a spy?" Miki laughed. "Is there a radioactive device underneath the I-Hop?" Miki tried a little flirtation to ease her attitude. Ron let out a nervous chuckle.

She glared at Ron. He looked down at the table liked a whipped pup. She whipped her head around at Miki.

"I am the girl who just buried her father," she replied without a hint of emotion. "I am Katherine Murray."

Miki felt horrible. He knew her history. She suffered through the train wreck that was her mother and the torments of her father. He was embarrassed over his cavalier sexual advances at the daughter of his late mentor. He was humbled by his missteps.

"Oh my God, I am so sorry. I had no idea. It has just been a rushed morning and I didn't know of his death. Ron and I got over here as soon as…"

"By rushed, do you mean hung over?" She hissed as she looked at Ron. He kept his head down and focused on the table.

"Excuse me," Miki mustered, praying for his sweet tea to arrive. He knew he needed an infusion of caffeine and sugar. She was correct. Miki's hangover was massive, but he was still reeling by the ugliness being spewed by such a gorgeous person. "Are you sure you're Chandler Murray's daughter? My law professor?"

"Yes, you arrogant ass. Did you think I concocted that story in order to stroll into an I-HOP to spend time with you and Rain Man over there?" she replied. She leaned back in her chair and took a sip from Ron's water. "You're just as advertised."

"Well, you aren't," Miki replied.

She set down the plastic glass with a hard thud. "Guess I will just have to spend hours in therapy learning to live with the fact that I didn't live up to your expectations. Or," she continued to drink Ron's water without any resistance from him, "I can just continue to live my life as a real lawyer in a really big law firm in a really big city making over $500,000 a year."

"I guess someone has to blow the boss," Miki fired back.

She chuckled. "On my death bed, I will want my entire time with you and Bob's Big Boy over here..."

"Hey," Ron looked up.

"Back." She finished.

"Somehow on your deathbed, I think you will see a lot of red and feel intense heat," Miki replied.

"Cute," she replied.

"So, Katherine?" Miki asked.

"Let's go with Miss Murray," she interrupted.

"No Mister in your life. What an absolute shock?" Miki replied.

Ron laughed.

"Why don't you just keep looking at the table before my law firm buys your firm out and then you are fat *and* unemployed," she snarled at Ron.

"Well you're about as charming as an angry yellow jacket, *Miss* Murray. Since you're being blunt, allow me to return the favor. What the fuck do you want?" Miki stared directly at her. He was not fazed by her beauty but was instead battling every urge to punch her freshly manicured face.

"I want to make my flight and leave you hicks to continue to rot away in this cesspool you charmingly call home." Katherine harbored a great deal anger at the state and town that dismantled her father. But she was equally angry with him. She blamed him for getting blindsided by the very political system that he helped shape during his time in the legislature.

"I think anyone who meets you down here will want to make sure that you make that flight as well," Miki replied.

"Ah, so now we have two things in common."

"What's the other? You have a penis?" Miki glanced down at her pelvic region. Ron laughed again only to be met by another hard glare from the unwanted tourist. He continued to look at the table.

"Don't mind him," Miki said pointing at Ron, "He gets intimidated by beautiful women unless he gets to bill his hourly rate. Although based on this pleasant exchange, beauty is truly only skin deep for you."

She ignored Miki's comments. "The other thing we have in common is that we are personal representatives for my father's estate. You and me, Whiskey Boy."

Miki was humbled by the appointment. He had not seen Chandler in years and yet, he wasn't forgotten. He also realized that based on his brief interlude with Katherine, Chandler probably knew that his only child was a bitch and simply didn't want her in charge.

"Don't get excited. You're not in the will. And actually, you are the successor personal representative which means you only administer the estate if I cannot or do not want to."

"I know. I took Wills and Estates in law school as well."

"Amazing, this state teaches more than racism and having sex with relatives."

Ron chuckled. They both stared at him. "That's not funny," Miki instructed.

"So, I have a proposal for you." She reached into her purse and pulled out a document. "You sign this order and I will pay you $5,000 to be the personal representative of the estate." She then threw him a $2,500 check.

Miki passed Ron the order. Ron finally looked up from the table.

"See, I told you. When he senses an opportunity to bill, he becomes immune to your looks," Miki said as he pointed to Ron.

"I see that." She glanced in Ron's direction. "Don't worry, it is properly executed. I had lawyers in my firm prepare it."

Miki looked at the check. "This ain't $5,00."

"Good to know that y'all are learning math down here," Katherine mocked.

"That's real funny." Miki paused. "But that still doesn't add another $2,500 to this check."

"You get the other half when the estate is closed and all assets are in my name. That represents about 10 times more than the normal fee. It is a sweet deal." She turned her attention to Ron. "Isn't it tons of fun?"

"Depends on how big the estate is," Ron replied.

"See, billable opportunity." Miki pointed at Ron.

"There is a safety deposit box and a parcel of land in Florida. All you have to do is close the box with the bank, do an inventory of its contents, and deed the parcel to me."

"Then $5,000 does sound reasonable," Ron said.

"So relieved that you agree," Katherine barked. "Because when I climb on that plane today, I hope it will be the last time I touch the soil of this God forsaken state."

"We're going to miss you!" Miki exclaimed with a Grinch-like grin.

"Frankly, if it weren't for the land in Florida, I would not have even come to his funeral."

"Your dad had land in Florida?" Ron asked. "He died as a ward of the state."

"My grandmother had a dream that she would retire and live by the ocean. So, many years ago she bought a ridiculous two-acre tract in the middle of nowhere. It only had trees and a view of the ocean. It was located in a then unknown area called Islamorada."

"Florida Keys," Ron interjected.

"Impressive." Katherine covered her mouth. "So they teach you Math and about the contiguous United States down here?"

"And your grandmother never got down there?" Ron asked.

"Nope." Katherine finished Ron's water. "But I am. I am going to work 10 more years, build a massive home down there and retire while the two of you are here toiling away in your miserable lives."

"Well, that is valuable information! I need to know where to send Christmas cards and shit like that. Gotta keep in touch. Because this has been an absolute pleasure," Miki replied.

"As much as I would love to stay here and envelope your smell of Bourbon-filled sweat and trade legal jabs with fat Lex Luther over there, I need to know if you will simply take my money," Katherine said as she slammed Ron's plastic glass to the table.

"You know, you came in here hot as hell. You smelled like coconut and cucumber. Now you are gross. Your once intoxicating scent fills my nasal cavities like the smell of sulfur," Miki fired back as he got inches from her face.

"Go easy." Ron grabbed Miki's shoulder and gently pushed back into his booth.

Miki regained his composure upon seeing the waitress arrive with their food. He squeezed the lemons into his tea and guzzled half of it. "Our food is here. I would ask you to join us but," Miki paused, "I would rather eat hot garbage alone than dine on a fine meal with you."

"Just take my fucking money and do what I ask." She held out the key to the safety deposit box.

"Miki, just do it. At least Chandler will have someone who cares about him to administer his final affairs," Ron said as he stared at the healthy breakfast before him.

"That's sweet," she said pointing at Ron's breakfast as ordered by Miki. "Why don't you go ahead and send back that half ass attempt of a diet order and get a plate of lard-ridden crap? We both know that you are dying to.

Miki snatched the key from her. She smiled as she reached for her business card from her Louis Vuitton purse.

"Here is my card. I won't give you my cell number. Just go through the switchboard and leave a message on my voicemail. But only call when it is absolutely necessary."

"Ah, Boston," Miki said as he looked at the card. "You may want to stay away from the Salem area. They tend to burn people like you up there."

She stood up without returning her chair to the patrons that she took it from. She looked at her Rolex and smiled again. "Well counselors, I am afraid that our time together has come to a merciful end. Good luck enduring the misery that is your lives down here. I must return to civilization." And she made her exit.

"You know they say that you can take the girl out of the South but not the South out of the girl. I don't think that applies to her," Ron observed.

Miki chuckled as he shoved his plate away. "I am not hungry. Do you…"

"Don't say it."

"Want it." Miki said with a smile. "Maybe a little afternoon snack later for you?"

The bank was Miki's first stop on Monday morning. As usual, there wasn't much going on at his office. Chandler's safety deposit box was located at his bank. Miki deposited Katherine's check and then retrieved the contents of the box. In it, Miki found a few Treasury bonds, a collection of old baseball cards, and a white expandable folder wrapped with a rubber band. The original band had long since vanished from overuse.

He cashed in the bonds and went to a local hobby shop to sell the cards for half of their value. He pocketed $7,000. Miki knew that it should have gone to Katherine as her share of the estate. He assumed that she would have used it to add yet another piece of furniture to what Miki knew was an already over-furnished million dollar condo. He relished stealing from her.

He threw the folder marked "Brown Recluse" in the back seat of his car.

CHAPTER SEVEN:
ELAD PATTERSON

Like any large corporation, Practical Solutions had a troubleshooting division known as the Progressive Rights Division. According to the tax returns, the division was dedicated to pairing companies in need of a tax deductible, charitable donation with third-world countries needing financial help.

There were no actual employees; rather, all work was outsourced to independent contractors. The company wanted to avoid any liability for the acts of these independent agents. The Progressive Rights Division existed to correct any errors made during the vetting process of a candidate. For example, a few years ago P.S. certified a potential gubernatorial candidate, only to discover she had a secret mistress that no one knew existed…mainly because it was her mother-in-law.

P.S. discovered this fact because of the long time maid in the candidate's family. The maid was fired and, more importantly, disgruntled. She had regional tabloids in a bidding war for her story. The bidding war was never won. The maid died in an unfortunate one-car collision before anyone could obtain the rights. P.S.'s CEO would brag to would-be clients, "our vetting was correct; it just needed a little push from Progressive Rights."

For the PRD (like the military, the company loved acronyms), Elad Patterson was its top "independent contractor." He was 5'10 with the build of a spaghetti noodle. He had a pale complexion tattooed with freckles. His thick set of hair was light orange. His lips were almost unperceivable, more pink than red with a thin brown birthmark extending the length of his lower lip.

His eyes were small and sunken into his head. Elad didn't mind that feature of his complexion because of his Gilbert's syndrome, a harmless liver condition that turns the whites of eyes yellow. But for Elad, it was just another item on the laundry list of his physical imperfections. There was only one that really disturbed him—his micropenis—an actual medical term meaning his erection is half the size of normal. According to his last measurement, he was precisely two and one-half inches when fully erect.

The only thing more grotesque than his appearance was his mind. Elad was a serial killer who simply found employment doing what he loved. Born and raised in Birmingham, Alabama, he was the fifth of seven children. He was raised as a strict Catholic but the power of Christ could not exorcise the demons in his soul. His classmates nicknamed him Lucy, short for Lucifer.

The signs were there well before graduating preschool. He was that kid who took a magnifying glass to ants and climbed trees to touch a nest of bird eggs to ward off the mother from returning.

The older he grew, the more pronounced his sinister acts became. He was the first suspect when a steel garbage drum was discovered in the woods. It was covered with a large piece of heavy plywood and several rocks. Animal control found the drum filled with the remains of several puppies and kittens drowned in a mixture of bleach and water. Elad found the strays, threw them into the drum, and then covered the top.

Elad was the first name to have been mentioned in the fictional game of "Who blew up the school?"

Elad was a junior in high school when he met the most significant male role model of his life. He was working part time as cashier/file clerk in a gun store with a gun range in the back. Ted Fellows was a frequent customer and, at that time, the top independent contractor with PRD. Fellows took an interest in Elad.

It didn't take much intuition to recognize that Elad was definitely a loner in this world. Ted Fellows was also a loner in high school. He was a late bloomer who didn't lose his virginity until 20 years old. But once he sprouted, Fellows unleashed his stored sexual frustrations on a different woman every week. With his dark hair and piercing blue eyes, he was a red neck version of James Bond. Elad was in awe of him and Fellows saw a chance to recruit new talent.

At first, it was the shooting range. Fellows was a sniper in the military and taught Elad how to shoot and handle a gun. Gradually, they spent time away from the shooting range. Elad felt like a friend with a major celebrity. Everywhere they went, Fellows was recognized and immediately welcomed. Fellows took him to bars and Elad would stare in amazement as Fellows had two or three women fawning over him. Most of the time, Fellows would get too drunk and Elad had to drive Fellows and his date home.

Elad would routinely pretend to fall sleep on the couch as a rouse to listen as Fellows took out years of frustrated teenage sexual energy on some lowly piece of Alabama white trash.

For Fellows, he had lived Elad's high school experience. He often thought what it would have been like to have a mentor like himself during those miserable years. He simply wanted to help but, instead, he unwittingly fertilized Elad's devilish soil.

He then proclaimed that Elad would lose his virginity before graduating high school.

"You will not be like me, Elad," Fellows blurted as he finished a fifth of Jack.

"Lad, all this time and you still mispronounce it. It is Lad. The "E" is silent."

"Then I should just call you E," Fellows joked, "and so, E, my good lad, we will get you laid!"

Fellows and Elad cruised the streets of Birmingham until they found just the right hooker. She was a darker skinned Hispanic teenager working the streets after dropping out of high school.

They went back to Fellows' place. While Fellow sat on the couch watching *Black Hawk Down* for the 50th time, Elad took the poor girl to the bedroom.

At first, Fellows dismissed her laughter as Elad's feeble attempts to pleasure her. But then he heard Elad scream, "Shut the fuck up!" That was followed by her quick, high-pitched female scream and a thud. It was silent after that.

Fellows jumped from the couch and began pounding on the locked bedroom door. It felt like an eternity before Elad opened it. His head hang down, chin to sternum. He never looked up. Fellows glanced at Elad and then turned his attention to the bed. It was empty. He looked closer and saw a small pool of blood on the floor at the base of the bed. He glared back at Elad. Again, there was no reaction.

Ted Fellows cautiously approached the pool of blood. He followed the stream of blood to the source. It was a three-inch gash in the girl's neck. Her naked body looked like it was painted in crimson red.

"What the fuck just happened?!" Fellows exclaimed.

Elad slowly lifted his head in her direction and let out a sigh. "I got underdressed and she started laughing at me. And, she wouldn't stop." Elad paused. "So, I made her stop." Elad's voice didn't match his appearance. It was a deep, almost baritone sound drenched in a thick Southern accent. It made his appearance even more eerie.

"So she saw your dick and you went OJ Simpson on her?" Fellows replied.

"Like I said, she wouldn't shut up," Elad whispered. He hung his head again.

Fellows went back to the living area to retrieve a bottle of Jack. He came back and took a hard swig.

"Is this your first time?" Fellows asked.

Elad paused. "Well, she and I didn't get actually get a chance to…"

"Killing, Elad. Not fucking. Is this your first time killing someone?"

"Oh. Yes. I have never done anything like this." Elad was embarrassed because he misunderstood the question.

Fellows took another hard swig. "You seem to be very apathetic." Elad looked confused by the statement. "That means unemotional. You're pretty unemotional."

"And other than one statement, so are you," Elad observed.

"Fair enough." Fellows studied the body. He then offered Elad a swig. "Here, take some. It'll calm your nerves."

"But my nerves are fine."

"I am sensing that," Fellows responded and then paused to soak in the blood bath that was once his bedroom. "So, where did you get the knife?"

Elad took another hit of the whiskey. He could feel the warmth of the alcohol roll down his throat and into his stomach. "You had it on your nightstand."

"Where did you put it?"

"I threw it out the window," Elad proclaimed.

"Never do that," Fellows cautioned. "You always take the weapon with you. It is almost impossible to convict without a weapon."

"Yes, sir."

"Elad, do you have any idea what I do for a living?" Fellows asked.

"No, sir."

"I work for a company. It's called PRD. It is a subsidiary of a larger corporation. Elad, do you know what subsidiary means?"

"Not really."

"That's okay because knowledge of vocabulary doesn't mean you're smart. Just means you can win a Spelling Bee."

Elad let out a much needed laugh.

"I didn't know what it meant before I started working for them, but now I do. And they pay me well and could possibly pay you well. But you would have to learn to contain your reactions."

"Yes, sir. Normally, I do, but she just pissed me off."

"Clearly," Fellows said as he widened his eyes. "But my company…"

"Subsidiary, you mean." Elad interrupted. It sounded like a Southern Barry White was talking.

"Yes." Fellow smiled, oblivious to the corpse on his bedroom floor. "My subsidiary will not pay for recklessness, which is what this is. You follow?"

"Yes, sir," Elad replied.

"I am actually a wealthy man." Elad looked around at the drab apartment.

"Oh don't let this fool you. I live modest and save. I am about five years away from retiring." Fellows grabbed the bottle from Elad and took a gulp.

"Really?"

"Yep. I figured I would get religious after I retire and ask for God's forgiveness and all that. Retire, repent and go to heaven." Fellows smiled.

"How do I get your job?" Elad asked.

"Well," Fellows took a long and deliberate sip from the bottle," You're about to find out. See, my company will not be happy with my retirement. You see, they don't like good folks to leave. We're kinda hard to come by."

"Yes, sir."

"We have a certain skill set that you won't find on Monster.com."

"I imagine not, sir."

"But," Fellows returned the bottle to Elad, "they will be a lot less unhappy if I find a replacement. I think that could be you."

"Me?" This was Elad's idol. He was glad just to be considered his lackey. And now, he was being asked to replace him? Elad couldn't contain his sinister smile.

Fellows retrieved a can of Kodiak Wintergreen dip from his back pocket. Again, he was the Alabama version of James Bond. He placed a large hunk between his gum and lip.

"Well, you just killed that young lady with the remorse of a great white."

"Yes, sir. I guess I am. Do you mind?" Elad motioned at the can. Fellows offered it to him. Elad took an even bigger chunk than Fellows and put it in his mouth. The fifth of Jack was gone. Elad used the bottle for his first spit and then handed it to Fellows.

Fellows looked at the body and remarked, "Boy, it took me years to learn how to react to killing someone the way you have." His first victim was a single car collision involving the maid of a future governor. "You have the heart of a killer. Most of those type of people go to jail, but listen to me and I can get you paid to do what you love."

Elad nodded as he grabbed the bottle for another spit.

"Well, are you in? I understand if you want to take some time to think about it because it is a lonely life and…"

"I am in," Elad interrupted. "I am definitely in. I have known for quite a while that I was destined for loneliness." Elad paused. "And, I am fine with it."

"Well alright." Fellows grinned.

"So when do we start?"

"We officially start after you graduate high school."

"Subsidiary," Elad interjected.

The subsidiary requires at least a high school degree."

"Yes, sir. I am two months away."

"But unofficially, we start tonight by cleaning up the remains of this poor soul." Fellows pointed to the body.

"Alright. Well, this is my first so I don't have a lot of…"

"Yeah, I figured that after you told me you threw the murder weapon outta the window," Fellows interrupted.

"Yes, sir." Elad was embarrassed by his mistake, the mistake of throwing the murder weapon from the window. The girl was of no consequence.

"So this is what we're gonna do." Fellows spit another stream of brown tobacco into the empty bottle of Jack. "Down the street there is a mom and pop service station. They rent U-Hauls there."

"Yes, sir."

"They don't have any cameras or surveillance. And this time of night, no one will be on the roads. We will go there and I will show you how to hot wire a car."

"Yes, sir."

"And then, we're going to come back here and move all my furniture into this living room area so we rip up all of the carpet in this bedroom."

"I follow." Elad nodded.

"And by we, I mean you." Fellows pointed at Elad.

"Yes, sir." Elad smiled.

"Then we will wrap up this young lady in that carpet and put her into the U-Haul."

"And by we, you mean me," Elad responded.

"Very good, Mr. Subsidiary." Fellows grinned. "Then, you will drive the U-Haul and follow me to an abandoned farm house about 100 miles from here."

"Yes, sir."

"There is a fresh roll of paper towels in my kitchen." Fellows paused. "What do you think we, and I mean you, should do next?" He wanted to test his protégé.

"I will unravel those paper towels and shove the first one into the gas tank of the U-Haul. I will unravel the entire roll and then light the last one. It will be like a long fuse attached to dynamite."

"Nicely done." Fellows grabbed his car keys and they embarked on the journey to dispose of Elad's first body. Elad would remember this moment when he used the same method to dispose of Fellows' body.

Elad made his name as PRD's best "independent contractor" in another gubernatorial election scandal. Elite vetted a candidate and informed its clients that he would be a perfect fit for their interests in a mid-western state. Their clients wanted a governor that would acquiesce to their demands for exorbitant tax incentives to build manufacturing plants in the state.

But the major issue was his opponent. He was a well-liked incumbent who raised the state's minimum wage law and lowered the restriction of union activity in the mostly Democratic state. The P.S. candidate was a ten-point underdog with the election only a month away. He was the first P.S. client to be vetted who would not win. The CEO proclaimed that it was a job for PRD. "That division will no longer be relegated to covering up our mistakes. That division will ensure that our candidates win."

Elad and Fellows designed the plan to destroy the opponent. The incumbent and his wife were squeaky clean but his 18-year-old son was a homosexual with a nasty drinking problem. The couple had used the struggles with their son's sobriety and acceptance of his lifestyle as a selling point in the previous election.

"We face challenges like all families and because of that, we know you need a government interested in helping you face the challenges of life." It was the signature line in the closing argument of each of the incumbent's debates.

Elad and Fellows scouted the governor's son for a week. They had heard that he had fallen off the wagon. The governor and his staff were too focused on the new agenda after the re-election. They were convinced of victory and no longer worried about the vices of his wayward son.

After following him to a local bar, Fellows approached him posing as a recent divorcee. His marriage ended when he told his wife that he was gay. Fellows, of course, was the only choice for the role. They wanted to entice the young man. Elad's physique would only repel him. After a few drinks, Fellows gained the trust of the incumbent's son. He told the young man of a shopping mall on the other side of town where he could let his hair down. Other than a few shops, it was essentially abandoned and became a meeting place for customers and male prostitutes. Elad used his connections with P.S. for undercover city cops to be in place when Fellows arrived with his guest. Elad also made sure that reporters from the state's largest newspaper were nearby to capture the drama.

The cops busted down the bathroom stall door to find the incumbent's son on the commode with a male prostitute performing oral sex. Two reporters stood on adjacent stalls taking phones on smartphones. It went viral before anyone was booked.

The story made headlines in every state paper and was featured on most political satire shows. The P.S. candidate won by nine points...a 19-point swing courtesy of PRD. And it gave Fellows the money he needed to retire. He announced his retirement to PRD the next day.

That night, Fellows and Elad celebrated the success of the score and Elad's succession. They frequented five different bars before ending the evening at Fellow's apartment. After consuming enough brown liquor to send a normal person to the hospital, Fellows announced that he was going to bed. Elad followed him.

Fellows fell on the floor as he tried to climb into bed. Elad whipped out his 9mm Beretta and put a bullet in his head. P.S. didn't want any loose ends. Fellows should have just left without announcing his departure. The succession was complete.

Eight years later and a month after Grafton learned of his appointment as a P.S. vetted candidate, Elad was at the Westin in downtown Charlotte for a meeting with his contact. Elad never met with the same person. Each day began with a phone call from P.S. A monotone, computer-generated voice would tell him the code word of the day. If he called into the agency or met with his contact, he would have to give the code word. Today's code word was "Omaha."

Elad stared from the window of his 11th floor suite, eyeing the peaceful skyline of the Queen City. His moment of solitude was interrupted by a knock at the door. Elad looked through the peephole. It was some nameless, faceless person from P.S. It was always a stranger. He never took the time to soak in their features. The conversation would be direct and quick and he would never see them again.

"Yes," Elad cautiously replied.

"Omaha," the stranger replied.

Elad opened the door. He was met with the normal reaction to his physical appearance, a mixture of pity and laughter. Not grotesque enough for pity, but just the right amount of ugly to cause a person to giggle.

"Why don't you take a seat?" Elad directed the stranger to the couch in the middle of the suite. Elad sat in the chair next to him. He took a bite from his overcooked, hotel hamburger.

"Man, that burger looks like shit," the stranger replied.

"Let's dispense with mindless chit-chat. That's for people that may actually see each other again. What do you have for me?" Elad coldly asked.

"Grafton Hood. Does that name ring a bell?" The stranger was agitated by Elad's abrupt response. His agitation caused him to forget the monster on the other end of the conversation.

"Yes. He's been vetted," Elad snapped at him. He paused as he grit his teeth in frustration. "Let's do this. You assume that I know much more than you and you tell me exactly what they want me to do. In turn, you can get the fuck outta here so I can choke down this shoe leather they call a burger."

Elad's beady, yellow eyes locked with the stranger. The stranger was petrified. He knew Elad's reputation and didn't want to risk offending him.

"There's a reporter in town," he stammered. "He's from some national tabloid. He's doing a piece on that serial killer." The stranger looked at the honor bar and spotted a bottle of Grey Goose. "Do you mind if I?" He pointed to the bottle. "I will pay you back."

"Sure, it's on the subsidiary's dime." Elad smirked. This stranger outweighed him by 75 pounds and was 4 inches taller. But if Elad farted without warning, the guy would have the rug drenched in piss. Everyone in PRD knew his reputation and the stranger was scared that he offended him. "You wanna tell me about this reporter, big boy?" Elad asked.

The stranger downed his mini bottle. "Right. Sorry about that. I just got a little nervous."

"Its all good." Elad toyed with him taking pleasure in his obvious discomfort.

The stranger settled. "He's here on a story about the Billy Idol killer. He's gonna interview a relative of a victim. You know about that?"

"Again, assume that I know everything."

"Right, sorry. Can I get another mini bottle?"

"Of course you can." Elad said as he handed the bottle to him. "The subsidiary takes care of its own. Right?" Elad grinned.

"Uh," the stranger stuttered, "yes sir, I guess they do." He finished the second bottle quicker than the first. "Anyway, our information indicates that this reporter believes he is onto a major story. It is a story that could dismantle Hood."

"And we cannot have our vetting process compromised, now can we?"

"No, sir. No, we cannot. And while we don't know the exact details, we know he is trying to sell this story to some of the major networks. He sees it as his Watergate. I guess he fancies himself as a some sorta Bob Woodward."

"Am I to guess that he is staying in this hotel?" Elad's Southern baritone resonated through the suite.

"Yes, sir."

"And I am to make contact and neutralize this would-be agitator?"

"Ah, yes. Yes, sir. And as quickly as possible because…"

Elad interrupted him, "Hood has the abortion bill drafted and ready to roll. And it has to get passed in order to validate the list." The stranger pointed for a third mini bottle. "I think you've had enough."

"Yes, sir."

"What's he look like?"

A few minutes later, Elad was at the lobby bar looking for his mark. He found him in about 30 seconds. He was just as the stranger described him. He was in his late 30s, bad

comb over with tortoise-framed glass. He was not attractive or unattractive. He was simply a face in the room. He was incessantly texting on his smartphone, sipping a glass of cheap Pinot Noir.

"Are you Riley Gaines?" Elad asked.

Riley looked up from his phone and stared at Elad. It was the same look of pity and laughter. Elad shook it off.

"Well, are you?" Elad continued

"Are you Pippi Longstocking's ugly cousin?" Gaines was on his fourth glass.

"Depends on if her cousin works for CNBC." Elad motioned for the bartender. "Can I get a double shot of Old Scout?"

Gaines stopped texting. "Bullshit, Red. Show me some fucking credentials."

Elad whipped out a freshly pressed set of fake credentials, courtesy of the stranger. He took a slow sip of his drink.

"Measure up for you?" Elad asked. Riley nodded. "So I hear you have a great story?"

"I do! Gonna interview a relative of a victim about the Billy Idol killings. Fucking cops won't disclose any details but she will." Gaines finished his glass of red. Elad had another waiting on him. "It is amazing what money will do. We pay her a few thousand bucks and she will let the entire nation know the intimate details of the death of her niece."

"Am I to assume that this is a niece she doesn't know too well?"

"Absolutely correct. Saw her twice in the last three years. But, she was invited to the funeral and her little sister, the mother of the victim, shared with her all of the horrid details. And now, she will share those sordid details to me and the entire nation."

"Very excited for you."

"You know why he is called the Billy Idol killer?"

"Not a clue?"

"It is because of the song. You know the Billy Idol song 'Eyes Without a Face.' Do you know that song?" Gaines took a sip of his newest glass of red. His teeth and tongue were stained red.

"Yes, an obscure 80s song that should not have been made. There were a lot of those. But that's not the story I am talking about."

"You are a really unattractive person," Gaines exclaimed.

"Yes, I am fully aware." Elad knew his prey was drunk. It was time to pounce. "Again, I am not here about the Idol killer story."

"Do you know that when the cops find the bodies there is a song by Billy Idol playing in the background?"

"Fascinating, but again, not here about that story." Elad replied calmly. He stopped drinking. It was time to focus.

"Hell, yes, it is fascinating," Gaines slurred, "It took me two months to track that down."

"Mr. Gaines!" Elad raised his voice to command his attention. He feared that Gaines would pass out at the stool.

"Yep. That's me." Gaines raised his hand.

"I am here, or should I say, that CNBC is here to talk with you about the other story. The one involving Grafton Hood."

Gaines perked from his drunken stopper. "Hood! That guy's a twisted piece of shit." He slammed down his last glass of red. Elad summoned the bartender for one more glass of red and the check.

"What makes you say that? He is a conservative, black Republican from the South. That is a rare and formidable combination. How could you bring him down?

Gaines motioned him to come closer and then whispered. The stench of the wine from Gaines' breath hit Elad like a punch. "I have a whole fucking file."

"Bullshit." Elad goaded him.

"Bull-yes!"

"Bull-yes! Where? Where do you have this supposed file?"

"In my room," Gaines whispered. "Shhhh," he said as he put his index finger over his lips. "It's a big secret."

"Well, CNBC hasn't broken anything of any substance in a while. Why don't you finish that glass of wine and let's head up there to see what you have? We pay well for a good story."

Gaines paused at the invitation.

"And we would of course give you credit for the story," Elad continued. "Maybe get you out of writing for that rag you call a newspaper. Unless you like that?"

"I would rather be a telemarketer for eternity than write for that piece of shit." Gaines finished his last glass of wine. "C'mon."

Gaines' room was two floors below Elad's room. It took Gaines three tries to get the room key in the door. Elad followed behind him. Gaines never noticed Elad slip on a pair of surgical gloves.

After a few seconds of fumbling through his half-opened suitcase, Gaines emerged with the file.

"Here it is!" Gaines exclaimed holding the file in his hands. "It even comes with a DVD."

"A DVD of what?"

"Why are your hands in their pockets? Are you cold?"

"Mr. Gaines, a DVD of what?" Elad calmly asked.

Gaines lost his train of thought about Elad's hands. "Huh…oh. A DVD of the interview of the creator of the file." Gaines proudly proclaimed.

"And who would that be?"

"Chandler Murray! Esquire!" Gaines proclaimed.

Elad snatched the file from his hands and began to study it.

"Why are you wearing gloves?" Gaines inquired.

"I got a cold," Elad brushed him off. He continued to examine the file. "Have you watched this DVD?"

"Yep. It explains everything." Gaines continued to stare at the gloves. "What kinda cold?"

Elad placed the file and DVD on the dresser next to him. "Has anyone else seen this?"

"No! This is my story!"

"So no one else saw it?" Elad inquired.

"Well, the guy who made it. But he's dead. I think he recorded it himself."

"So just you and a dead guy? That's all?"

"Yep. So how much is this worth? A million, maybe two?"

"Oh, it is worth a lot." Elad replied in a monotone voice. He reached into his back pocket and retrieved an oyster knife. "Now, let's talk about this Idol killer."

Gaines eyes widened at the sight of the knife. "What?"

"The Idol killer. You know 'Eyes Without A Face.' Why do they call him that, again?"

"You're not from CNBC," Gaines slurred.

"Nope."

"Are you the guy? Are you the Idol killer?"

"No, I am not." Elad inched closer. "But I know what he does. Let's see if I can recreate that for you." Elad punched Gaines in the face with his right hand. Gaines hit the floor. Elad kicked him in the face, shattering his nose. Gaines was out cold.

"According to the files I have read, the killer knocks out his victims using physical force," Elad lectured to the unconscious body. "He then takes what the authorities believe is an oyster knife or sharpened spoon," he continued to lecture, "and removes their eyes."

Gaines' body convulsed as Elad methodically removed his eyes. Elad causally dropped the eyes onto Gaines' chest. "And hence, 'Eyes Without a Face'." Elad grabbed the file and causally left the room. He grabbed his cell phone and called P.S.

"We have a problem."

CHAPTER EIGHT:
STORM FROM BELOW

It was the last legislative session of Grafton's eight-year run as governor. The session was in full swing. Grafton had called a press conference to help the most important legislation of his political life gain traction. He stood at the statehouse stairs and stared at the sky.

A supercell is the scientific term for the most powerful thunderstorm. A supercell forming in early February is a rare event, but on this mild winter morning, one had formed and hovered directly over the state's capital. There was not a hint of blue in the sky. The rain had not started, but the roar of thunder alerted everyone that it was imminent.

The crackle of lightening made the hairs of the spectators stand on end. Everyone anxiously awaited Grafton's speech. They knew that rain could explode from above at any time, but they were willing to endure. Finally, they had someone to voice their position. Grafton was going to be a voice of power rather than compromise. There were 2,000 in attendance, all dressed totally in black and armed with black umbrellas to ward off the first signs of rain. There would be nothing that could dampen their spirits.

With the state capital as his backdrop, Grafton stood at the podium. In his black Armani suit, he was dressed for a funeral rather than a press conference. He tapped the microphones, more for effect than to ensure that they worked. Grafton cleared his throat and began his speech. There were no note cards or screens to lead him. He had memorized it three weeks ago. Now was the time to deliver.

"This isn't a speech," he paused, "it's a eulogy. A eulogy to express the sorrow for the loss of our moral standards."

The crowd responded with applause. The cameras rolled.

"Who here agrees that the line between what is right and what is wrong is more blurred than ever?"

The crowded resounded in unison with a "Yes!" There was a roar of thunder followed by a quick strike of lightening.

"And when we see the centerfielder drop an easy fly ball, we all wonder, why didn't he catch that?! Well, we shouldn't blame him too much because we are all dropping fly balls. We drop fly balls by allowing the Who here believes that the moral compass of our society is leading us to the agenda of the far left," Grafton paused again for effect. "Liberals...there, we'll say it. These liberals through social media and certain 'news' networks are leading us closer to their agenda rather than the agenda espoused by our forefathers in the Constitution and Declaration of Independence."

The crowd erupted.

"I don't believe that our forefathers, the authors of the greatest written documents since the Bible, envisioned that their words would be perversely interpreted to erode our moral fabric the way that these liberals have advocated!"

The almost all-white audience was overjoyed to hear those words uttered by their black, conservative governor.

"No! I don't think that Ben Franklin and Thomas Jefferson wrote the documents that created this country in order to forsake God and allow Americans to thrive on the desires of human flesh!"

You could barely hear Grafton over the din of applause and cheering. He raised his hands to quiet his supporters. The crowd hushed but still hung on his every word. The press corp continued to span its cameras between Grafton and the crowd.

With his low voice booming over the speakers, Grafton continued. "I think that they created those cherished documents to avoid the rule of a tyrannical government from far away. But now," Grafton paused again, "we now face a tyranny from within. It is a tyranny from people using the words of our forefathers, words crafted to free us, to imprison us in a world with no moral limits or boundaries."

The cameras continued to capture the crowd. The crowd exploded. Grafton had to silence them again.

"They have twisted our Bill of Rights to brainwash those in power to adhere to the standards of a loud but very small minority of people. We have been force-fed a moral agenda that offends the very being that created our planet! We are now required to tolerate more of what should be, and used to be, intolerable."

Grafton paused and took a sip of water from his Styrofoam cup. He laughed. "Those liberals are more offended by this Styrofoam cup than what is being broadcast on the airwaves of our nation."

The crowded laughed.

"That seems simple but just look back at history to see the standards of various civilizations. You only have to look at what they deemed entertainment to gauge the moral barometer of the people. Romans threw Christians in the Coliseum to be mauled by lions. And now our standard of entertainment is a steady diet of sex and violence streaming through our airwaves to be viewed by any child with the ability to turn on a television set. They are watching shows which have their own ratings…or rather, warnings!"

The crowd continued to laugh and cheer.

"Do you think our parents had ratings on their TV shows? No! And when I want to watch our national pastime on TV, I have to tell my children to leave the room when the commercials come on. How do you explain to a ten-year old why the blue pill is so important to a middle age man and his wife?!"

Grafton chuckled at his remark, just as he rehearsed. Plus, he had no children. "But knowing our liberal minority, we will soon see those same blue pill commercials showing a man and his husband!

Another laugh from the crowd followed by a roll of thunder from above.

Grafton took another sip of water. He held the Styrofoam cup up to the audience. Let's go green with our morality instead of just the environment!"

His supporters again erupted with applause and cheering—all captured by the press corp's cameras.

He raised his hands to hush them. Grafton pointed with his index finger extended. "Our society is the beach and the sea is morality, and we have been at low tide for far too long! Our beach needs to be cleansed by the sea of morality. We don't need to hold it at bay with concrete walls and bags of sand piled on by the liberals."

The cameras were focused on Grafton as he dictated from his bully pulpit. The press corp realized that this was not a press conference but rather his call to arms.

"And that cleansing starts with securing the most basic, fundamental right. It is the right to live. We have allowed our beach to be cluttered by the dead bodies of children. We have watched our elected officials accept a sadistic interpretation of our Bill of Rights to give people the inalienable right to kill a child!"

The crowd could not be contained; it was comprised only of supporters. Grafton had leaked out the contents of his speech to a select few religious leaders and other conservative minded groups.

He had to shout above their cheers. "Call me old school, but I don't think that Valley Forge was fought to allow us the right to kill an unborn child! And that same Bill of Rights also says that we don't have to just watch. We can change it!"

He waited and raised his hands to silence them again.

"That is why we are dressed in black. We are here to mourn the souls of millions of unborn children—not fetuses, but children. These are children that have been killed using our own Constitution as a sword to kill an unprotected, innocent life. Those liberals kill that life under the cloak of freedom and then they twist our Bill of Rights to vacuum the remains from the womb of his or her mother."

The press captured images of men and women crying over the image painted by his speech. The first raindrops finally began to fall, but no one raised an umbrella.

With his index finger raised upward, he continued. "This rain is a sign from above. It is like the liberals in this country. It may try to interfere with what we are supposed to do but"—another pause for affect—"it will not stop us. We will reclaim our beach and it starts by outlawing that abomination of a law allowing people to kill children. That is the first step in allowing the sea of morality to enter our shores!"

This time Grafton waited for the applause to quiet. He wanted the cameras to capture their enthusiasm. Grafton had also instructed his staff as to the placement of press cameras. All of the cameras were at ground level, making the crowd look several times larger than its actual size.

The rain started to pelt down like liquid marbles, but no one was leaving. They finally raised their black umbrellas in defiance. The crowds danced in joy to Grafton's every word.

One of Grafton's aides raised an umbrella to shield the governor. "I have proposed legislation to outlaw all abortions in this state! With no, and I mean *no*, exceptions! And while some see abortion as an antiquated political issue,"—another pause for effect—"to me, the murder of children will never be deemed an antiquated political issue!"

The crowd was in a perpetual state of unwavering support. The people in the back could barely hear him. The rain was becoming more pronounced. It soaked the statehouse grounds.

"And I know I will have a fight, but it is a fight from the same people who scream to protect the life of a serial rapist from execution. But they scream with a raspy tone. Their tone is raspy because their voice is hoarse from yelling to proclaim the right to kill a child." Grafton soaked in the applause. He once again did not silence them. "And to that end, I have proposed legislation that will really just piss them off."

Grafton laughed on cue and the crowd laughed with him.

"All abortions, and I am mean *all* abortions, will become illegal. If you are doctor that performs an abortion under my legislation, you have killed someone. That is a capital offense which means you will get the death penalty!"

The huddled, wet masses of 2,000 sounded like 10,000. Grafton had to shout above them.

"And if you are the mother who aborts her child, then the same charge! Capital offense! Death penalty!"

The thunder of support from the crowd far exceeded the thunder from above. Grafton had to scream into the microphone but, even then, it sounded like a whisper.

"We're going to let the sea of morality storm our beaches like our soldiers did in Normandy. Those were men who fought to protect a Bill of Rights that defined our children as children and not as biological objects. And we will continue their fight against genocide. But not the genocide of others, but the genocide of American children!"

Grafton could barely see the crowd through the sheets of water flowing from above. He waved off the umbrella offered and raised both arms. "We will protect our children!" He gave the crowd one last wave and left the podium.

He was quickly ushered into a black Cadillac Escalade parked about 100 yards away.

Pontet was in the rear seat of the car waiting for his arrival. He was on the phone trying to guide the feed of Grafton's speech to the major news networks. He ended his call as soon as Grafton sat down.

"Pretty bold, Governor," Pontet said in his most sarcastic of tones. He followed it with a smile that made Grafton want to break his nose.

"Fuck you."

"Hey, c'mon! What you said was inspirational. Look at that crowd. They are ready to kill any doctor who looks at a newborn the wrong way!" Pontet pointed to the huddled masses of hatred.

Grafton politely waved at his supporters and gave a false grin as they drove off. "You told me abortion was the issue so I wanted to make sure I didn't just give it lip service."

"Mission accomplished. No half-ass in that speech." Pontet smiled as he took as swig of gin from his silver flask. He offered some to Grafton but was waved off. "It could also be political suicide."

"Please," Grafton responded.

"You are proposing legislation to kill a mother who aborts a child conceived of rape and the doctor that helps her. All the while you proclaimed that anyone who disagrees with you is a Nazi."

"In this state, I could probably get re-elected or sent to the U.S. Senate for that legislation." Grafton stared out of the window. "But that's not what I want."

"Then what do you want, Governor Hood?" Pontet asked.

Grafton glared at him. "I want support from our boys in Atlanta for what I am doing. This is the only visible coverage of my efforts and I had to orchestrate the damn thing. If I am their real candidate, then where is the backing? Answer me that, Ginhead?"

Pontet took another sip from the flask. "This is your state. Why should they have to help you control your own fucking state? I am guessing that is their response."

"Because they get paid to back a winning candidate." Grafton's anger began to boil and he slapped the flask of gin from Pontet's hand. "I am the first black governor of this state, and want to be first black Republican in the White House. And that is something that the boys in Atlanta should want as much as me."

Pontet picked up his flask and calmly took another sip. "Grafton, your anger will catch up with you."

"Whatever. Let's not worry about my anger issues. Let's focus on getting the support of your company to match my efforts to get this propaganda passed. You know this legislation is bogged down, don't you?"

"Committee. Yes, we know." Pontet drank the last of his flask. "Julius Spring, right?"

"Yes, exactly. Senator Julius, pain in my ass, Spring. I didn't even know that the South created grey haired, white liberals."

"Well, he is the senior Democrat in the statehouse. What did you expect—his support?" Pontet raised his eyebrow. "I trust you *didn't* count on that especially now that you have branded a Swastika on the cheeks of his major political supporters."

"Well, I needed to do something to gain momentum for the bill. I have to thwart his efforts to bury this bill in a subcommittee. I need help."

"Again, that sounds like a you problem. If you cannot control your own state, then how can you lead a nation?" Pontet retorted.

Grafton grit his teeth. "Well, it is not exactly a tax reduction bill. I am trying to resurrect an issue that was placed in the political graveyard more than a decade ago." Grafton's anger was brewing again.

"You're not going to slap my flask again, are you?" Pontet placed his flask near his chest.

"Shut up."

Pontet reached into his leather briefcase and retrieved a manila folder. He tossed it into Grafton's lap. "This may help."

Grafton reviewed the contents. "Who is Miki Martin?"

"No, the question is who is Ron Poe?"

"Well, according to this, he is Martin's best friend."

"And Poe is the son-in-law of Senator Spring."

"And according to the file, this Martin fellow is a low-level scoundrel."

Pontet nodded. "Exactly. Maybe use this to gain leverage with Spring? At least enough to get your legislation to a vote on the floor."

Grafton continued to review the file. "Doubt it. But you know I will try."

"Oh, I know you will exploit every piece of information to your benefit." Pontet paused. Do you see anything else of interest in that file?"

"You tell me."

"Sullivan's Island. He had some trouble on Sullivan's Island."

"So?" Grafton asked.

"We have some lose ends on Sullivan's—rather, Charleston, to be precise."

"Does the P.S. know?"

"Well they do now. Murray made a fucking file." Pontet leaned over and stared directly into Hood's eyes. He was not afraid of any reaction at this point.

Grafton sat still. "I can take care of this," he said in almost a whisper, his voice tired from the speech.

"Yeah, and I heard that eight fucking years ago." Pontet said in disgust.

"What are they going to do?"

"Hood, you just need to get this legislation passed. I didn't show you that file as a leg up. I wanted you to see how easy it is to find anything about anyone. Are you reading me now?"

Grafton nodded.

"You've been vetted. You're the choice"

Grafton breathed an internal sigh of relief.

"And while this Charleston issue is unexpected, they cannot go back on their support of you. They cannot be wrong. They can never be wrong." Pontet continued.

"So, what's the plan?" Grafton asked.

"The plan is to announce your candidacy in June for next year's election. So," Pontet pointed at Hood, "you need to make good on your promise. Deliver the legislation. Because if you let them down, then not only will they not fix this issue, they will actually expose it to teach others a lesson about disappointing the organization."

"I understand," Grafton calmly replied.

"And don't worry, they will uphold their end of the deal. They have fixed bigger messes than this before."

"How?" Grafton couldn't help but ask.

"That's not your concern. They have the right man for the job. Now, you need to show that you're the right man for this job." Pontet pointed to the state house in the distance as the car continued to travel. "Just get it passed."

CHAPTER NINE:
NATURAL REACTION

It was 2:00 in the morning and Miki's alarm went off. It was time to pick up Gabbie. Miki had passed out only three hours before. He gingerly sat up in bed and slowly put both feet on the floor. He had a 50/50 chance of standing or falling flat on his face. But she would be waiting, so he had to risk it. Miki stood up. He was a little unsteady but at least he was standing.

"Success," he said aloud. He grabbed his only clean pair of pants—blue jeans he had worn for the last three days. He scoured the floor for a shirt that didn't smell of sweat and alcohol. Another success—he found a white, button-down Polo, normally reserved for court. Given his paucity of courtroom appearances, those shirts were always in abundance.

He guzzled a bottle of water and took another with him for the road. That was enough to make the trek to her. She could drive back.

It was almost 2:30 a.m. Miki vigilantly watched the highway for cops. At this late hour, it would not take much to get pulled. While he was sober enough by his standards to drive, he knew that law enforcement would have an entirely different opinion. There were no cop cars on the road but he noticed a white Ford pick-up truck in his rear view mirror. It had been following him since he left the house. He figured it was a private investigator following one of his married girlfriends. He chuckled to himself until he saw the truck pull into the strip club parking lot after him. Two large white men got out and walked toward him.

"Uh oh," Miki said to himself. He got out of the car and rapidly made his way to Gabbie's place of employment.

He didn't look back but could sense that they were following him. He made his way to the bar and then glanced at the door. The men causally entered but did not make eye contact with him. They deliberately made their way to a satellite stage and fixed their attention on the half-naked performer.

"What's got you in such a rush, Miki?" The bartender asked. Miki was of course on a first name basis with all of the bartenders.

"Huh?" Miki turned his attention to the bartender. "Um…nothing…I guess. I don't know." He continued to glance at the men.

"What are you drinking tonight?" the bartender asked.

"Give me a Maker's and Coke."

"Double with the Maker's?"

"Of course." Miki shook his head at the silliness of the question. "Where is Gabbie?"

"Oh, she pulled some grandfatherly-looking fellow to the back area about an hour ago. He had a wad of cash, which means of course…"

"That she now has a wad of cash," Miki said with a smile.

"Which means y'all have a wad of cash. Quite the couple from what I hear."

"Yeah, yeah, yeah." Miki brushed it off. "We're in love." He chuckled as he downed the first of four drinks during the next hour. Each drink was stronger than the previous. Miki continued to watch the men that followed him. They would occasionally stare in his direction, then quickly focus their attention back to the stage. Gabbie finally appeared from the VIP room and made a beeline to Miki.

"Hey babe, what's up?" She said as she wrapped her arms around him and kissed him on the cheek.

"These assholes over there," Miki slurred. "They have been staring at me all night."

Gabbie looked in their direction and caught their eye. They quickly turned their heads to the so-called talent on the stage. "Well, you haven't been here all night." She turned and gave him another kiss. "And maybe they are just jealous that you are with such a hot piece of ass."

"No, no, no!" Miki almost yelled.

"I am not a hot piece of ass?" Gabbie was trying to defuse him. She had been with him enough to know when the belligerent stage of intoxication was approaching.

"No babe, not at all. You're the hottest." Miki belted in a garbled tone. "It is just that these assholes have been spying on me all night!" Miki shouted and pointed in their direction.

The men looked at him and then quickly looked away. The bartender motioned for a bouncer to come over. He happily obliged. He had a crush on Gabbie for the past several months and hated the sight of Miki at the club.

Gabbie stepped in front of the bouncer before he could grab Miki. "He's fine!" She waved him away. "He's just fine!" She glared at the bartender. She turned her attention to Miki. "C'mon Big Boy, let's get you home before you do any more damage," Gabbie said. She grabbed Miki and escorted him toward the entrance. She was more like a crutch than an escort.

"Wow, you're strong!" Miki said as he grabbed her waist.

"And you're drunk. Now that we have that established, can we just leave?" Gabbie replied.

"I am going to tear that up when we get home." Miki slapped her on the ass and stared at the bouncer as they passed by him.

"I am sure you will," Gabbie said with a grin.

Between Miki's exchange with the bouncer and Gabbie desperately trying not to let him fall over, no one noticed that the men had paid their bill and were following them outside.

Miki and Gabbie approached the passenger side of his car. "I am thinking that…" Miki couldn't finish his sentence.

"That I should drive," Gabbie interrupted.

"We are so in tune with each other," Miki replied.

"Yeah," Gabbie exhaled and she tried to open the car door while holding Miki upright, "must be love," she sarcastically replied.

"Hey!" One of the men exclaimed from a few feet back. They were two white males. One was tall and skinny; the other was built like a refrigerator.

Gabbie ignored them as she tried to pour Miki into the car.

"Hey, half-breed! I am talking to you and your mouthy little friend there!" the refrigerator exclaimed.

"Half-breed!" Miki attempted to stand on his own but looked like he was trying to balance on a surfboard in water.

Gabbie tried to step in. "Listen guys, if I so much as scream, these bouncers will make sure that your evening ends in a miserably uncomfortable position. They are jacked on nothing but steroids and pent up testosterone. They relish a chance to save a stripper. Just let us go home and call it an evening."

"You think your bouncers can beat up a bullet?" The little one pulled out a 9-mm pistol. "You think they are jacked up enough to do that? You fucking whore."

Miki stared at the gun. His nerves took over. He did the only thing he knew to do in the situation. He didn't try to control it but simply succumbed to his natural impulse. He just closed his eyes and let it unfold.

A stream of vomit flowed from Miki's mouth and landed directly in the face of the refrigerator. It hit him with the force of a fire hose.

"Holy shit!" the thin one exclaimed. In his excitement to avoid Miki's grotesque attack, he moved away from the refrigerator. "Dude, what in the hell did you do?" He used the gun as a pointer to show his friend's face, which was covered by the better part of Miki's evening. Then in a flash, his finger slipped, discharging the gun. The bullet entered his colleague's forehead and exited the back of his skull. His lifeless body fell backwards.

There was an eternal pause as everyone attempted to comprehend what just happened.

Gabbie, Miki and the little one stared at each other. Each was equally amazed and scared by the unexpected end of the confrontation. No one knew what to do. They remained in a silent pose.

Miki finally broke the stalemate by wiping his chin. He had regained full sobriety between the release of alcohol and excitement of watching a man get shot. He kept his eyes on the gun.

"Listen, let's just all calm down. It was a simple accident. I am sure that if we just call the cops and explain the situation…" The thin one turned and darted into the night before Miki could finish his sentence." Or you could do that?" Miki pointed in his direction.

Gabbie turned her head in all directions like an owl. "We need to go!"

"Huh?"

"No one saw us. No one heard us. We need to leave. We need to leave!" Gabbie was forcibly pushing Miki into his car.

Miki resisted her efforts. "No! Wait a minute. We need to stick around and tell them what happened. Believe me, I know. Running from it will only make it worse."

"I don't have time for the lawyer response."

"That's not necessarily a lawyer response," Miki replied.

"Oh, you have personal experience in dealing with a dead body?"

Miki paused. "Not saying whether I do or don't. I am just saying that running is not a good idea."

"Well that is definitely a lawyer response." Gabbie continued to push him into his car. "Listen, I don't know much but I do know that cops don't like strip clubs. They don't like strippers. They don't like lawyers and they really don't like dead bodies."

Miki just listened as he stared at the body.

"And we have all of those elements right here. So I am thinking that the cops are not really going to just interview us and let us go for the evening." Gabbie finally got the passenger door opened and used her body to thrust Miki into the seat. "So, unless you want to get arrested and spend the next few years explaining to some public defender how you killed a man with vomit, then I suggest that we go!"

She slammed the car door and climbed into the driver's seat. She raced 30 miles from the scene and found the most deserted exit offering a hotel. After about two hours of restlessness, sleep finally overcame Miki and Gabbie for a few hours. He was the first to wake up.

Miki shoved Gabbie in the shoulder to wake her up. After 20 seconds, she responded.

"What?" Gabbie growled. "What the hell? What time is it?"

"Noon. I have been awake since 9. Thought I would let you sleep some." Miki sipped on the horrible concoction called "coffee" as offered by their motel.

"Well, keep thinking and let me keep sleeping." Gabbie turned her head back into the pillow.

Miki continued to shove her shoulder.

"Whaaaaat?!"

Miki pointed to the television. Gabbie rubbed her eyes and tried to focus.

The screen showed clips from Grafton Hood's previous speech being interpreted by national commentators dissecting every political consequence of such a bold speech. It was a national weekend broadcast. Hood appeared on the panel to discuss and defend his latest bill. Gabbie was unimpressed. "That's what's-his-bucket talking about how he will kill people who kill babies. So what?" Gabbie said as she threw arms at the television.

"That is a national show. Wait for the cutaway to the local feed in a second."

Gabbie continued to watch as the national show faded to a local bulletin.

A young baby-faced local news anchor appeared. "And that was this state's governor defending his controversial and potentially groundbreaking new anti-abortion bill. And just as controversial and groundbreaking is our latest story," his face beamed with pride over the copy her wrote, "A lawyer is wanted for murder!"

Gabbie sat up with her elbows on her knees. She was glued to the set.

"No one knows much except that the shooting occurred outside of the "O" Club. It is known as a female adult entertainment club, according to authorities. The police will not reveal his name but they are asking for anyone who knows a white lawyer that may have frequented or been at that club last night to come forward. He is over 6 feet tall with olive complexion and dark hair. If anyone knows of any lawyer fitting this description, please contact the police."

The anchor paused for effect. "I know that we all have lawyer jokes and that it only takes one bad apple to ruin the barrel, but let's all work together to get this bad apple from the barrel. Now, back to your regularly scheduled broadcast." The studio personnel refrained from laughter until they were off air.

"See I told you!" Miki exclaimed.

"Told me what?"

"That we should have called the cops and handled it the right way!"

"You were in a strip club with a stripper when someone got killed. You really think they were just going to interview you and let you go?"

Miki shook his head. "Gabbie, as much as I would love to sit here and play crossfire with you about how about we should have handled this problem... this," he pointed to the television," this is a problem."

"You cannot tell me that you are the only lawyer matching the description as espoused by that half-ass Walter Cronkite?" She pointed to the television with a sly grin.

"Don't even try brevity with me right now!" Miki fired back. "I need to make a call."

"Huh? Who?"

"Someone who can help," Miki responded.

It was Sunday afternoon. While Ron's beautifully aged wife played mixed double tennis, Ron was sharing time between his Sunday billable hours and taking care of his 12-year-old and 6-year-old.

"Hey, what are you doing?" Miki causally asked.

"No, the question is what are you doing?" Ron asked.

"Excuse me?" Miki asked.

"What the hell, Miki? I get a call at 9:00 this morning from the local prosecutor asking about you."

"Huh?"

"Don't huh me, Miki! Not just any local prosecutor but the chief prosecutor. He's asking questions about you and a shooting outside of a strip club. I mean, what the fuck? Didn't you get enough of this shit with Sullivan's Island?"

Miki had no response.

Ron eased back. He had come on too strong. "Listen, I am not trying to bring up the past, but you have made some serious waves." Ron listened, hoping for a response that would exonerate his friend. That would not come. "Miki?"

"It was…it is…just a big misunderstanding. We were at the club and these two guys…" Miki calmly replied.

The lawyer in Ron took over. "Hold on. Just hold on. You know I want to help."

Ron's friendship with Miki was deeper than any other in in his life. Ron took Miki into his home when he was castigated from everyone else. He gave Miki shelter from his indiscretions on the coast—even when everyone urged him to abandon his law school buddy. Miki was his one constant. His parents and even his wife had an agenda for him and his life, but Miki didn't. He simply loved Ron for being Ron.

"I know that Ron," Miki replied.

"I do want to help. So the less I know, the better. You following my drift, counselor?"

"I do." Miki said as he looked over at Gabbie. She was intently following Miki's side of the conversation.

"This alleged crime occurred in the wee hours of the morning and yet, the chief prosecutor for the county is calling me early in the morning. A crime with no real witnesses and a dead man that no one has yet to claim." Ron paused." The chief prosecutor is calling me to ask about you."

"I would call that a little unorthodox," Miki replied.

Ron chuckled. "That's putting it mildly."

"So what do we now, counselor?" Miki asked.

"Well, you haven't been charged with anything."

"Yeah."

"Something doesn't seem right. I think you need to hide out until we can figure all this out. Again, you haven't been charged."

"Where? I am not exactly sitting on a mountain of real estate."

"My wife's family had a housekeeper. She was in the family for years. They felt that they owed her something and they needed a property tax break. They deeded a house to her. She passed away and left everything to some wayward son in New York. He never probated the estate so that house sits there, empty."

"Where is it?"

"You're gonna love this one. It is just outside of Charleston on the Isle of Palms."

"Just next to Sullivan's Island," Miki said as he shook his head.

"The key is underneath the couch shell on the front porch. Call me when you get there, but don't use your cell phone. Call me at the office." Ron promptly hung up.

The next morning, Miki visited a former client who was a low-end, used car dealer. He sold his car for $7,000 and a 1985 Harley Davidson Screaming Eagle. Miki grabbed his belongings from the car and threw them in an old school book bag. With Gabbie straddled to his back, Miki climbed aboard the motorcycle and raced toward the coast. Once the place he escaped from...now it was the place he was escaping to.

In those belongings was the folder marked "Brown Recluse."

CHAPTER TEN:
INTERNAL INVESTIGATIONS

While Practical Solutions had Elad as a strong arm, Grafton was saddled with Tybee Peppers. He was 6'3 feet tall and bore a stark resemblance to a cross between Paul Newman and Robert Redford. God blessed Tybee with good looks to compensate for his lack of intelligence. He was also the sole heir to one of the wealthiest families in South Carolina.

The Peppers' family was a red neck dynasty. For over half a century, it owned timber rights covering two-thirds of a western rural county in the state. The family used the wealth from timber to purchase grocery stores, gas stations and even car dealerships in the three neighboring counties. All of the counties were economic deserts relying on the Peppers' business ventures to survive. It was a modern Southern form of impoverished servitude. For generations, the Peppers lived in and controlled the corridor known as the armpit of the state.

In order to make living in the "pit" more palatable, Tybee's father built an estate befitting of American royalty. He took a tour of the Biltmore Estates and came back with the idea for the Peppers Estates. It covered over

1,000 acres and bordered parts of the Salkehatchie River. The outside of the home was an exact replica of the White House.

Tybee's father was a lawyer. He grew tired of the mendacity of wealthy living amongst the nation's poorest and aspired for a professional reputation. Tybee's father turned over the day-to-day operations of the multi-million dollar family business to a team of accountants from Charlotte. Thanks to a large donation to Grafton, he was now a state judge. He was Grafton's last appointment before being elected governor.

While God blessed the Peppers' family with wealth, he did not bless them with fertility. Tybee's father and Tybee were the last living heirs of the Peppers' fortune. Each generation had produced only one male and that male managed to marry an only child with no real family. After Tybee's father, known as "Senior" because Tybee was a junior, Tybee would be in charge of the family empire. And that scared the hell out of Senior.

Tybee gained his place on Grafton's staff through a round of golf between Grafton and Senior.

There was a large product's liability case set to try next week in front of Senior. The corporate defense firm needed a victory to keep its largest client. Grafton needed to show everyone that he still maintained control over the judges even after their appointment. He also needed a sizeable donation from the firm to assist with the retirement of his re-election debt. The firm was prepared to make the donation, provided that it had the resources. That was code for "if we keep our largest client then we can help you out."

Grafton needed Senior to help the defense firm. It was a civil suit. A father had lost his wife and two children in a home fire caused by a faulty switch in the family car parked in the garage. The father had escaped but his family burned.

Grafton wasn't concerned with the administration of justice. He just wanted the donation. Grafton had set up the meeting. It was a Par 3 and Senior grabbed his 7-Iron Callaway Apex from his bag.

"He's just a complete worthless piece of white trash shit," he said.

"Who, Senior?" Grafton replied.

"My son, and I hate the name 'Senior.' It just reminds me that I have a son as worthless as him." He fired a shot within 15 feet of the hole.

"Nice," Grafton observed.

"He's had everything handed to him on a golden fucking platter. But he would rather kill a deer and tell off-color jokes."

Grafton took his shot but made sure it was at least 30 feet from the hole. He was here to convince his appointee to circumvent the justice system, not to show him up.

"Doesn't he work in the family business?"

"Yeah, he manages the truck schedules at one of our lumbar yards. The boy can't spell algebra but he's somehow using math to determine when our trucks arrive at the right place with the right load."

"Maybe his talents lay elsewhere."

"Sure. You know any profession where the qualifications are killing animals and bragging about your family's wealth?"

"Well," Grafton paused, "his, I guess. It seems to pay pretty well." Grafton and Senior enjoyed a chuckle.

"Yes, I guess it does," Senior replied. "Maybe if I could get the boy out of here. Let him start hanging around more successful folks who won't pay him homage because of his family name, actually make him work for it."

"So, you're thinking a position in the capital. Maybe a post on my staff?" Grafton asked.

"Governor, I could never ask that of you. I can't back the boy. He's a cross between Jethro Bodine and Chris Farley in Tommy Boy. You'd be assuming a lot by taking him on."

"I would be doing it as a favor to you."

"And a mighty big one at that." Senior laughed as he putted for birdie. "One I wouldn't forget."

"One that you may be able to repay sooner rather than later. You have a big civil case before you next week? A products case about a car catching on fire."

"I do." Senior tried to hide his surprise about Grafton's knowledge of his upcoming docket. "Bad case in a bad venue. I am surprised the defense hasn't tried to settle."

"I have heard that. I have also heard that there is a motion by the defense firm to essentially dismiss the case?"

"There is," Senior calmly replied. At this point, he wasn't surprise by Grafton's knowledge—he was impressed.

"Well, if that motion were granted," Grafton paused as he putted within two feet of the hole (he didn't want to match Senior's birdie), "then that defense firm would be very grateful in terms of donating to my retirement of debt campaign."

"Oh, would they now?" Senior watched Grafton complete his par. "And this post for Tybee?"

"He would head my own security task force known as Internal Investigations. He would have a title, credentials, and report to only one person." Grafton grinned. "The governor of our fair state."

Tybee's father used the reams of legal authority supplied by the defense firm to support his decision to dismiss the case of the widower with two dead children. And Tybee got his appointment.

Embarrassed by his last conversation with Pontet, Grafton knew he had failed to cover his tracks. More importantly, he felt Pontet had the upper hand. He decided to correct his own mistakes without Pontet's help. He enlisted Tybee to clean up the mess. They were charged with killing Miki and Gabbie, which was of course an utter failure. Incensed, P.S. dispatched Elad to interview

Grafton's Internal Investigations team to assess the collateral damage from the failed attempt and assure that it didn't happen again.

It was 6:30 in the morning. Elad picked a gas station coffee diner located 70 miles from the capital. He was seated at a booth sipping on his second cup of bad coffee when Tybee and his second-in-command arrived. They were late for the meeting.

Tybee arrived with a black male. They searched the restaurant until Tybee's colleague pointed out Elad seated in the corner. Tybee waved. Elad continued to look down.

"Hi!" Tybee exclaimed. His accomplice slid into the booth next to Tybee and across from Elad.

"You match the description," Elad said as he pointed to Tybee, "but who is this?" Elad pointed to the sidekick.

Elad's cold demeanor and appearance took Tybee aback. He stared into his yellow eyes. "Excuse me?"

Elad glared back at Tybee and pointed to his companion. "Who the fuck is this?" he growled.

The baritone voice startled him. "Umm, this is John...John," he stammered.

"And why is he here?"

"He's my second-in-command."

"In command of what? Dumb assholes? Are you in command of those? Because I don't think you could command an army to open a paper bag."

Tybee was shocked—not even the Governor addressed him in such a manner.

"Listen, you don't have to worry about me because I won't say a word," John replied. He held his hands up in an act of surrender. "I promise that I don't know a thing."

"You don't know anything. Well, clearly you would fit right into any army in this one's command." Elad pointed to Tybee.

"Excuse me. Do you know who are talking to? I am the head of the governor's security force."

"Yeah, I know that. And I also know that your family owns this gas station. Did you know that?" Tybee looked around in bewilderment. "I didn't think you did."

"I'm sorry. We didn't catch your name," John interjected to deflect attention from Tybee who was as aggressive as a wounded rabbit at this point.

"My name is Shut the Fuck Up. You want me to spell it for you?" Elad replied as he raised his middle finger. "You need to write that down?"

John leaned back in his seat. "I'm not trying to offend. We were told to meet a political advisor for the governor and I just wanted to make sure we were in the right spot."

Tybee sat in silence. He was glad that John was taking the lead to talk with the stranger.

"Name is Elad, and that's all you need to know."

"Fair enough," John replied.

"Now, let me ask some questions. Who told you to take out Martin and the girl?"

Everyone looked at Tybee, who was frozen. His mind

was still trying to comprehend how the stranger knew him and still had the audacity to address him like a child.

John interjected again. "It was Hood."

"Thought you didn't know shit?"

"Needed to make sure we knew how we were talking to," John quickly retorted.

"So you know me and know who I am?" Elad asked.

"Yes, we do. Like he said," John nodded toward his superior, "we work with the governor's security force. We have to know."

"Tybee, can you at least join this conversation? Yes?" Elad asked. He could sense Tybee's partner wanting to inject a response. He pointed to John. "Let him answer."

"Hood wanted us to take care of it," Tybee finally sputtered.

Elad turned his attention back to Tybee. "Don't speak his name again."

Tybee frantically nodded.

"How did you find the men? What's their connection to you?"

Tybee and John needed a good answer to this question. Elad was ordered to eliminate any potential risks to the governor. He had a 9-mm pointed at Tybee under the table. He had unholstered his weapon when they first sat. Elad already played the scenario in his mind—shoot Tybee first and then the companion (whom he didn't expect). There was only one other person at the station, a cashier. He would shoot her on the way out, grab the video feed and race away. All of that was about to transpire if he wasn't given a satisfactory answer to his question.

"Well, who were they?" Elad pressed.

Tybee remained silent, clueless as to his brush with death. John mercifully responded. "They were nobodies. No family other than a few kids that they have never seen in order to avoid paying child support."

"How'd you know them?" Elad's finger was rubbing against the trigger.

"I used to be in law enforcement," John quickly responded.

"Where?"

"On the coast. Out of state." John paused. "I knew them from that. They were just a couple of career drunks, in and out of prison all the time on a DUI or assault and battery. I offered them each $5,000 to do the job, which clearly didn't go so well."

"Clearly," Elad replied.

"We're going to start looking for the other guy to make sure he doesn't talk."

"Don't bother," Elad said. Tybee and John stared at him dumbfounded. "He is already dead."

"So, you already knew who they were? Then why question us?" John asked. Tybee remained silent in a conversation that was well outside his mental acuity.

"Needed to make sure that you guys were actually dumb rather than just playing dumb. And the verdict is in." Tybee and John looked at each other. "You're just dumb." Elad holstered his weapon. "And whose act of brilliance was it to leak this crime to the press, including Martin's name?"

"Oh, that was mine," Tybee proudly proclaimed.

"Naturally." Elad shook his head. "Now all of law enforcement will be searching for him. Not just me."

"Don't you mean us?" Tybee asked.

"No, turd wad. I don't. I mean me." Elad slowly got out of the booth and leaned over into Tybee's face. His coffee breath enveloped Tybee's senses. "I don't want either one of you doing anything unless I tell you to. From here on out, I am in charge."

"What about the Governor?" Tybee asked. John let out a sigh of exasperation over his superior's question. He just wanted Elad to leave.

"Unless it is mindless and menial, then you don't do it. You don't do anything that requires any mental effort on your part. Is that clear?" Elad was almost nose-to-nose with Tybee. "You understand me, don't you John?"

John nodded.

"Keep this one by your side." Elad pointed to John and leaned into Tybee's ear. "He just saved your life today." Elad then calmly walked out of the gas station and into his car.

"Jesus, what was that all about? Who is that guy?" Tybee asked John.

"Clearly someone with a different agenda than ours," John answered.

"What did he mean by you saved my life?" Tybee

asked.

John knew the answer as soon as he heard the question, but shrugged it off. John knew of Practical Solution as a rumor with no substance. He also knew that today he had just met the substance. There was no sense in educating Tybee. He was a soul that gained more from life through ignorance rather than knowledge.

And how did you know who he was?" Tybee asked.

"Huh?"

"You told him that you knew who he was. How did you know that?"

"Oh, I probably overheard Governor Hood say it on the phone or something."

Tybee mindlessly accepted the answer. "So do we follow up with that lead? The last person we know Martin talked with?" Tybee asked.

"No. I guess not. I reckon our friend Elad will have a conversation with Mr. Poe."

CHAPTER ELEVEN:
LUNCH

Grafton had a speaking engagement at a local middle school. It was a Social Studies class and he was assigned to educate and inspire a class of inner school youth about how a bill becomes a law. Cameras clicked and rolled as he spoke to the children. There were local and national news agencies hanging on his every word. His speech to gain support for his anti-abortion legislation had thrust him onto the national scene. He gained his instant fame the old fashioned way, by making yourself a polarizing figure.

"Now, children," Grafton's voice reverberated through the crowd, "does anyone know how a bill becomes a law?"

One innocent 7th grader raised a hand.

"Yes, you! What do you think?" Hood barked.

"It has to pass both houses and then it goes to the governor," the young girl stammered.

Grafton smiled as he nodded with approval. "That is a very good answer. But it is a little more complicated."

The little girl sat mesmerized that the governor of the state was responding to her. She was beaming with pride.

"She is correct for the most part." He reached down and rubbed her head. He continued to maintain his focus at the cameras. Hood soaked up every second of media attention.

"There is a bit more. I write a bill and it is read to the entire House of Representatives and then it is sent to a committee. Then that committee decides whether or not it can be brought back before the House. That committee can really control the future of your bill. And if it ever gets back from committee, it goes back to the House."

Grafton continued to focus on the camera.

"The bill must then survive a second, and even a third," Grafton counted with his fingers, "reading before the entire House. That means the entire House must agree to pass it before it will go to the Senate. And only then, after it passes the Senate, will it come before me to be signed as a law. So that committee is important to the life of that bill."

"Wow," said the little girl that answered his question.

"Wow is right, sweetheart," Grafton again tapped her on the head. "And I have a bill that can't even past a committee. What do you think of that?"

"Boo!" exclaimed his middle school audience.

"Boo is right. Boo is exactly right," Grafton laughed at his young audience. "And you," Grafton shouted above their voices, "you need to tell your parents just that. Will you do that? Will you do that for your governor?"

"Yes!" They shouted.

Hood tried to quiet them like he did the crowd on the statehouse grounds. "I know you will. I know you will. And now, I have to get back to my job and you have to get back to your school work."

That also was met with a resounding "Boo!"

"But do me one favor. Look at all those cameras and shout…shout as loud as you can…Go Hood Go! Can you do that as I leave today?"

"Go Hood Go!!!" The kids exclaimed.

Grafton smiled as he was escorted from the school into his car. His driver met him with a cell phone in hand. Pontet was on the other end.

"Nice. I am watching it live on CNN," he said.

"Your approval warms my heart," Grafton replied.

"If you can't get the parents, then why not their kids? Too bad that you will be completely irrelevant by the time *they* can vote."

"You're as funny as suicide. Why is it that you called?"

"To let you know that Practical Solutions has made contact with your band of rejects from the Island of Misfit Rednecks."

"Yes, I heard from Peppers. He met Elad."

"Yes, he did," Pontet snapped. "Listen, I know you hate that you are somehow beholden to me, but think of the bigger picture here. This is a royal fucking mess, and by royal mess, I mean someone blew up the sewage station. And you're trying to clean it up with a sponge."

Pontet fumed. "You need to leave the cleanup to the professionals."

"I don't need a fucking lecture. I understand that!" Grafton seethed.

"Just simmer down, big boy. That lack of self-control will be the death of you." Grafton didn't reply. "Where do you stand with getting this bill out of committee and back to the House floor?"

"I am meeting with Spring in about 30 minutes for lunch. Thanks to my Island of Misfit Rednecks, I may have leverage to sway him…"

"Sway him? Is that a 'Grafton term' for force?" Pontet interrupted.

"To assist in the passage of my bill from committee and back onto the House floor," Grafton continued.

Julius Spring was in his mid 60s. He was 5'6 with a hunched back. His once flowing blonde locks were reduced to a flaking bald scalp surrounded by a thin, grey band of hair. To most folks, he was a sweet elderly man who took his cap off inside and made sure that he opened the door for a lady.

To those in politics, he was the elder Democratic leader of the State Senate. His family had made enough money from textile mills to buy an island off the shore of Bermuda. He was a dangerous politician because he didn't need politics for money or power—he actually wanted to make a difference. Spring was an old school Democrat. He believed all underdogs deserved a fighting change against the establishment, but that didn't mean simply giving them a government check.

Spring despised Grafton.

Just before Grafton was elected Governor, he spent three years in the State Senate. He served as head of the judiciary committee. The committee was designed to screen those individuals seeking appointment from the state legislature to become state court judges. It was a gateway of sorts to weed through any undesirable individuals seeking to become judges. The committee was designed to ensure that only individuals of strong moral character and great legal minds were considered as candidates for judgeships.

A judge can influence a jury verdict through his or her evidentiary rulings or his or her demeanor toward either party. This means influencing the outcome of trials of criminals facing the death penalty or severely injured individuals relying on civil compensation to simply survive. While it was not as prestigious as its federal counterpart, a state judge still enjoyed a great deal of power. The committee was supposed to be a defense against attempts by the corrupt to seize control of such power. And the committee functioned exactly as intended until Grafton became head.

Grafton knew that there were many corporations and large law firms that would bid against each other in order to control the appointment of a judge. They would love to have their hand-picked candidate in a black robe. Through his minions of so-called political staff, he made it known that the appointment of state court judges was definitely up for sale. It was $150,000 to receive the blessing of his committee and an additional $250,000 if the candidate was actually appointed.

And in typical Grafton fashion, he took it to the next level. He was receiving more requests for judicial appointments than could be filled. He quickly sized up the problem—there were not enough openings to fill. As a Republican, he could not advocate tax increases to raise money necessary to hire more judges to create more openings, so he decided to force the retirement of sitting judges.

He made personal phone call to those judges whose terms were nearing the end. If they sought reappointment, the committee would not endorse them. And Spring's sister received that phone call despite the respect her brother enjoyed in the Legislature.

"Listen, you are welcome to run for another appointment, but I just cannot back you. My committee seeks to invigorate the judiciary with some new blood—judges that are in tune with the notion that this nation is tired of runaway verdicts and lawyers looking to make a quick buck because of a simple fender bender."

She simply listened in silent awe. She had heard rumblings about Grafton's phone calls. He had been deemed the Grim Reaper for sitting judges. She assumed that her brother's status gave her immunity from Grafton's touch. She was wrong.

"People are tired of their insurance rates going up just to make the fat wallets of trial lawyers even fatter. We need a change. Now, you are welcome to seek a reappointment and you may win. But if you don't…"

His touch was upon her.

"…then you will have to go back to private practice and appear before the very same judge that you opposed in the appointment hearings. I don't know the law, but I know people. I have a feeling that you will have some real tough sledding appearing before a person that you opposed. But there is an alternative."

"Which is?" she whispered.

"Now, if you don't seek reappointment and just retire, then I could talk to some folks on the Budget and Control Board. These are the folks that control your retirement from the state. They would probably allow you to take early retirement, and forgo private practice."

She relented. "Sure, Governor. Sure."

Grafton knew her personal history but did not care. She had recently lost her husband of almost 40 years to Alzheimer's. It was an excruciating three-year battle. He devolved from a successful real estate broker to a man who needed his adult diapers changed by her. After his death, she immersed herself in her work. It was the only thing that helped her deal with the pain of his agonizing loss. With the loss of her job, she would lose all hope of a normal life. Spring's sister put a bullet in her head within ten minutes of the conversation.

Grafton had the audacity to attend the funeral to show his respects. He received a cool $250,000 for the appointment of her replacement, Tybee's father.

On this day, Spring and Hood met for lunch to discuss the legislation slowed down in a committee controlled by Spring. They met in one of the oldest restaurants in the Capitol. It was caked in wood and serviced by a kitchen so small that it was only practical to elves. Most claimed that the worn leather seats predated the Civil Rights. Still, it was a lunch staple for politicians and lobbyists. The owner insisted that they have a table in full view of everyone. He wanted to make sure that his customers knew that the two most powerful people in the state dined at his place.

"I am sorry I am late," Grafton said as he sat down. He had just hung up the phone with Pontet.

Spring studied his lunch companion. He noticed Grafton's Canali wool suit. It fit him perfectly. Spring's suit belonged to his grandfather. The bow tie was his father's favorite.

"I just got here myself, Governor." Spring looked at the menu.

The waiter nervously approached under the watchful eye of the owner. Grafton interrupted him before he could launch into his spiel about the specials. "I just want a water and house salad."

Spring glanced up from the menu.

"I am sorry, Senator. You're not ready."

"No, no, no." Spring smiled as he looked up from the menu. "I can get it together. Let me have your pork lion and a sweet tea. Extra lemons," Spring responded.

Hood glanced around the restaurant and politely waved to the politicos desperately trying to get his attention. They all knew him and he didn't recognize any of them.

"It has been a while since we have had lunch, Senator."

Spring chuckled. "Well, that's because you haven't needed anything from me until now."

Hood smiled. He actually admired Spring as a political foe. He always thought that Spring could have been a nationally prominent figure in politics if he had been willing to abandon his adherence to being a man of the people. It had cost Spring a lot of powerful allies and even more special interest money.

"Always blunt and to the point. A rare combination for a Southern politician," Hood replied.

"Well, Governor, let me be even more blunt. "You don't want to be at lunch with me anymore than I want to be here with you," Spring smiled as he delivered the insulting truth. "We've been doing this dance since you were first elected to the House."

"And you tried to get me to cross party lines and I refused. You've always hated me for that."

"Oh, Grafton, my feelings for you run deeper than just that initial rebuke of my offer," Spring laughed. "Besides, the past is the past. Why am I here? What do you want?" Spring asked as he squeezed a third lemon into his glass of Southern table wine.

"My bill," Hood replied.

"What about it?"

"It is still buried in a committee controlled by you. I cannot get a second reading on the House floor while it remains in committee."

"Well, I think they are probably a little troubled by the content of the legislation, Governor," Spring said shaking his head in disbelief over Hood's surprise.

"I know that it is aggressive."

"Aggressive? A bill designed to kill single mothers and doctors if they engage in a medical procedure. This bill is well beyond the realm of aggressive—it is barbaric," Spring replied.

"Maybe, to some. But to others, it is exactly what this country needs. It deserves to at least get a debate in the light of day rather than be shelved in a dark basement because a few of your colleagues deem it too harsh."

"Sir, you think I am the reason that your bill is still in committee?"

"Of course I do. I could propose the Yellow Pages as legislation and get at least a second reading within a week. So I know you're behind this."

Spring didn't react to the accusation. He just listened.

"You and I both know that there is a reason I have presented such a bill. You know that this is an important piece of legislation for me. Had any other person proposed it, you would have it rushed to a second reading and you would have crucified the author in the media."

"So you agree that your bill is somewhat absurd?"

"No, not at all. In fact, I think it has a chance to become law if I am allowed a fair chance. Which you won't allow." Grafton paused. "What is that slogan you use in your campaigns? Oh that's right. 'Not a check but a fair chance to earn one!' Why can't I get that fair chance?"

"Governor, fair chance implies a level playing field. We all know that anyone who plays ball with you is not playing on a level field."

"Now you do sound like a politician. You're dodging the accusation. You are opposing this legislation not based on your perceived notion of its obscenity, but instead because I have proposed it."

For Spring, talking to Hood was akin to drinking hot vinegar and he had been dealing with the taste since they sat down. Grafton was absolutely correct with his assessment, but there was no way Spring would let him know that. At this point, Spring just wanted to leave the table and regroup with his allies to ensure that the bill stayed in committee. Spring knew that there must have been something huge riding on the proposal of this bill and its ratification as law. This bill needed to remain in the basement of the legislature.

"Governor, if you have problems with the members of that committee and how they are treating this bill, then by all means, talk with them directly."

"Oh, I plan to. That is the reason I called this lunch. I wanted to give you a chance to address your troops before hearing from me."

"Sir, I don't have any troops," Spring casually replied.

"And neither do I," Hood sarcastically responded. "Are you curious to hear what I have to say or shall we choke down this lunch in a pretended atmosphere of civility?"

"Governor, like anyone in this state, I am always curious to hear what you have to say."

"Well, there are five members of that committee. I know I have one vote. So that means I need two," Grafton said as he held up his fingers. "And I know that two of the remaining four members of Spring Army are seeking re-election in the fall."

"Spring Army. Very clever."

"I will assure you those members will face stiff opposition in their re-election bid. I will tell them that they will find their opposition to be well organized and very well financed."

"No doubt from your days as Chairman of Senate Judiciary Committee."

Grafton ignore the jab. "I promise if this bill doesn't find its way to the House floor, then it will be the last meaningful vote that they ever cast. I will tie their political futures to the future of this bill."

"Ah, you will threaten them. Force their votes. Hardly the democratic result envisioned by our forefathers as you so eloquently referred to in your speech in the rain."

"I am fighting against your tyranny. I think our fore-fathers would understand. And I will also tell them one other thing."

"What would that be? Threaten their families?"

"No, not their families. But maybe your family."

Spring stopped in mid-sip of his tea. He placed the glass down and glared at Grafton.

"Do you know Miki Martin?"

Spring didn't respond. He continued to stare at Grafton. If he had been 20 years younger, he would have thrown his political career to the side to punch Grafton in the face.

"I know that you do. He's the best friend to your son-in-law. Ron Poe…correct? I hear that your grandchildren even refer to him as uncle."

"What about him?" Spring quipped.

"Well, according to my sources, he's the unnamed suspect in the recent murder that occurred outside of a strip club in the city."

"By sources, do you mean Peppers' half-wit son? He's in charge of your famed Internal Investigations." Another dig at the Peppers' appointment to the post of Spring's deceased sister.

Hood ignored the jab. "I hardly think anyone will care where the information was gathered. They will only be interested to know that the 'uncle' of your grandchildren is wanted for murder."

Spring took another sip of his tea. He carefully put the glass on the table and rubbed his chin. "So unless this bill gets out of committee, then two very good—no, *great*—representatives will face a hotly contested and probably nasty re-election bid. And, you will make sure that the entire state knows that my grandchildren have a close connection with a man wanted for murder." Spring paused. "I guess I was right all along."

"How so?"

"This bill is critically important to you. You want to ensure its survival even at the risk of threatening the family of the senior Senator of this State's Legislature."

Grafton continued to press forward. "Your son-in-law is a partner in a very prominent and conservative insurance defense law firm, correct? Don't think his firm will want a partner that consorts with such people as this Martin character."

"And his children…"

"Your grandchildren," Grafton interrupted.

"Will have to deal with the press backlash from such a low rent story."

"Isn't one of *your* children in high school? Kids that age can be really cruel with this kind of stuff," Hood replied.

And like his sister, Spring relented. "Yes, they can, Governor. Yes, they can."

"Senator, it just makes sense to give the bill a chance and to just stay out of the way. I will be out of this state in a few months and you will have all of your troops in order to tackle the next administration. And," Grafton took a sip of his water, "you won't have to worry about your family dealing with any of this mess."

"I won't help you get this thing passed in the Senate. There is no way that will happen." Spring was emphatic.

"Oh, I know that. It would be political death for you to do that. According to my research, most of your constituents would be prosecuted under my bill. So, I don't expect that. I just need it out of committee and let me worry about the rest."

The waiter finally arrived with the lunches.

"I will have to take mine to go. I am sorry. I have a pressing meeting that I just remembered. I hope you understand, Governor." Spring put on a political façade for the waiter.

"I absolutely do. We are in session. There is much to do." Grafton followed Spring's lead in a charade of civility.

The waiter stood dumbfounded with dishes in each hand. He was in awe over the individuals he was serving and not smart enough to react to the unexpected request of Spring to take his lunch to go.

Spring snapped to get his attention. "Son, just put my lunch in a box and I will take it to go. You can meet me at the door to give it to me." He reached in his pocket and retrieved a $20 bill to pay his meal.

"I would offer to pay for your lunch but with the new ethic's reform bill, I cannot do that."

"Yes, it has proved to be a very powerful piece of legislation," Spring smirked.

Grafton and Spring rose from the table at the same time. Grafton extended his hand. Spring took it and gave him a firm, hard shake. If Spring had the strength, he would have broken every bone in Grafton's hand.

Grafton fought off the temptation to wince from the shake. He grinned instead. "Senator, I look forward to a spirited debate about my bill on the Senate floor."

"Well, Governor, that will be up to the House. I think your bill is due for its second reading soon. Correct?"

"I hope so. It is bogged down in committee but they are supposed to vote on it this afternoon."

Spring released his grip. "From what I hear, it should pass the committee and move for its second reading. Good luck with your bill, Governor." The hot vinegar was burning down his throat.

Grafton sat down to dine alone. He immediately picked up his phone and dialed Pontet.

"It is outta committee," he said, taking a fork filled of arugula.

"Well, that took long enough," Potent replied.

"Spring isn't dumb and doesn't like me."

"Well, who does, Grafton?" Pontet asked.

"It's after noon, shouldn't you be drunk by now?" Grafton retorted.

"You're not done with him. The Senate will be the real battle."

"Oh, you think?" Grafton shook his head at the obviousness of the statement. "But I may have a pressure point in that regard?"

"What's that?"

"This Martin guy. He's a real hot button issue for Spring."

"Yeah, that's funny because he could be a hot button issue for you if we don't catch him."

"Well, whatever we do, we just need to link him to that murder."

"You mean Peppers' failed attempt to fix the problem," Pontet laughed.

"Laugh it up. That attempt may give me the leverage to get this bill passed. We just need to connect this Martin kid to the killing."

"You just focus on the bill. We will focus on Miki Martin."

CHAPTER TWELVE:
EIGHT YEARS AGO, PART II

Miki was awoken by the monotone voice of a local newscaster broadcasting through the television set he forgot to turn off before passing out the night before.

"And on the local political front, Governor Graton Hood's controversial anti-abortion bill surprisingly passed through committee with a favorable ruling and has been given its second reading on the House floor. While it has shocked many that the bill made it to the House floor, most believe that even Governor Hood will not be able to find a way to help his bill navigate the treacherous political canals that await him in the Senate."

"Treacherous political canals? Pulitzer material, my friend," Miki said as he promptly turned the channel to ESPN. He slowly rose from bed and staggered his way into the kitchen to brew an insanely strong batch of coffee. It was 3:00 in the afternoon and he couldn't decide whether he was still a little drunk or just suffering a mammoth hangover. Miki needed a cup of coffee that could run a small lawnmower in order to regain his senses.

For the past three weeks, Miki and Gabbie had been guests of the Spring family beach house, courtesy of Poe's invite. It was a two story, modest beach home built in the 1960s. The bottom story was once a make shift garage which was converted to a living area about 20 years ago. It was the prototypical Isle of Palms beach home until Hurricane Hugo. The home somehow survived the Charleston makeover and was now surrounded by multi-million dollar homes that dwarfed it. The home was a brownstone located in a block of skyscrapers. It was cloaked from the street by a series of large oleanders and a tapestry of Jasmine woven through the staircase leading to the front door on the upstairs screened porch.

Everyday was like a vacation for Miki and Gabbie. They would begin drinking at 3:00 p.m. (as soon as they woke up) and didn't end until 5:00 a.m. There was no ritual or schedule. Life was consumed with drinking, sex and the occasional meal, generally when a hangover could not be cured by coffee. Not unlike Miki's life before, except now he wasn't working and was wanted by the law.

He paid slight attention to the mouthpiece spewing through the boob tube as he read the newspaper on his phone to see if there was any mention of the murder investigation in the Capital city. Surprisingly, there was nothing. He then grabbed Ron's post card resting on the dinning room table.

It instructed Miki to call him at the firm every Tuesday and Thursday at 4:30 p.m. The postcard gave him the location of an actual working payphone located outside a local dive bar on the island. He could call from there. It was Tuesday. Miki finished his diesel-like cup of coffee and headed down the street to make his phone call. Gabbie continued to sleep as Miki kissed her head and slipped out of the door.

Miki was given Poe's direct dial to the firm and got him on the second ring.

"Hello," Ron answered.

"Hey, how goes life in the billable lane?" Miki tried to fake some form of normalcy more for Ron's sake than his own.

"As always, measured in .2 increments. How are you holding up?"

"I am a wanted by law enforcement, once again. I try to stay buzzed or drunk to forget reality."

"Well, you've had some practice at all that."

"Yeah," Miki laughed, "I am pretty good at it. So, what you have you heard?" Miki was sipping on a vodka-water he grabbed from the bar before making the call.

"Officially? The same as before…crickets. Nothing."

"What about the prosecutor that initially called me?"

"Same. Crickets. I have tried calling and texting him," Ron paused. "Same with the press, nothing. Your so-called story hasn't been in the papers since you left. But they do have their hands filled with covering that Hood bill."

"Saw something about that this morning," Miki replied as he took another sip of his drink. "Maybe that means that they are looking somewhere else. Maybe I am in the clear."

"Don't think so," Ron responded.

"Huh? Why do you say that?"

"One of the firm's partners is on the Bar's Committee on Character and Fitness. He told me that they suspended your license yesterday."

"Well, I figured that was coming based on my last brush with them. I didn't report the crime."

"More than that, there have been some odd phone calls."

"Who?" Miki asked. He waited for the answer before taking another sip.

"Your mom and your dad. They called me."

"What did Crazy and Crazier want?" Miki chuckled. "Haven't they done enough?"

"They each reported the same thing in totally different phone calls. They had been personally approached by a member from the state's law enforcement."

"Personally approached? You mean this guy met with them face-to-face?"

"Yes, some guy named Peppers visited them a couple of days ago. On a Saturday."

"Ok…"Miki took a long pause as he tried to process the information. "Just that one guy."

"No, he brought someone with him. But they didn't catch his name. Said he was a black man."

"What were they asking?"

"The normal shit, I guess. Hell, I don't know. I don't know anything about criminal law."

"Well, me neither," Miki retorted.

"Except how to violate it?"

"Funny, Ron. Real fucking funny," Miki hissed.

"I'm sorry man. I'm just trying to keep things as light as possible. I have never aided in hiding a wanted felon from law enforcement."

Miki felt guilty. Unlike Miki, Ron actually had a life worth losing and was risking it in order to help his friend. Miki could never begrudge Ron if he decided to turn him in. He tried to play off his outburst. Like any man, light humor is sometimes better than an apology.

"Well, at least I don't cut your bills!

Ron laughed. Apology accepted. "You probably would if I sent you one."

"So, what did they ask my parents?" Miki sipped his drink.

"The last time they saw you. Last time they talked to you. Do they know anything about your girlfriend?"

"Girlfriend? They thought if I had a girlfriend that I would actually introduce her to them?" Miki laughed. "How did Ozzie and Harriet respond?"

"The truth. They had not seen you in several years. Your parental alienation actually worked to your benefit."

"Yeah, but it still concerns me. How did they even know how to find that pair of misfits? Dad lives in a deer stand and Mom leads a lifestyle that most gypsies would consider nomadic."

"Don't know about all that, but they were grilled about the girl. I am assuming she was the one in the parking lot."

"Yes, she is indeed the closet thing resembling a girl-friend in my life." Miki responded.

"It is all very strange. They are looking for you but not using local media or law enforcement to find you."

"But they have a state investigator to make an out-of-town trip to question my parents," Miki replied. This time he gulped down the rest of his drink.

Ron paused. "Miki, I don't know if you are making things worse by running or whether you need to come home, hire a good lawyer and face the music."

"Face the music?" Miki asked sarcastically.

"You know what I mean," Ron answered.

"Listen, I have faced that music once before and the dance sucked." Ron was silent. That, coupled with Ron's other statement, caused Miki to think. Maybe his friend's desire to help was now outpaced by his logical decision to turn Miki in. "Ron, I know you are worried. And maybe you should distance yourself from all of this," Miki replied.

"That's not what I am saying. That's not what I am saying at all." Ron felt badly. His friend was in real trouble and Ron represented his only chance at salvation.

"You've done plenty. I can take care of myself. You don't need to wade any deeper into these waters."

"Miki, I would let you know if this was too much heat for me. And right now, it is not. But you're correct, at some point it may become too much. But as long as I am willing to help, then you need to take it. Plus," Ron paused, "it's free."

Miki laughed. Apology accepted even though Miki knew none was needed. "Let me go—some of the locals are starting to stare. I don't think they've ever seen a person actually use a pay phone."

"Alright, talk to you on Thursday."

"Sounds good but, by the way, this was bullshit advice so don't bill me for this call."

Ron laughed as he hung up.

After his conversation with Ron, Miki ventured into the bar and downed three more vodkas. He then walked to a neighboring liquor store and bought a bottle of George Dickel before heading back to Gabbie. It was near dark and he was the liquor store's last customer.

She was sitting on the front porch snacking on a sub sandwich from the local gas station. Last night was brutal and she needed to eat away her hangover. It was her first meal in two days. She looked up as Miki entered through the screen door.

"How'd it go with Mr. Poe?" She asked.

Miki didn't responded. He placed the bottle of liquor on the porch table and headed to the kitchen. He returned with two glasses and proceeded to fill each to the rim.

"That well, huh?" She took the glass Miki handed to her but didn't take a sip. "You're going to have to give me a break tonight. Last night was a tough one."

"Well, my law license has been suspended and state law enforcement questioned my parents about my girlfriend." Miki pointed to her.

"Girlfriend? Wow! I need to update my Facebook page." Gabbie smiled. It was not a joking situation but she could tell that Miki was already drunk and a serious conversation would not be remembered at this point. She would just playfully jab at him until he passed out.

"Yeah, just don't tag me in it."

Gabbie laughed and thought, "he's probably consumed enough alcohol to put an elephant in a stupor but still has a one liner in him. "

"Doesn't sound like he's told you anything we didn't already know," she replied. "You're wanted for murder, they took your law license and interviewed your parents. I kinda figured all that before you spoke with him."

"Bet you did," Miki slurred. "You're a smart girl. Why do you make a living spinning on a pole?" Miki tried to bring his drink to his mouth. It was like watching an airplane landing in a strong wind—back and forth. Gabbie smiled as she watched him struggle for a few seconds. She finally relented and pushed the bottom of the glass to guide it for a smooth landing.

"Tell you what," Gabbie waited until he finished his drink, "you answer my question first and then I will answer yours."

"What's yours?!" Miki rose his empty glass as if giving a toast.

"Why are you a drunk? Why have you pissed away a degree that most people would give their left arm for?"

"That's two questions." Miki waved his index and middle finger.

"And somehow, I think they have the same answer."

Miki put his glass on the table and sighed. He started to speak and then stopped. "I don't think I am drunk enough to tell you all that."

"For most people, you probably would be, but for you," Gabbie poured him another glass of Dickel, "not just yet."

He took the pour in one solid gulp and slammed the glass down. He looked at her and down at the glass. She poured him another.

"Okay Sailor, that's it. You're cut off. Anymore and I will need subtitles to understand you." She put the bottle on the floor out of his reach. "So, what happened?"

Miki sighed. He had not told the story in over five years. But even in his state, he could remember every detail. "It was eight years ago, on Sullivan's Island. The island right next to us." Miki pointed in the wrong direction.

"Okay." Gabbie intently listened.

"I just finished settling another big case. I was on my way to being named partner."

"Sounds like you were a great lawyer," Gabbie interjected.

"Oh, I was. I was tremendous." Miki sighed again. "But the problem was, I knew it. And that night was my night to celebrate me...my prowess as a trial lawyer. I was a rock star."

Miki took a sip of his drink.

"And I met this woman. Her name was Athena Newton. I will never forget that name as long as I live. She was stunning," Miki took another sip, "and we hit it off."

"Not a surprise."

"She was part Asian. She was so hot." Miki reached for another sip but Gabbie stopped him.

"Slow down or I will need those subtitles. And don't you want me to hear your story?" She smiled. Gabbie played cool but she was dying to know what exactly caused the downfall of this man. She only knew a drunk with tremendous potential. She wanted to know what actually got him to this state. She had not cared this much about another person since Savannah."

"Yep, right. Gonna get my questions answered." Miki pointed at her with a wink. "So we decide to grab a couple of drinks and walk on the beach. And honestly, that is all I remember of that night."

Gabbie continued to listen.

"But the next day, I do remember all of that. It was a game changer." He looked at the glass and then at her as if asking for permission for another sip. She allowed it.

"What happened?"

"Well, I woke up in the dunes and she was nowhere to be found. It was Saturday so I didn't have to worry about missing work. I still had on my dress shirt and tie from the day before. I looked like a successful homeless person making his way over the dunes."

Gabbie smiled at the image.

"I found my car, drove home and took a shower. As soon as I got out, my doorbell rang. It was a black man who said he was a cop."

"Ok."

"I will never forget his eyes. I had never seen such anger in someone. I had represented people who lost loved ones in wrecks and because of faulty products. I had seen anger and pain…but never like that."

Gabbie continued to listen, hoping he would not pass out before the end.

"So, he introduced himself as Detective Newton. Evidently, her father was a cop and came to ask questions about his daughter. She had been missing since last night."

"How did he know about you?"

"He had questioned the bartender from the night before. Like I said, I was letting everyone at the bar know exactly who I was and all that I had accomplished. That bartender remembered me very well."

"Not exactly under the radar."

"Hardly." Miki sighed. Even drunk, it was hard to tell the story. "So I am sitting there in my robe, just out of the shower. My normally sharp legal mind was blunt from the night before. I had this unrelenting headache. I just started answering his questions without even thinking."

"Normally you would have reacted differently?"

"Of course, I would have closed the door and told him to talk with my lawyer. But instead, I sat there and started telling him everything. I told him how we met, how we had some drinks and how we went down to the beach. He had in front of him the last person to have seen his missing daughter."

"So you knew you were being interrogated by this missing woman's father."

"Yes, but it wasn't registering until...you know the radios that cops have on the uniforms?"

Gabbie nodded. "I am keenly aware of those. I have heard my name mentioned over them." She smiled.

"Well, his radio goes off. It states that a woman matching his daughter's description had just been found. But it didn't say woman, it said body."

"Oh, shit," Gabbie replied.

"Which is almost exactly what I did all over myself. It was when I heard the word 'body' that I realized I was in trouble. But before I could utter another word, I was face down on my hardwoods."

"He arrested you, I assume," Gabbie replied.

"Oh, he arrested the fuck out of me. It still amazes me how quickly I was thrown into the back of the patrol car and read my Miranda rights. Ten minutes ago I am showering in my $10,000 Hansgrohe, and now, I am heading to jail."

"Life can literally change in a matter of minutes, sometimes even seconds," Gabbie observed. Miki nodded. "What did they book you on?"

"Suspicion of murder."

Gabbie continued to listen.

"Then I did what I should have done when her dad darkened my doorstep. I lawyered up. One of our firm's criminal lawyers got involved. He was one of the best in the state. He had us on the offensive from the beginning."

"How?"

"Well, he already had planned to bury any statements made to her dad before my Miranda rights were given. And my law firm had already reached out to sources at the Bar to leave my license alone. They also made sure that my name wasn't mentioned on any of the press leaks."

"There was actually a time in your life when you were part of the 'haves' versus the 'have nots'?" Gabbie acted shocked.

"Hell, yeah. My firm stood behind me. Our senior partner was threatening the county sheriff with a civil suit if the charges were not dismissed. He told him that they were singling out me and our firm over the death of a woman who got drunk and drowned." Miki took his last sip. "And all that was working until the results of the autopsy were released."

"What were they?"

"Athena had been brutally beaten and raped before her death. The trauma on her body revealed that this poor woman had endured a physical experience that was simply obscene. The county coroner opined that she actually died from excessive blood loss from her vagina and anus rather than drowning."

"Dear God." Gabbie exhaled.

"All of a sudden, everyone in my corner scattered. I was no longer seen as a sympathetic person who simply had a drink with the wrong person at the wrong time. I was viewed as successful man with a terrible dark side." He stared into space. His eyes watered and a single tear rolled down his cheek.

Gabbie stared at him. He was completely exposed. It was the most intimacy she had ever experienced with another person.

Miki wiped his eyes and continued. "So my lawyer, who desperately wanted to run from the case but knew he was on the hook to represent me, demanded a DNA test to match the blood and sperm found on the victim. That was the time I was actually the most scared."

"Why?"

"I didn't remember anything from that night. As absurd as it sounds, I had convinced myself that anything was possible. What if they somehow found physical evidence of me on the victim?"

"And?"

"No match. There was no physical evidence linking me to the brutality that woman suffered. But the damage was done. It is hard to survive being associated with such a thing."

"Did they ever find who did it?"

"No, no they didn't. But her father always thought I had something to do with it. He put the nail in my coffin."

"How?"

"He found a way to get some of my hair. Don't know how. Maybe on my robe or maybe he went back into my home when I was at jail to do his own investigation. He took that sample and had a 10-panel hair follicle test done."

"Trying to dig up some dirt on you?"

"Probably. I am not sure that would have been admissible, but it couldn't hurt. Inadmissible great evidence can go a long way."

"Did you test positive?"

"Oh, yeah. Remember, I was a rock star." Miki looked at his empty glass but Gabbie shook her head. There would be no more for him. "Cocaine, marijuana. And her father made sure that those results were leaked to members of my firm and the SC Bar."

"Which led to you being fired?"

"Like a SCUD missile. And the Bar told me that while I had not violated the law and could not necessarily be disciplined, if I ran into any more trouble then I would be disbarred." Miki laughed.

"What's so funny?"

"There was a time that losing my license would have been a death sentence. But after that event, I could have given a shit less. At least it would be a sign that I need to do something else with my life. I haven't had a sign in my life in years."

"Most of us haven't," Gabbie replied.

"I get fired from the firm and my reputation in Charleston is ruined. That's when I decide to set up shop in our state's capitol." Gabbie poured him one last shot. She figured he deserved and needed it.

Miki took the shot and dropped the glass. It amazingly didn't shatter on the floor. Miki smiled at the glass and then back at Gabbie.

"That glass is like us," he slurred.

"How so?" She leaned over and put her hands on his cheeks.

"We may get banged around but we don't shatter, even though it may be better if we had." Miki rubbed her cheek with the top of his hand. She acquiesced to his touch. "Too bad."

"What's too bad, Mr. Martin?" Gabbie said with an adoring glow. "

"If I weren't a drunk and you weren't a stripper, we could have really been something." Miki leaned back away from her. "But then again, if I weren't a drunk and you weren't a stripper, then we would not have met." He grinned. "Life's such a paradox." He finally relented and passed out.

Gabbie gently tapped him on the shoulder and led him from the chair and into bed. Miki crumbled without taking off his clothes. He had endured enough life for the day. She kissed him on the head and closed the bedroom door.

She found herself in unfamiliar position—sobriety at night. She was still wired from listening to Miki's story.

She was trying to digest it when the folder marked Brown Recluse caught her attention again. It had accompanied them on their journey but she had never asked about its contents. She just assumed it was something work-related. But Miki's story left her wanting to learn more about him. Even something as trivial as seeing what he does during work.

She grabbed the folder and opened it. A DVD-marked Report of Findings fell to the ground. She ignored the written contents of the folder and scoured the living room for a player. It was buried under a slue of DVDs marked Spring Family Vacation I, II, and all the way up to IV.

Gabbie put in the disc and watched the contents unfold on the TV screen. She didn't blink through the entire showing. She watched it four more times that night.

Perhaps this Miki's chance at salvation.

CHAPTER THIRTEEN:
LAY THE TRAP

Julius Spring was at his family's lake house for the weekend. With the legislative session in full swing, he was focused on thwarting Grafton's efforts to have his legislation passed. He had made more headway than even Spring anticipated. He wasn't surprised by Grafton's willingness to gain political ground at the cost of his own state's reputation. He knew that passage of the bill would result in detrimental ramifications for the state. There would be corporate and public backlash. There would be millions spent in legal bills to defend the legislation…not to mention the loss of massive federal funding if such a bill was passed. Grafton had blind-sided him with the information regarding Miki. Spring blamed himself for the potential havoc his state was getting ready to face.

Sharon White was a native to Spring's home county. They shared a long history. At 45, she was the only black female to head a state law enforcement agency. After her mother passed, her grandfather raised her. She never knew her real father. White grew up on government subsidies. She ate thanks to food stamps and her health care was provided through Medicaid. Unlike some, her reliance on the government strengthened her resolve to make sure she would never need another handout. It also instilled a sense of duty to the state that essentially helped raise her.

She was a brilliant woman. She graduated magna cum laude from high school and earned a scholarship to the state's largest university. The scholarship was named after and funded by the Spring family. In college, she focused on grades and extracurricular activities rather than friends and drinking. She graduated top in her class with a Criminal Justice degree and went to work for the FBI.

At 5'5 and weighing 110 pounds, she resembled a model rather than a federal law enforcement officer. The FBI assigned her to a desk job, and that simply did not suit her. So Sharon White returned home and became the first black female sheriff's deputy in Spring's home county.

For the first couple of years, White's profession was uneventful and, as she would describe in her best selling autobiography, repetitive. She spent her days and nights arresting former high school classmates for public intoxication or domestic violence. There was no crystal meth… that took too much math and science. But that all changed in her third year as a deputy.

It was in the early morning hours of a night shift patrol when White was toned out. Headquarters had received a phone call from an elderly woman claiming to hear screams of children coming from the woods in her backyard. While the poor old soul was prone to call 911 for conversation because she was lonely, she never made a prank call. White was suspicious that perhaps it was the howl of a lonely dog or coyote. She pulled into the driveway with her headlights glaring into the backwoods of the woman's property.

"It came from back there," the elderly woman exclaimed from her front porch. She pointed in the direction of the woods. "I heard them! I heard them screaming and then they stopped. I think they're hurt!"

"Ok ma'am. It's okay. Just go back inside and I will check it out." The lady obliged. Sharon held her flashlight next to her ear and headed into the darkened forest of trees. She proceeded cautiously, continuously flashing her light between her feet and the tree line. As each moment passed, she became more confident that she would only find wildlife and this was a waste of time. That changed when she saw the first body hanging from the tree.

There were two black children swinging from ropes attached to the limb of a 100-year-old oak tree. She recognized them from the area. They were brother and sister. She was ten and he was eight. Like Sharon, they were raised by their grandfather, as their parents skipped out shortly after the youngest was born.

Within ten minutes, every available emergency vehicle owned by the county illuminated the forest. Then, over her radio, she heard that the grandfather of the children had called in. He reported a break-in at his home. He stated that two white males wearing white hoods knocked him out and he awoke to find his grandchildren missing.

The next morning the county was covered with FBI. The crime made national headlines. "An Old School Hanging in an Old School County!" Julius Spring was mortified. He was inundated with calls from every major civil rights organization. He was receiving calls from Democratic leaders on a national stage. He was facing political death merely because of his home county.

Sharon watched as FBI subjected the county's white population to an inquisition. She heard of threats of income tax audits and prison if people did not cooperate. She learned that they had narrowed the lead to four self-professed racists with an affinity toward drinking and driving but not violence.

While the FBI and nation focused on the racial tone of the crime, she focused on the crime. As she observed the autopsy, there was one thing that stuck out in her mind—there was no sign of struggle from the children other than marks that were attributed to them trying to break free of the rope. She said they were lured into the woods by someone they knew. But no one listened. There was no one else to lure them.

Sharon played a hunch. She interviewed the only insurance agent of the entire county. She learned that approximately six months ago, the grandfather of the children had taken out a million dollar insurance policy on each life. It was a term policy that cost him less than

$50. With a little more digging, she learned that their grandfather had lost his job and owed some local bookies over $50,000.

She didn't share any of that information with the feds. Instead, she interviewed the grandfather, videotaping the interview. She told him that it was all routine—just needed to tie up some loose ends.

After approximately three minutes of mundane questions, she showed him the insurance information and asked him why he would take out such a policy. He dropped to his knees and sobbed uncontrollably. It was a complete and unforced confession. There had been a break-in that night and he was knocked out. But it was from people seeking payment for past due gambling debts. They had been breaking down the door and beating him unconsciousness for over the past month. He took advantage of the opportunity to stage their deaths.

There wasn't a closed mouth in the room when Sharon shared her video with the FBI. Sharon finally received a real job offer from the FBI. She rose to the rank of Senior Special Agent and was involved with every major hate crime investigation in the nation. After a few years with the FBI, Spring made her an offer that she could not refuse. She would run the state's law enforcement agency. Sharon did not have the patience to withstand the politics involved with being promoted to director of the FBI.

Grafton won the governorship a year after her appointment. He knew White was a Spring ally, but did not have the political moxie to have her removed. He instead was reduced to employing Peppers as a part of his security detail to keep an eye on her. Up until Grafton's recent lunch with Spring, Peppers was of no consequence. But the information about Miki was the reason for meeting with Sharon at his family's mountain house.

It was a mid-morning meeting. The sun's reflection off the lake was almost blinding. He sat under the shade of the gazebo at the base of his dock awaiting the arrival of his guest. Sharon strolled to the dock wearing a pair of jeans and green turtle neck. It was far cry from her normal business attire worn for lectures on her autobiography or appearances on countless news shows sharing her experience with the FBI.

She had turned down countless offers to be a professor or fulltime legal analyst on a multitude of news shows. She had even turned down an offer to host her own show dedicated to the investigation of hate crimes. She still felt a duty to her home state and the Senator that brought her to the proverbial "ball." But her professional success caused her to view her role as the state's top law enforcement agent as part-time.

"Senator Spring," she greeted him.

Spring rose to give her a hug. "Miss White." They sat down in the Adirondacks facing toward the lake. "You want some coffee?" Spring said as he sipped on his second cup of the morning.

"Oh no, thank you though. I try to limit myself to one cup. I find that a person with my energy level doesn't need any additional help. Fine line between energetic and jittery." Sharon smiled.

"Well, based on all your television interviews, and speaking engagements, it seems that you have mastered that fine line. You are quite the darling of law enforcement." Spring took another sip from his cup.

"I don't know about all that Senator," Sharon responded.

"No, no. It's true. I don't think I could watch a television news program cover a hate crime without you being interviewed as an expert. I trust you get paid for that."

"Oh, Senator, I don't think it is that widespread. Besides, I think I am just easy on the eyes, so to speak. They like that." Sharon gave a sheepish grin.

"Maybe," Spring returned the grin. "But whatever it is, it sure seems to keep you busy."

"Never too busy to make time for you though," Sharon replied. They had not met on a weekend since he courted her for the position. And she had never been to his lake house. She knew there was a hidden agenda. She was relieved, and concerned, that he was so willing to forgo the normal politico chit-chat and get right to the point. White thought back to her Shakespeare, "something was rotten in the state of Denmark."

"I don't know about that," Spring snapped.

White looked concerned. That was the closest he had ever come to insulting her. "How do mean, Senator?" She couldn't conceal the agitation in her voice. Her tours on the lecture circuit were met with adulation. She wasn't used to scorn.

"Peppers," Spring coldly replied.

"Grafton's lap dog," she countered.

"From what I hear, yes."

"Is that why I am here on a Saturday morning?" Sharon was shocked. "What has that little pup done to garner your attention?"

"What do you know of Miki Martin?"

"Honestly, not much. I know that there is a folder on my desk with his name on it. But I've between the two coasts over the last couple of weeks and just haven't had a chance to…"

Spring interrupted. "Well, I need you." Sharon stared in amazement. Spring never needed anyone. "I need you to look at it and look into it."

"Well, of course."

"Sharon, I know that you aren't long for this state. I know that your aspirations are far greater than what this state can offer you."

"Senator." She acted humbled and embarrassed, but he was correct.

"But while you're here, Sharon, while you are on this post, I do need you to be focused," Spring continued.

"Yes, sir."

"I know that occasionally I will be bitten by a dog. But I just don't expect it to be a dog in my back yard."

Sharon nodded. "I will look at the file later, but am I to assume that Peppers found some information that you weren't expecting?"

"This Martin fellow is the prime suspect in that strip club murder and he's best friends with my son-in-law."

Sharon continued to nod.

"These are things that I would have expected for you to tell me." Spring paused. "Not things to learn from Grafton via Peppers."

Sharon continued to nod. She wasn't versed in being a political ally but she knew what it meant to be loyal. Spring had never asked her to manipulate her position except as it related to shielding him from Grafton. She failed.

"Well, can't I simply fire him?" Sharon replied. "Governor's security detail is still in my realm."

"Maybe, but I don't want that."

"Ok. May I ask why? I can place my own people on this investigation. We can make sure that Martin's connection to your son-in-law never sees the light day. It has nothing to do with the criminal investigation."

"I do appreciate that, Sharon," Spring pretended, but it was too late for that. If she had not appeared on so many mid-morning talk shows, then he would not be in this position. "But with Peppers, I have an avenue to know exactly what Grafton is doing. Without him, I then have to worry about not only finding out what he is doing but finding a way to discover it."

"The better between two evils is the evil that is known," Sharon replied.

"Exactly."

"Well, I know that Peppers has his own right-hand man. A fellow named John."

"Last name?"

"Not off the top of my head, but I can find out."

"Sharon, you have a lot of opportunities before you and plenty of resources to help you and potentially others advance. Maybe you could lure him into our camp with the promise of something more."

"I can do that. I could make a phone call and get that guy a great job with the feds tomorrow."

"Well, let's not do that just yet. Save it until he gives us some inside information on Grafton."

"Yes Sir, Senator."

* * *

Ron Poe had just finished another brutal day of hourly billing. He had been at the office for 12 hours and was only able to bill 8. It was his night to watch his 12-year-old and six-year-old. His wife was playing a match in her mixed couples' tennis league. It was really her escape from being a stay-at-home mother of three. She and another male member of the league had been engaging in a dangerous game of flirtation. Lil knew that she would never allow it to advance to the next level, but this was a fact she did not share with her male counterpart. She adored the attention and did not want their exchanges to end.

While she played her game of cat and mouse, Ron sat in the stands of a multi-field baseball complex along with the other parents—all cheering and yelling to press their children to attain the athletic success that they did not achieve as a child. On this night, his 12-year-old was riding the bench while his six-year-old was camped at a playground 20 yards away.

As Ron Poe was shifting his head from the baseball game and his youngest, his nose was filled with the scent of Saint Laurent Black Opium perfume. He spun his head to the right to find the source. It belonged to a long-legged brunette in her mid-30s. She wore a black P.A.R.O.S.H skirt and red Eltro neck sweater. She did not fit the mold of the other baseball moms in the stands. And, she was seated right next to him.

"I'm sorry. Am I crowding your space?" she asked him.

"No, no. Not at all." Ron was paralyzed just as he was in the I-HOP with Miki and Chandler's daughter. He nervously twirled his wedding band.

"You have a son that plays, I take it?" she asked.

"Um, yes. Yes, I do."

"What position?" She continued.

"The bench," Ron replied as he pointed toward the dugout.

She let out a beautifully feminine laugh. Poe was nervous. It had been years since he engaged a beautiful woman other than his wife in conversation. He felt like a high school freshman talking to a senior on the cheerleading squad.

"Well, I didn't know that the bench was a position," she replied.

"Yeah, it doesn't get the same attention as those on the field positions," Poe said.

The woman laughed again. Poe's stomach sank in anticipation of her reaction to his next one-liner.

"But my son must be pretty good at it because he's the only one allowed to play that position."

She laughed harder than the previous laughs. Poe was basking in his success of charming the gorgeous woman.

"I am sure that he appreciates you coming to his games," she replied.

"I guess so because he plays the position so well that he starts every game at it."

She continued to laugh, her brown eyes locked with Poe's. His insecurities about his weight and appearance disappeared. Poe was a lawyer and knew how to read people. This woman was interested in him. He also enjoyed the attention. He hadn't received much since his wife started tennis.

"Do you come to these 12-year-old fast pitch games for enjoyment?" he asked.

He grinned as she giggled at this response.

"Or do you actually have a son that plays?" he continued.

"No. I haven't ventured down that road. I leave that to my sister. I promised my nephew that I would watch him. That is what a favorite aunt does."

"Which one is he?" Ron pointed to the field.

"He's the handsome young lad playing third base for the other team. Have ya'll played them before?"

"No. That team is from another league. We only play them once a season unless we make the playoffs."

She already knew that.

"Is that your only son?" she asked.

"No," he replied.

She already knew that as well.

"I have a high schooler whom I rarely see because he doesn't acknowledge that he has parents."

She resumed her flirtatious laughter.

"And a six-year-old named Justin. He's right over there at the play..." Ron turned his head in the direction of his youngest. He wasn't there.

She was looking at the playground with him but more importantly, she was also observing his reaction.

"Wait a minute. Where is he?" Ron switched into Daddy mode. The woman that consumed his attention for the past few minutes was erased from his mind. His stomach sank once again, but it had nothing to do with nervousness. This was pure fear.

Ron jumped from the stand and made his way through the crowd of people swarming the baseball fields. He arrived at the playground but Justin was not there.

"Justin!" He shouted. He tried to calm himself at first. Perhaps, he wondered to the concession stand or was simply watching another game. "Justin!"

He walked briskly toward the concession stand. He wasn't there. Ron scoured the crowd looking for his son. What Ron usually perceived as a normal crowd of parents scattered amongst the complex now appeared as a massive sea of people taking up every ounce of clear space.

"Justin! Justin!" The fear in his voice pierced the ear of every parent that heard him. People began to turn their heads in his direction.

Ron ran to each of the five ball fields in the complex, screaming Justin's name.

Other parents came to his aid. He could see the concern in their eyes. They were watching a parent enduring the ultimate nightmare—a missing child.

He enlisted the help of several other parents as they dispersed amongst the complex shouting "Justin!" One parent volunteered to check the parking lot and another parent volunteered to go to the gate of the complex and monitor any cars that were leaving.

It had been ten minutes, but to Poe it felt like a day. With each passing second, his mind filled with dark thoughts of a stranger restraining his child as he whisked him away. He tried to shake off the thoughts and remain focused on finding his son. But he was overwhelmed by the reality that his boy had been abducted. He was abducted because his dad was flirting with some stranger. How would he explain that to his wife? To his other children?

His mind continued to wander to unspeakable places. What would they do to his son? Was his son in pain?

Was he crying? Was he crying for his dad? The tears began to well in his eyes. He held his breath and then he let out one last loud scream "Justin!" It didn't come from his lungs or his diaphragm. It came from his soul. It also strained his vocal chords.

Now, he felt truly helpless. He could not find his son and was unable to scream above a raspy whisper.

Just as the public announcer called Justin's name to tell him his father was looking for him, his cloud of despair was lifted. He saw a single arm raised in the air waving at him. At the base of the arm was Justin. They were walking toward him. Ron sprinted to them.

"Justin," Poe grabbed his son with both arms and lifted him in the air. "Oh, my God, Justin." The tears were streaming down his face.

"Daddy, why are you wet?" Justin asked as he felt his fathers sweat-soaked body against him. "And why are you crying?"

"Buddy, you scared me to death. Where did you go?"

"I don't know. Some man came and got me. He told me that you wanted to see me at one of the ball fields over there." Justin stared back at his father. "You are really wet!"

Ron glared at the stranger that brought his child back to him.

"Oh, that man wasn't me," Elad said.

Ron's anger subsided at the answer. Elad was dressed in a suit and tie. He certainly did not fit the description of a kidnapper. Poe continued to bear hug his son.

"Daddy, that's too tight. And you're wet! Yuck!" Justin exclaimed.

"I saw him walking with an unsavory-looking fellow. And I don't know, you see all those news articles and I guess your senses get heightened. Something just didn't look right. You know?" Elad replied.

"Absolutely," Ron whispered. His voice was gone.

"So I went up to the guy and started asking questions about the complex and where certain ball fields were located. And this guy couldn't give me any answers. And I thought that was odd. He's here with a kid and knows nothing about this place."

"Right," Ron nodded.

"So that's when I asked this little guy," Elad rubbed Justin's cheek, "How does your dad not know about the baseball fields? And that's when he told me that the man wasn't his father and that his father was over there."

"Is that what you told him, buddy?" Ron asked his son.

"Uh-huh," Justin said. His attention was now focused at the concession stand. "Can I get a Coke?"

"So I looked at the guy, he just looked at me and then he took off running. That's when I heard you let out that scream."

"Yeah, I let out a scream alright." Ron rubbed his voice box.

"That was loud, Daddy," Justin chimed.

"It sure was. You sounded like Mel Gibson from *Braveheart*." Elad smiled.

Ron chuckled. It was a much-needed moment of laughter. "I don't know how to thank you. What's your name?"

Elad grinned. "I know that this will sound a little odd but I would rather not say and I actually have to get going."

Ron was perplexed by the answer.

Elad pointed to a van parked in the lot near the fields. "You see that van there?"

"Yes," Ron replied.

"It is a surveillance van. And I am a PI. It's a divorce case. The wife thinks her husband is using his son's baseball games as an excuse to meet up with his paramour. We have the entire area under watch. That's how my eye caught your son and the guy."

"I gotcha." Ron was consumed with the elation of finding his son. He didn't care how he got him back.

"Dad, I'm thirsty. Can we get a Coke? Maybe a candy bar?" Justin said as he kissed his dad on the cheek.

It was the best kiss that Poe ever felt.

"Dad, I am going to leave you with him," Elad instructed. "And I am going to get back to work."

"Well, thank you. Thank you very much," Ron said as he extended his hand to Elad.

"Of course, I am just glad that it all ended well." Elad turned and made his way toward the van.

One of the parents had called the police and they just arrived. Elad quickly drove off.

The next morning at work, Ron fielded a phone call from a man who identified himself as "John" working with state law enforcement.

"Mr. Poe, this is simply a routine follow-up to the events last night."

"Well, I told the police all that I know. I am not sure why y'all are involved?"

"Mr. Poe, you are the son-in-law of a well-known political figure in the state and his grandson was almost abducted. We just wanted to follow up to see if you can offer any clues as to who would have done this."

"I have no idea. Like I said, a stranger took him and then he was returned by a man who said that he was a private investigator. I gave the description to the cops."

"Right, a strange-looking redheaded fellow. We got that. Let me ask you something and this may be off the beaten path, but what do you know about Miki Martin?"

Ron looked down at his phone. The display showed "Caller ID Blocked."

"I'm sorry, who did you say you were again?"

"I told you. I am John with state law enforcement. So...Mr. Martin? We know you are friends. Can you give me any information as to his whereabouts?"

Ron was caught off guard by the question. "Miki? What does he have to do with any of this? I don't." His lawyer instincts took over, "Sir, I am going to need your last name and badge number before we continue any further with this conversation."

John hung up. Ron's head ran wild with thoughts of how Miki's whereabouts were somehow connected to last night's episode. What was Miki involved with?

John immediately called Elad and relayed to him the brief conversation.

"Sounds like he knows Martin's locale," Elad said.

"Yeah, that was my thought."

"Now I just have to get it from him."

CHAPTER FOURTEEN:
SPACE OUTSIDE OF THE "T"

Grafton's bill was headed for a second reading on the House floor. This was the biggest hurdle for passage and he anticipated a lengthy heated debate. Essentially, a bill must have three readings in the House and must pass each reading before being presented to the Senate. Once the bill hits the Senate, it must then pass another three readings. At that point, the bill will be presented to the governor to sign into law.

The second reading is the most critical. For most bills, the third reading is merely a formality. Once Grafton got passage from the House, then he only needed to focus on the Senate. Grafton's lunch with Spring allowed his bill to escape committee and head to the House floor and then to the Senate. Now, it was time for him to secure the necessary votes to pass each reading in the House and Senate.

There are 124 House members and 46 members of the Senate. Grafton's magic numbers were 75 in the House and 24 in the Senate. He needed 25 more House members and another 15 in the Senate in order to get the bill in front of him for signature. He needed more votes and knew exactly where to go to get them.

Whenever he faced a contested battle with legislation, Grafton always told his staffers to look to the area outside the "T." He coined the phrase during his first gubernatorial race.

South Carolina is bounded by Tennessee on the northwest and the Atlantic Ocean on the east. Georgia is to the south and North Carolina to the north. If you were to draw a line from the west of the state to the east, then you would hit Greenville, Columbia and, finally, Charleston.

Greenville was the technological epicenter of the state thanks to a multi-billion dollar automobile plant built over a decade ago. Columbia was the state's capitol and home to the largest university. Charleston was the economic jewel of the state, created through a mixture of tourism—including renowned restaurants and chefs—one of the busiest ports on the eastern seaboard, and large manufacturing plants.

Myrtle Beach was to the north of Charleston and Hilton Head to her south. Myrtle Beach was a tourist mecca; wealthy retirees from across the nation inhabited Hilton Head. Drawing a line from Myrtle Beach to Hilton Head completed the top of Grafton's "T."

Grafton viewed the "T" as representing 90 percent of the state's wealth. It was the area outside of the "T" that Grafton termed as the land that time forgot. This area was comprised of small rural counties that had not changed in the last 50 years.

Manufacturing and textile plants that once fed these counties had been outsourced to foreign countries. There were no powerful unions to keep industry in the state. The businesses simply picked up stakes and followed the cheaper labor. A large group of barren counties was left in the wake of the mass exodus.

The only form of industry in these counties consisted of a few Wal-Marts scattered across Grafton's self-described hinterlands. There were no major interstates but rather a maze of two-lane country roads bounded by rows of cotton, tobacco fields or Kudzu-infested forests. There were no subdivisions created by national builders but rather rows of mobile homes. For these counties, a tourist was considered someone who was lost.

The public schools were starved because there was no money in the county coffers to educate its own citizens. One of the counties had actually sued the state, seeking state money to allow the county to meet the minimum standards for public education. It lost the suit thanks to Grafton's use of state funds to employ the best attorneys to fight the action.

People imprisoned in a jail cell of poverty and lack of education inhabited the area outside the "T."

For Grafton, these people and their representatives were easily swayed by the promise of government funding. He likened it to his own personal oil well and he had the rig to drill it—state funding. He had employed this rig in his election bid and again, when he needed votes to pass legislation.

But for this particular legislation, he knew that the drilling would be tough. This was not a bill that representatives of this area embraced. The socioeconomics of their constituents matched the vast majority of people who had abortions. He had attempted to reach out for support but was quickly rebuked at every turn. Grafton would need something huge to land these votes.

Grafton and Pontet organized a meeting of 25 House representatives and 15 Senators from the area outside of the "T"—the number of votes he needed to allow his bill to pass. It was one Grafton's "meetings that did not actually occur." The legislature had recessed for the week and Grafton invited this group to meet him in the basement of a local church whose pastor was one of his biggest supporters. He advertised it as a planning session to help these representatives with re-election bid.

Rather than continue to try to pick them off one at a time, Grafton wanted to make one sweeping proposal that would capture all of the votes. If it didn't work, then he would resort to personal promises or extortion, depending on the circumstances. But that would take time, and he needed this bill passed during this session.

With a card table serving as a makeshift podium, Grafton's audience squirmed in discomfort in their plastic folding chairs. They had just left the session and were dressed in suits and ties or dresses and high heels. The representatives were chatting with each other about the less than modest accommodations of the meeting. It was the storage area of the church housing extra chairs and cookware for the monthly pancake supper.

There was a sea of waving hands as the representatives tried to ward off the heat caused by the lack of ventilation. The representatives had been in the room for 30 minutes as they waited for last-minute stragglers to arrive.

Pontet and Grafton were huddled together, scanning their audience. Pontet nodded to the figure standing by the doorway.

"Who is that?" Pontet asked.

"That's Peppers' lap dog...John something," Grafton replied.

"Why's he here?"

"Well, I need some form of security. I couldn't exactly have my security detail in attendance for this meeting. Don't need this leaking out."

"I reckon not," Pontet chuckled.

"Alright, let's get started," said Grafton as he raised his hand to get his audience's attention. "Ladies and Gentlemen, if I could have your attention."

The representatives became silent but did not stop fanning their faces.

"First, I would like to thank you for meeting with me today."

"Governor, I know we don't represent the economic powerhouse counties of the state but couldn't we at least meet in a place with some air conditioning," a female House member said.

Her statement was met with laughter and nods.

Grafton laughed along with his audience. "Well, I guess this is what happens when I plan an event versus letting my staff plan it," Grafton smiled.

His audience laughed at his attempt at self-deprecating humor.

"But I wanted to make sure that we could meet without the distraction of press or other representatives. I wanted an honest discussion about not only your political futures, but the futures of your constituents."

The audience was silent. They knew this was no planning session. It was part of Grafton's plan to press them about support for his bill. No one in the room intended to support his plan, but curiosity motivated their decision to attend. What could Grafton have in his bag of tricks that would cause them to support a bill that their constituents so vehemently opposed?

"Governor, I am hot and tired. Let's cut to the chase—why are we really here?" a male House member asked. The audience nodded in approval of the direct question.

Grafton chuckled. "Well, so much for delicately easing you into a discussion." Grafton looked at Pontet. Pontet simply raised his eyebrows as if to say, "This is your show...good luck." Grafton focused his attention back on the audience. "I am here to ask you to support my bill."

His audience shook their heads.

"Governor, you know that we just cannot do that," a House member exclaimed.

"No, you can do it. You just don't want to," Grafton replied.

The audience grew restless and frustrated. They mumbled to one another about Grafton's incredulous request.

"Can you believe him? Brings us to a church basement to ask us to support this thing," one representative exclaimed.

"Well, of course he would. He doesn't want to get embarrassed in public by asking us to support this thing," another replied.

"I think he turned the air conditioning off just to try to sweat us out," a voice blurted out.

"He wouldn't treat any other representatives this way!" another representative observed.

"That's for damn sure!" someone replied.

Pontet looked at Grafton and continued to raise his eyebrows as if to say, "Hope you know what you are doing."

"Ladies and Gentlemen, you can do this. You just don't want to. There is a difference," Grafton raised his voice to regain their attention.

"It don't matter whether we can't or won't. It simply ain't gonna happen. We have to live with our constituents. And they don't want this bill," said a House member.

"Governor, he's right. How the hell do you propose that we vote for this bill and then explain it to our hometown folks?" another female house member chimed.

"Exactly! Our folks get nothing from the state!" exclaimed the first representative who spoke.

He was rapidly losing his audience. Every time someone spoke up, the crowd was getting more riled up. He noticed that a few representatives were beginning to stand up as if to leave. Grafton wanted to be more delicate in his offer to them but he feared that they would simply walk out. The passage of his bill hinged on the approval of these representatives. With passage came the support of Practical Solutions and with that, the White House. He needed to keep them in the room.

"What if your folks were to get one billion dollars in state funding?" Grafton yelled above the din of his grumbling audience.

Everyone hushed. The sea of waving hands and discontent was replaced with the whites of wide eyes looking at him in disbelief.

"Have your attention now?" Grafton smirked.

"How? We've been begging for state funding for 20 years. We've been crawling through the desert searching for a drop of water and meanwhile, the "T" counties are so wet that they're filling up swimming pools. You gonna change that?" questioned a male House member.

"By making Senator Spring an offer he cannot refuse," Grafton replied.

Spring was not only the senior Democratic Senator but he was also the unofficial political leader of the area outside of the "T." His home county was part of it.

"I am ready to file proposed legislation known as the Growth & Development Act. In our state, there is a $500 cap on the sales tax for cars and boats. Whether you buy a Hyundai or a Mercedes, you pay $500 as sales tax. Under this legislation, I would change that tax to 5 percent of the sales price. This would raise $100 million per year."

Continued silence. All eyes were on him.

"Under my bill, this $100 million would be disbursed to the 15 most economically disadvantaged counties in the state. The distribution would come in the form of road construction, new schools, and creation of a state-supported technical college system dedicated to your counties."

"You said a billion dollars?" a House member asked.

"I did. We will dedicate that $100 million to your counties for the next 10 years. After that, the legislation will be re-examined."

"Yeah, but who says that the legislation won't be re-pealed next year?" a Senator asked.

"Because of the money waiting on the sideline. There are companies that would love to invest in your counties but don't. And why?" Grafton gazed at his audience. "They still look at this state as being run by a bunch of backwards rednecks, spitting tobacco and waiving a Rebel flag. This legislation changes all of that."

"How?" the same Senator questioned.

The audience anxiously awaited his response.

"Because these companies waiting on the sidelines perceive our unwillingness to help your counties as our desire to maintain the status quo. When we show those companies that we are willing to help...to be progressive...then they will march in full force. Your counties will become new, self-sustaining marketplaces that haven't been open in decades. Once that ball rolls, no one will want to or be able to stop that economic steamroll."

They quietly digested the offer with apparent approval.

Finally, one of the less politically savvy representatives spoke up. He was just elected last fall and this was his first session. He was a young white male who was more comfortable on his farm than the statehouse floor. But he wanted something more for his infant son and thought being a representative was a great place to start.

The freshman representative simply wanted to make sure that he understood the proposal.

"So, if we want this money, then we need to support your abortion bill?"

Grafton hesitated. There is nothing worse in politics than a "yes" or "no" question. Grafton quickly glanced at Pontet for guidance. Pontet was stunned over the turn of events. Grafton had turned a raging wildfire into a smoldering campfire. Pontet simply shook his head as if to say, "Whatever you think, Mr. President."

"Yes, that is exactly what I am saying. My abortion bill passes and I file the Growth and Development Act."

His audience openly nodded at one another... overwhelming approval of his proposal.

The newbie asked another blunt question. "I just don't understand why you wouldn't do this for us without having to say "Yes" to that bill, Mr. Governor. Why can't you just help us out?"

The audience turned their heads back to the governor, awaiting his return volley to their freshman colleague.

Grafton stared at his interrogator. "I am sorry, but I forget your name."

"Representative Luther from District 57," he replied.

"Well, Representative Luther, this has been a fairly blunt meeting and I am going to make it even more direct. I am the only person who can help your counties achieve resurrection and enter the 21st century. You will live your entire life without encountering another governor who can wield the power necessary to save your counties."

Grafton left his makeshift podium and walked toward the freshman. He was close to securing victory and this upstart was now his only obstacle. Now was not the time for diplomacy, it was a time for intimidation. He now was face-to-face with Luther.

"I control facets of this state you don't even know exist," he whispered in his ear. John had waltzed over in case there was a potential security issue and also as an intimidation tactic. "I will have control over this state long after I leave office and for many years to come. And while that may not concern you, it may concern your son. You don't want your son to begin his young life with me as an enemy, or do you?"

The audience strained to her their conversation. John heard every word.

Grafton pulled away and addressed the crowd again like a ringmaster. "And so, Representative Luther, you will learn there are no gifts in politics, only offers and compromise. So this is my offer, if you are willing to compromise. And the question is, are you willing to compromise?"

Luther gulped. "Yes sir," he meekly replied.

The room erupted in applause. Grafton had pulled it off. He spent the next 45 minutes personally shaking the hand of each attendee and shoring up the votes that would pass his bill.

Pontet smiled as he shook his head in awe of Grafton's feat. He quietly approached John.

"Your Peppers' guy, aren't you?" Pontet asked.

"Yes sir," John replied.

"John?" Pontet asked.

"Sessions. John Sessions."

"Is this your first time seeing Grafton in action?"

"No sir, I have seen him in action before," Sessions calmly replied.

"Pretty impressive, huh?"

"Oh, yes sir. Governor Hood always finds a way to get what he wants," John replied with a slight grin.

CHAPTER FIFTEEN:
CHANDLER'S FOLDER

It was the end of Miki's first full week of sobriety in nearly a decade. Gabbie forced him under the promise that she had information that could change his life. She wanted his mind and body clear. She had now watched the DVD over 10 times and scoured the folder to make sense of what she had seen. It was too much for her to comprehend. She needed help, but not from a drunk. She needed Miki to become the lawyer he once was and was probably meant to be.

Miki was astounded by his muscle memory. Despite the daily physical onslaught of alcohol, he was able to run five miles after his first day without a drink. He could feel his physique tightening. Physically, he felt tremendous, but mentally, he was weaker than a kitten. He did not have his chemical concoction of alcohol and antidepressants to ward off the depression that filled his mind. He had wasted so much of his life. He had no wife, no children. The only mark that he had even existed was the carbon footprint that he would leave on this planet. Miki spent every waking moment dissecting every mistake and character flaw with laser-like precision. It was an unrelenting exercise in self-reflection that taxed his soul. Gabbie would find him sitting in a chair, staring at the floor. He looked as if he were watching a movie. For Miki, he was watching the movie of his life in his mind, and it was the scariest horror flick he had ever seen.

Unfortunately, the night did not provide a refuge for Miki's depression. Like an alarm, Miki awoke at 2:00 a.m. every day, scared about his present situation. He was gripped in fear over what would happen when, not if, but when they were caught. Miki knew that they could not continue this run forever. How would it end? Gabbie tried to soothe him back to sleep—sometimes through sex but mainly just holding him while he cried.

Gabbie was on a different road of self-reflection. Up until Miki, she assumed that she would never be anything more than a sex tool for men. But now, she had become an emotional partner rather than just a physical one. She knew that without her, Miki would probably have taken his life or simply drank himself to death. He needed her and because of that, she had lowered her emotional walls to care for him. It was something that she thought had long been abandoned, her ability to care for someone else. They were both traveling on a road of self-discovery albeit on much different paths. That odyssey would continue for them with the contents of Chandler's folder.

She found Miki sitting alone in the dark. The television was turned off as he was replaying his mental movie again. She walked to him with the white folder in one hand.

"Miki?" Gabbie called to him. She snapped her fingers in his face to release him from his trance. He looked up at her.

"Yeah," he said in a soft tone. His eyes were tired and his face was sunken. His shoulder and back were hunched over.

"Why don't you take an intermission? Let's watch something more real," she said holding the DVD in her hand. He looked at the disk. "And no, it's not porn," she said with a slight grin.

She turned on the TV and inserted the DVD. Miki looked at the image on the screen and immediately sat up. It was Chandler Murray staring at him.

"If you are watching this, then I am dead," Chandler said. "Now, I of course don't know how I died but it may or may not be related to what I am about to tell you and what is contained in this folder." Chandler displayed a folder—the same folder that Gabbie had in her hands. Miki reached for it.

"Not just yet, keep watching," Gabbie replied as she moved the folder out of Miki's reach.

"Hell, I don't even know who my audience is for this DVD or if it will ever see the light of day. My daughter hasn't been in my life for years. If she discovered this folder, then it is probably at the bottom of a trashcan."

Chandler paused and breathed in deeply.

"I lost my daughter and didn't do anything to deserve it." Chandler started to tear up. His mind was painted in images of a sweet nine-year-old girl who looked at her dad as if he built the world. That little girl had grown into a woman that was so ashamed of her father that she ran away from him long ago.

Chandler regained his composure. "But perhaps she has given this package to you, Miki, as I directed."

Miki could feel the goose bumps across his arms upon hearing his name mentioned by his late mentor.

"That is what I asked for her to do. And perhaps, you are somewhere in your life that you can help my legacy. Hopefully, you are. All I really have is hope and while it hasn't served me well in life," Chandler paused, "maybe it can in death."

"Where did you get..." Miki tried to ask.

Gabbie interrupted him. "Just watch."

"After I got disbarred, I spent the first few years trying to connect Grafton to the fellow who ended my legal career. I heard some rumor that he was the cause of it all, but I could never trace anything to him. And then I caught a break."

Miki stared in disbelief at the image on the screen. He never thought he would see him again.

"I was driving taxi cabs for a living. It was about seven or eight years ago when I picked up this fare. It was 3:00 in the afternoon and he was stumbling drunk. I had to help him into the car. I wasn't so much surprised about him being drunk. I mean, I am taxi driver. Over two-thirds of my fares are drunk. But I was surprised because he was a cop."

Gabbie and Miki continued to watch intently.

"And I know he was a cop because I picked him up from the station house. He was actually dressed in his uniform. He had shown up for work piss-ass drunk, again. And while it wasn't the first time, it was the last time. They had just fired him."

Chandler paused for a moment and scratched his chin. He was gathering his thoughts to continue his monologue.

"As soon as I got him in the cab, I turned on the radio. I just wanted some noise to distract us both from the so-called white elephant in the cab. Then, on the radio, we hear the voice of Grafton Hood, our esteemed Governor."

Miki leaned forward toward the screen.

"Well, the cop hears Hood's voice and flips out. He bangs at the Plexiglass that separates the front and back seats. I thought he was going to break it. And the whole time, he is screaming 'Turn that shit off!', which I promptly did. And then all of a sudden, he slumps back in the seat and it looked like he passed out. Such a surreal moment having a cop dressed in his uniform passed out in the back seat of a cab."

Chandler chuckled as he thought of it.

"But he didn't pass out. Nope. He had a lot to say. I guess the combination of alcohol, hearing Hood's voice and losing his job created some sort of pixie dust that transformed my cab into a confessional and made me the priest."

Chandler paused again.

"The cop kept going on and on about Grafton Hood. He kept saying how he hated Hood and that Hood was the anti-Christ. I tried to ignore him and get to our destination as fast as possible. But the cop was unrelenting in his confession."

Miki turned up the volume on the television.

"The cop told me that he was responsible for the death of a woman. He told me that his mother worked with the state. He said that she was diagnosed with uterine cancer. It was stage II and she had a 45 percent chance of survival only if she received good treatment. Luckily, her job provided great health insurance. So things looked promising. "

Chandler paused and took a sip from his bottled water. "He then told me about his phone call from Grafton Hood. He said he didn't know Hood and was shocked by the call. The cop said that Hood was very direct. He needed someone taken out. Hood then instructed the cop that he would be the person to assist Hood in this mission."

Chandler took another sip of water.

"The cop of course refused and threatened to expose the conversation to his superiors and press." Chandler chuckled. "Rookie response. As I have come to discover, Grafton doesn't ask anyone to do anything, unless he knows he can make 'em do it. "

Chandler smiled and nodded at his last statement.

"So the cop has to endure a ten-minute lecture from Grafton about uterine cancer. Grafton informed the cop of the significance of the different stages. Grafton went into great detail about the treatment that is most effective for a person classified as stage II. He talked about the various treatments available through her insurance and her being eligible for treatment from cancer centers around the country, provided," Chandler paused, "that she knows the right people to talk to you."

"Grafton being the right person, of course," Miki whispered in response.

"Grafton, of course, offered to help him get his mother that treatment, but also told the cop the other alternative. Not only would he not help, he would instead have her fired. Then she would have no insurance and no treatment. Classic Grafton. Help me and your mother survives; don't and she dies."

Gabbie and Miki shook their heads. They knew nothing of Grafton except he was the governor. Chandler was once again teaching his favorite student.

"Grafton even tells the cop that his mother has been effectively terminated because of supposed 'downsizing' and that the paperwork had been signed and was just sitting on Grafton's desk. But he was giving the cop the chance to change all that."

Miki is taken aback when Chandler appears to stare Miki directly in the eyes and speaks to him directly. "This is important, Miki. You get a real insight about this man. Grafton probably created the downsizing, causing innocent folks to lose their jobs, in order to let him blackmail this cop. You see that?"

"Yes," Miki replied, forgetting that he was conversing with a dead man.

Chandler thumbed through the folder that was now in Gabbie's hands. He grabbed a sheet of paper.

"There is a lot of information in there which substantiates what I have told you and what I am getting ready to tell you. I trust that what is now in my hands has made it to your hands." He showed the papers toward the camera. "This is a printout from the state database as to employees and budgetary cuts for the past several years." He pointed to one page. "This is the name of the cop's mother, Aisha Watson. She was one of ten employees to survive a massive layoff in her division. It was the same year that the cop had his conversation with Grafton."

Gabbie had also pulled out the same page from the folder and showed the highlighted name to Miki.

"After I dropped off the cop, I decided to befriend him so I could get more information. Every time we met, I tried to create the confessional pixie dust. We always had a drink. I would mention Grafton Hood and then ask questions about his job loss and search for new employment. It worked every time."

Chandler thumbed through the folder and pulled out a few newspaper clippings.

"The cop told me how he coerced two black males serving time at the Department of Juvenile Justice to help him take out this person. He promised to have them released if they would kill this person and make it look like a random crime. So they raped and killed that poor woman. Her name is in the newspaper clipping that the cop actually gave me."

Chandler held the clipping to the camera.

"Her name was Athena Newton."

Miki's mind could not process what Chandler just said. He turned to Gabbie. "Rewind that!" he growled.

Gabbie held the same clipping in her hand. The name was highlighted. "Let's just pause it." She showed him the clipping. "You heard correctly. Athena Newton. Just keep watching it. We can rewind it later," Gabbie responded.

"I don't know how much more I can comprehend right now. Little fixated on the fact that our esteemed governor may have derailed my life. Lot going on upstairs right now," Miki fired back.

"I get that. Just keep watching," Gabbie said.

Miki reluctantly relented and focused back on the screen. Chandler continued his story.

"There is another news article in here about the death of a disgraced police officer. It was a one-car collision—alcohol was involved. The officer's name was Christopher Watson. It says he was pre-deceased by his mother, Aisha. She succumbed to cancer. There is another state printout in here showing where she was terminated from her job two years after the death of Athena Newton. And there is one other article."

Chandler shifted through the clippings and held one to the camera.

"This article describes the death of two inmates that were arrested on a botched carjacking. There was a fire at the jail and they were amongst the five convicts to perish in the blaze. The cause was unknown. The prison records showed that they were released earlier under the direction of Officer Christopher Watson. These were the men that killed Athena."

Gabbie continued to show Miki the documents being referenced by Chandler on the screen. His mind was swimming in confusion and anger. Chandler continued to search the folder and found one final article.

"This shows the one connection between Athena and Grafton. They knew each other. It's a picture of the employees of Charleston City Hall. They are receiving some civic award from some hospitality organization."

Chandler pointed to two people pictured in the article.

"That is Grafton Hood, and that is Athena Newton standing right next to him. Unfortunately, that is the only connection I could discover after many years of research. They simply worked together 20 or so years ago."

Chandler carefully placed the documents back into the folder. He took his time to organize the placement of each.

"I have tried to peddle this video and copies of the folder to lower end reporters. But no one seems that interested. It is all too farfetched. Plus, I have to be careful with sharing this information. Grafton's reach extends into every nook and cranny of this state. Who knows—

perhaps you're watching this video without me because I showed it to the wrong people."

Miki continued to look at the documents Gabbie handed him.

"Miki, you are not the cause of your professional demise. But you are the cause of your personal demise. Your poor reaction to a bad situation is your own fault. But maybe this will allow you a resurrection of sorts."

"Perhaps," Miki said as he stared at the screen. He felt as though he were part of a real conversation.

"I don't know what you will do with this information. But heed my warning. Grafton Hood has the ability to carry out *any* act he deems necessary." Chandler glared at the camera. "If you are going to chase this down, go into it knowing that your adversary is devoid of human compassion and any semblance of moral decency. He is the closest thing to pure evil I have ever seen."

Chandler placed the neatly organized white folder in his lap. He then stared directly at Miki again.

"Good luck, Miki."

The screen went black. Gabbie and Miki sat in silence for a few minutes. Miki began to pore over every document in the folder.

Gabbie broke the silence. "Miki, I know what you are thinking but now is not exactly the time to begin a quest to topple our governor. Kinda gotta a lot going on right now. You know...with avoiding the law and murder charges?"

"Are you fucking kidding me? Now is the perfect time to do it. This connection between Grafton and Athena may be our ticket out of this misery. Shit, I could kill a hundred birds with one stone! Absolved from connections with a murder I had nothing to do with…get back my career…my life."

"What about the murder that you did have something to do with?"

"Exactly!" Miki exclaimed. "Maybe those two thugs were sent because they think I know what Chandler knew. Make that connection and all of this goes away. "

"Let's pump your brakes a little. Think about what you actually have, the mutterings of a disgraced lawyer with a bunch of articles about dead people and state layoffs. Hardly the smoking gun."

"Fine, Gabbie. Let's look at our choices. We stay on the run together and forever. We can wander from place to place for an eternity smiling at the end of each night because we we're still free and then scared shitless every morning because today may be the day we get caught."

"It beats jail," Gabbie replied.

"Sure, we have our *freedom*, Braveheart. You know he gets caught and disemboweled at the end of the movie," Miki replied.

"I wasn't even born when that movie was made so I have no idea what you are talking about," Gabbie fired back.

"It means that we will get caught. We will get arrested. It is going to happen. We aren't that good."

"How so?" Gabbie asked.

"Well, we kinda stick out in a crowd. The police are looking for a man in his mid-40s and a gorgeous woman of Korean/Black descent. We don't exactly blend in. They won't need a picture of us in the Post Office."

"Then we can go our separate ways," Gabbie said in almost a whisper. She had to contain the tears. She didn't want for him to see any weakness.

Miki looked at her. He wouldn't entertain a notion of her not being in his life. The video had buoyed his spirits, but he still was motionally fragile. He couldn't fathom the thought of going through his daily emotional torment alone. She was his oasis and he needed her.

"Well, that's a horrible idea," Miki replied. "If we're together, then I can contain all of the risks which could get me caught. I know what you are doing and I know what I am doing. But if we're apart, then I lose that control. I have no say as to what you are doing. So I will have to worry everyday about whether you have gotten caught and how that can lead to me."

Gabbie stood silent.

"So separating is not an option. And being on the run forever is not feasible."

"And I disagree with sticking around to chase down this theory," Gabbie said. "I say we make like a tree, get the fuck out of the country."

"But if we track this down, we can lead a life without fear. I have been living in fear since Athena's death and I hate it. I'd rather be in jail than lead this life."

"Let's see you say that the first time you bend over for the soap," Gabbie replied.

"Gabbie, this is a do over. We have been given a chance at a do over in life. Those don't just come along and when they do, you're gonna have to take some risk."

"Yeah, like jail, loss of personal freedom, anal raping…" Gabbie replied.

"I get it. There is a lot to risk, but the upside," Miki paused. "Well, the upside is outrageously phenomenal. Think about it."

"I have," Gabbie said hesitantly.

"No, you really haven't," replied Miki. "The most powerful man in this state's history, and maybe someday in the world, has had people killed to bury the very information that we could discover. What if we found that information? Do you know how much power we would have? That's like Watergate power."

Gabbie listened in silent disbelief. She was seeing a person she had not met. Miki was sober and confident, and he was making a great argument to his jury.

Miki sighed. "I am tired of being part of the weak and huddled masses. Save that shit for the Statute of Liberty rather than my life's motto."

Gabbie chuckled.

"I have done enough time at Camp Have Not. I want to be part of Camp Have because I lived in that camp. And let me tell you," Miki paused, "it is great!"

Miki was speaking with the charm and passion of a great trial lawyer. Highlighting the pronunciation of each syllable with the precision of an Oscar winning actor. His hand movements were perfectly timed and placed. It was a skill set that had not been part of his repertoire for a long time. But like his muscle memory, it came back very quickly.

"So? Are you in?" Miki asked with a slight but very confident grin.

Gabbie reached into her jeans pocket and pulled out a yellow sticky note. She handed it to Miki.

Miki examined it. "It's dated six months ago."

"The video is two years old. This is the only document in the folder which is newer than the video," she replied.

"DSS. Harold and Jennifer Beckwith. Summerville." Miki read it aloud. "Were you going to hide this from me?" Miki asked.

"No, I was going to give it to you. I just hadn't decided whether I would give it to you as I left or when we got started on chasing this down," Gabbie replied.

"And?"

"How far away is Summerville?" Gabbie said.

"30 minutes."

CHAPTER SIXTEEN:
SPRING THE TRAP

Ron Poe had finished another day on the billable treadmill. His life was measured in billable hours. Even in his free time, he was thinking about how many billable hours he was missing. Every moment away from work was a moment that could go toward fulfilling his annual quota.

It was late at night. He had to make up time because of missed work during the week. He covered his son's baseball games while his wife was playing tennis. She had started a mixed couples' tennis league about three months ago and it seemed to consume her. He had noticed her weight loss and she was wearing underwear that would make a Victoria Secret's model blush.

He quizzed some of his divorce lawyer buddies about mixed couples' tennis. They told him it was essentially a Match.com for married folks. Ron's responsibilities as a father and billing machine helped distract his concern about his wife's new hobby. But it was always in the back of mind.

Ron walked through the parking garage to his new 5 series BMW. With a push of a button on the key chain, the car beeped and the lights flashed. He stopped in his tracks. Next to his car was parked a van. It was the same van he saw at his son's baseball game when he went missing.

He then felt the presence of a stranger approaching to his left. He turned to find a strikingly beautiful woman. She was the woman from the game. But she wasn't alone. There was a man next to her.

"You recognize me?" Elad asked as he approached Ron.

"Uh, yes," Ron was taken aback. "You found my son the other night, and you...I met you at the game as well," he said as he pointed to the woman.

"Actually, I took him," Elad replied.

"Excuse me," Ron replied.

"Here, let me show you something," said the woman as she approached Ron with her phone.

Ron backed up. "Why don't y'all just stay here while I call the police? Then you can show all of this to whomever you want." He reached for his cell phone.

"Ron, just relax and let the lady show you something. And then you can call the police. If we meant you harm then that would have already happened," Elad said.

"How the hell do you know my..." Ron was interrupted.

"Look at this," the woman shoved her phone into Ron's face. He looked at the images. It was his home.

"That's my house," he replied.

"Yes, it is," she replied. She started to click through various images showing the inside and outside of his home.

"How is my house on your phone?"

"When I took your son and you started to look for him, she grabbed your phone and hacked into it. It seems that you have surveillance cameras set in your home and you can access them through your phone," Elad answered.

"How did you know that?"

"Because we have been to your home," Elad replied.

Ron's eyes widened. "Why don't I just call the cops and let them sort through all this," Ron said as he started to dial 911.

"You push one fucking button on that phone and you will never see your family alive again," Elad said in a tone that sent chills up Ron's spine.

"He's very serious. You may want to put the phone down and listen to us," the woman said. Ron had not noticed that she pulled a 9-millimeter from her purse.

Ron lowered the phone. "Why? Are you going to kill me?"

"Yes," Elad said with a slight chuckle. "We will kill you and put you in that van. I will drive that van to Charleston and dump it into the Ashley River. She," Elad pointed to his partner, "will drive your car home when we know everyone is there," Elad paused.

The woman waved her phone with the images of his home in Ron's face. She had a slight smirk on her face.

"And she will put a bullet in the head of each of your family members. She will then erase the cameras in your home, just as we have erased the cameras in this parking garage, and no one will know what the fuck happened," Elad concluded.

Ron held the phone to his waist. He had seen movies about kidnapping but never envisioned himself in such a situation. His mind was rejecting the reality that now confronted him and he was paralyzed in a state of shock.

"Ron...Ron," the woman snapped her fingers, "I am going to lower my weapon, but if you dial one number then you know the short existence that awaits you and your family. Yes?"

Ron nodded and shook his head. He was still trying to regain his senses.

"Trying to get a handle on the situation, Mr. Lawyer? Trying to figure out what we want?" Elad approached Ron. He casually brushed the dust off the shoulder pad of Ron's Armani suit. "Ronnie, I am going to be blunt with you. I am just going to tell you what it will take for me not to kill your children. You okay with that kind of candor?"

Ron glanced at Elad's hand as it brushed his shoulder. He prayed for the strength and skill to rip Elad's hand from the wrist and shove it in his mouth. But he knew that prayer would not be answered. He needed to act like a lawyer and not a UFC fighter. This meant he needed to "say little, let your adversary talk a lot and act based on your adversary's missteps."

"Sure," Ron replied.

"I need to find Miki Martin," Elad nodded again, "you know who that is, correct?"

"Yeah, but why do you think I can lead you to him?" Ron responded.

"Ronnie...Ronnie...Ronnie," Elad raised his voice as he moved his hand from Ron's shoulder to the back of his neck. He gave it a firm grab and leaned close into his face. They were almost nose-to-nose.

"I know about your wife," Elad whispered.

"What?" Ron tried to wiggle his neck from Elad's grasp but to no avail.

"Your wife and the tennis," Elad said as he released his grip. "Do you want to know who the guy is? This is the guy that she has fucked in your marital bed. The same bed your children crawled into last Sunday when you decided to sleep in, miss church and have family time instead."

Ron was nauseated. He felt like he took a punch to the gut and a strong knee to the groin. He was enduring the gamut of the worst emotions—fear, jealously, and heartache. It was a trifecta of misery pulsing through Ron's soul. He had no retort.

Elad put his hand on Ron's shoulder as if consoling an old friend. "Listen, I know this is a lot coming at you. Cheating wife, strangers threatening the life of your family. Its a lot to digest," Elad said in a apathetic tone. "But the important thing to focus on is that we are very serious. Nod if you agree."

Ron slowly nodded.

"Good. Good, Ronnie. I saw you playing catch with your son in the back yard a couple of days," Elad paused.

"I would hate to have to cut his little head off. But that will be your choice."

The image of his youngest child suffering such an unspeakable crime rolled through his head. He closed his eyes and mustered the strength to finally speak. "What do you need for me to do?" Ron growled.

"Ronnie!" Elad gently tapped him on the cheek. "I've already told you that. Miki Martin. You know where he is, correct?"

Ron cautiously nodded.

"We're going to meet you in this garage on Friday. Two days from now," the woman interjected.

Elad was pissed that she interrupted his interchange with Poe.

"You will come with us and we will meet with Martin at a time and place that you will arrange," the woman said.

"How do I know that we will be safe after you meet with Martin?" Ron said as he glared at Elad.

Elad chuckled. "Well, you really don't. But you do know what will happen if we don't meet with Martin," Elad hissed. He grabbed the back of Ron's neck again and drew him close to his face. "And please understand, I will know if you contact the cops and I will kill your family just before I leave the country. Martin meeting with us is your only way out of this." Elad pointed to the woman's phone. There was an image of his wife tucking their youngest into bed. "So, can I count on your cooperation?"

Ron nodded.

Elad released his grip. "Great! It's gonna be a weekend trip so you will have to come up with some excuse for your wife," Elad said with a grin. "But I have a feeling that she won't ask too many questions. I am sure she won't be lonely or bored without you." Elad winked.

Ron looked at both of them. "Are y'all done with me?"

"Yes sir, Mr. Poe. You are free to GTFOH," Elad responded.

Ron raised an eyebrow at the response.

"Get the fuck outta here," Elad said as he pointed to Ron's BMW.

Ron staggered to his car trying to comprehend what had just occurred. He had to find a way to reach Miki although he wasn't sure what he would tell him. He was not prepared to exchange another person's life for his own.

Elad and his accomplice waited for Ron to leave before they walked toward the van. Elad climbed into the driver's seat and started the ignition.

"You think he will talk?" she asked.

"Oh, I hope so. Otherwise I have to kill his brood and find another avenue to Martin. That would be a huge pain in the ass," Elad casually said.

"Yeah," the woman responded. "Who are you calling?"

Elad had the cell phone to his ear. "Oh, people with a higher pay grade than us. Checking in," Elad replied.

"What kind of gun did you whip out?" Elad said with a laugh. "I didn't see that coming."

"This," she pulled out her 9-millimeter. "It's a CZ 75. I love this gun," she said with a smile.

Elad had the phone squeezed between his shoulder and ear. "That's nice. Let me hold it." She gave him the gun. "Wow, very light."

A voice answered on the other end of the call with a simple "Yes."

Elad spoke into the phone. "I think we are good on this end. We have the information and should have everything secured within a couple of days. But I just want to clarify something," Elad finished.

Another abrupt "Yes" followed from the phone.

"No loose ends, correct?"

There was pause on the other and then a response. "Yes, no loose ends." There was another pause. "Anything else?"

"No sir, I will call you when I have more information." The phone went dead.

Elad put the cell phone down and in one fluid motion he placed the muzzle of her gun against her left temple. The last words she heard were, "You talk too much." Her lifeless body slumped in the seat. It was surreal the calm manner in which Elad maneuvered her body into the back of the van and opened the dash box to retrieve a box of wipes to clean the passenger side window.

* * *

For the first time since their arrival at the beach house, someone knocked at the door. It was a Federal Express delivery person. Miki and Gabbie watched undetected. They were cloaked in the teal green Pottery Barn drapes of the front bedroom window.

They waited a full five minutes after the Fed Ex truck pulled away from the driveway before Gabbie snuck onto the front porch and snatched the letter-sized delivery.

"It's addressed to you but there is no return address," Gabbie said as she handed it to Miki.

Miki ripped open the package to reveal a single sheet of paper. It was Poe's handwriting. It read: CALL ME AT THE OFFICE TOMORROW AT 10 A.M. TELL THEM IT IS GROVER JASPER. LONG-TIME CLIENT. HAVE THEM INTERRUPT ME. RP.

Gabbie read it over his shoulder. "Ron?"

"Yeah," Miki replied. His mind raced with reasons to motivate Ron to contact him. He had to focus on their mission. He shook his head in an effort to clear it from the thoughts generated by the message. He stared back at Gabbie. "Now, back to...where were we?"

"Oh, trying to break into the Department of Social Services to get information about the Beckwiths? You know they're not just gonna let us waltz in and type the name into the computer," Gabbie responded. "It's that whole 9/11 thing and security."

"Stating the obvious, that's always helpful."

"Still don't see a connection between DSS, the Beckwiths, Newton and Grafton," Gabbie said.

"Not going to know that until we figure out the connection between those people and DSS. So how do we figure that out?" Miki responded.

Gabbie just shrugged her shoulders.

Miki thought for a second. "We need access to a phone. Didn't you buy a couple of burners last week?"

"Yeah, they're in my bag. Why?"

"Let's get the number to DSS. I have an idea," Miki responded.

"You're going to call them and just ask about these people?" Gabbie asked.

"Yep," Miki replied with a grin. "Can you get them on the line?"

"Sure boss. I will get them on the line. Anything else like some coffee or a doughnut," Gabbie fired back.

"Just get them on the damn phone, Gabbie."

Gabbie called information and had DSS on the line within a few seconds.

All lawyers must do pro bono work. This is essentially working for free. As a lawyer, you can pick whether to represent criminals for free or do free civil work. If you pick free civil work, then you represent people in family court. Generally, people in family court get free representation if they're facing an action filed by DSS for the termination of parental rights. It is an action filed by DSS to terminate a person's rights to his or her child based on failure to support or to visit the child. DSS must terminate those rights in order to allow the child to be adopted. Once the child is adopted, it is no longer a ward of the state and DSS doesn't have to foot the bill to raise the child.

Miki was appointed to a termination case. Through that case, he became acquainted with a law firm in the state that represented parents seeking to adopt children. It was a well-known firm and they would regularly call DSS as the first step in vetting potential clients desiring to adopt children. The firm's name was always recognized by any DSS case worker. It was a firm that helped to get children off the DSS payroll through adoption.

As soon as DSS answered, Miki asked for the first available caseworker.

"Hey, this is Cameron with the Harnett Law Firm. We are just trying to get some background on a couple of potential parents," Miki said.

"Absolutely, anything we can do to help y'all," the caseworker responded. "What are the names?"

"Beckwith. Harold and Jennifer Beckwith," Miki responded as he grinned at Gabbie.

Gabbie just shook her head. She hated and loved it when he was right.

There was a pause at the other end of the line. "Oh. Have y'all not done any background checks on these folks?" the caseworker said.

"Not really. They just walked in with a wad of money. My boss told me to do a quick reference check," Miki played along.

"Well, they were foster parents. But they're off our list. And have been for some period of time," the caseworker replied.

"Foster parents? Really?" Miki asked as he looked at Gabbie. "How'd they get off your list?"

"I can't tell you that. That information is blocked."

"I gotcha. Damn HIPPA," Miki said with a laugh knowing that law had nothing to do with her inability to disclose the information.

The caseworker laughed with him. She had no clue about HIPPA, but was talking with a lawyer and didn't want to appear ignorant.

"Do you have a recent address? Just so I can verify that these are the same folks?" Miki asked.

"Um, yeah. Yeah, we do. Evidently, one of them is on food stamps. You ready?"

"Sure," Miki responded with confidence.

"1428 Forrest Trail…Lot 102…Summerville," the caseworker replied.

"That's just outside of Charleston, correct?" Miki asked.

"Yeah, that's right. Does that match your records?"

"Yep, that's them," Miki wanted to end the conversation as soon possible. He was still amazed that his rouse worked. "I guess they're out. Thanks for the help."

Miki hung up the phone before she could say goodbye. He looked at Gabbie with a chagrin that enveloped his entire face.

"What?" Gabbie grimaced.

"So you're just gonna call DSS?" Miki mocked her as he waved his head back and forth. He then looked down at the address and back at her. "You wanna go to a trailer park?"?

"Pretty much raised in them," Gabbie replied.

"Who says you can't go home again, Gabbie," Miki said as he stood up and grabbed the keys to the motorcycle.

There are two types of trailer parks—those with homes that are technically manufactured homes because they are made off-site, but are affixed to the land. And then there are parks with homes that still have wheels and an axle. With the right hitch and truck, you can move the home. The one Miki and Gabbie were heading to was the latter.

Before reaching the park, they drove to the closest second-hand clothing store and found outfits suitable for a job interview. They could not attempt an interrogation dressed for a Jimmy Buffet concert. Miki wore a grey suit made in the 1990s and Gabbie wore a dress that was no longer fashionable at Wal-Mart. But it did the trick and they looked professional, especially for their destination. Miki parked the motorcycle at the front of the entrance of the trailer park rather than in the front lawn area of lot 102.

"Why you parking all the way up here?" Gabbie asked.

"We're trying to establish some amount of credibility. It may be hard to do that if we're dressed for church and riding a Harley. We'll have to walk the rest of the way."

They walked down the dirt road through the park until reaching lot 102. It was a 30-year-old single wide metal structure, but the axle was still in place. Miki banged on the cheap aluminum door with a 12-inch diamond-shaped window. He anxiously awaited the response. The exact type he assumed would answer the door greeted him.

In the doorway stood Harold Beckwith, in all his glory. He was clad in a "Speak English or Go Home" T-shirt and jeans that were probably at least a decade old. His gut obviated the need for a belt and, judging from his five-day-old beard, he was saving money on razors. It was 3:00 p.m. but Miki surmised that Harold wasn't working today, or any other day this week—or month. The television from the living area spewed sounds of yet another lawyer ad looking for wreck cases from the unemployed.

"Yeah," Harold greeted his guests, "what do you want?"

"Mr. Beckwith?" Miki responded.

"Yeah."

"You are Harold Beckwith?" Miki asked.

"Yeah, who the hell are you?" Beckwith moved closer toward Miki.

"He's Chandler Murray with the Murray Detective Agency. And I am his associate. DSS sent us down here to ask you some questions about Athena Newton," Gabbie interjected.

Miki had to bite his inside lip to keep from smiling. "Murray Detective Agency, nice," he thought to himself.

"Wait, DSS sent you? I thought we cleared that shit up years ago," Beckwith responded.

"Well, Mr. Beckwith, they are DSS and sometimes it takes them a while to catch up," she said with a disarming smile. Beckwith could not help but return the smile to the gorgeous woman on his doorstep. "What do you know about Athena Newton?" Gabbie pressed ahead.

"I don't know nothing about her. I thought you were here about that baby thing," Harold responded.

"Harry! Harry! Who the hell is that?" yelled a high-pitched feminine voice drenched in an unmistakable accent of trailer park trash.

Like Harry, her appearance was exactly as Miki assumed it would be. Jennifer Beckwith was pushing 50 but dressed like a 20 year-old—but unfortunately, she could not pull it off. She had a thick head of hair mixed with jet-black roots and blonde highlights. The tattoo of an Indian feather on her neck hinted that her alcohol-ravaged body was covered by more ink.

"Harry! What the hell do they want?" She screeched as she pulled the freshly lit Marlboro Red from her lips and nicotine-stained teeth.

"DSS sent them. They're here about that baby," Harold answered.

"That baby! That was over 20 years. We answered all your questions. Why y'all back here now? They cleared us of everything," she directed her comments to Miki.

"Well, we have some more questions, ma'am. That's why we are here," Gabbie responded.

"I ain't talking to you, Half-Breed. Damn half-breed baby is the reason for all this shit. And we didn't do a damn thing, I have the fucking paperwork to prove it," Jennifer said as she walked toward Gabbie.

"What the fuck did you just say, you inbred douche bag?" Gabbie fired back.

For one brief moment in time, Harold and Miki had a common goal—stop their women from fighting. Harold gently pulled his wife back by her shoulders and Miki put his arm across Gabbie's chest as if they had come to a sudden stop in a car.

"Okay there, *Detective.*" Miki glared at her. "Let's just calm down and remember why we're here."

"Yeah, honey, the man is right—let's just calm down. You get arrested and you lose your probation," Harold said.

"Three hots and a cot may be an improvement over this place," Gabbie huffed.

"Okay ladies, as much as Harry and I here would love to see a good cat fight," he winked at Harry as if they were buddies at a bar and Harry smiled, "why don't we get down to business so we can leave y'all alone. Can we see this paperwork?"

"Well, I thought that you would have had it. But if getting the paperwork will get this nigger off my property, then fine. Fine. I will get it." Jennifer withdrew into the trailer.

"Your property, my ass. Probably three months behind in rent, low-rent whore," Gabbie whispered.

"Simmer, Detective," Miki whispered.

"What did she say?" Harold asked.

"Low-rent door. Your landlord should have that fixed for you," Miki replied.

"I agree. I've been on him about a shit ton with this place."

"Here, here's the entire fucking file," Jennifer returned. "Didn't want that damn half breed anyway. And we didn't touch her!"

Miki grabbed the file and scanned the first page. One name jumped at him. Athena Newton. It was listed under Mother's name.

"What do you know about the mother? Athena Newton?" Miki asked. Gabbie tried to grab the folder but Miki moved it from her reach.

"Not much. Probably more than I should. She came to visit the kid a couple of times. She worked in Charleston. Said that she got pregnant with a co-worker's baby but he didn't want to help. So she put her up for adoption," Jennifer answered as she lit another cigarette.

"And the abuse charge? Where'd that come from?" Miki asked.

Gabbie listened intently.

"I don't know! Look at the file. It was unfounded. The kid was with us for less than a year. The mother visits us a few times and the next thing I know, we're charged with abuse. And the kid is taken away."

"Funny thing is that the mom shows up to visit her daughter and doesn't even know that she had been taken away," Harold chimed.

"Yeah, exactly." Jennifer exhaled smoke from her nose. "If we did something to that girl, you would think that the momma would have known something."

"You keep calling her a half-breed. Why is that?" Miki asked.

"She was part black and part Asian. Kinda like your partner there," Jennifer said as she pointed to Gabbie.

"And under child's name, it says Gabriele. Is that what you called her?" Miki continued.

Gabbie stared at Miki with her mouth open.

"No. We couldn't pronounce that," she replied.

"Yeah, we just called her Gabbie," Harold injected.

CHAPTER SEVENTEEN:
CONVERSATIONS

Julius Spring was concerned. Hood's bill passed the House and was heading towards its first reading in the Senate. If it passed a first reading, then it was only two steps away from Grafton's desk—a second and then perfunctory third reading in the Senate. It should not have gotten this far, but what concerned him more was the silence.

Spring anticipated contact from fellow legislators trying to orchestrate a debate against the bill. Just one debate could result in an amendment that would send the bill back to committee, effectively killing it before Grafton's term expired. But no one was reaching out to him. He was the elder statesman of the legislature, the unofficial Godfather. A bill of this magnitude should have inundated his office with calls from fellow legislators. Normally, every legislative member would have sought his opinion. His phone should have been ringing off the hook, but instead, it was deadly silent.

Spring tried to convince himself that the bill was so outlandish that it would never pass. This would explain the dearth of calls to his office. Why would anyone need his input about voting for such an outrageous bill? But then again, he knew Grafton. This legislation was important.

Spring and he had many battles in the legislature. While they disliked each other as adversaries, there was a mutual respect. They represented the heads of the state's most powerful political bodies. They knew there would be times when they needed a favor from the other. So while their battles were intense, they weren't intense enough to completely alienate the other. But Grafton crossed that line...he threatened Spring's family. Perhaps it was because his term was ending and he didn't need Spring anymore or, perhaps, he was pulling out all the stops to pass this bill.

Spring was convinced it was the latter and as he debated his next move, his phone finally rang. It wasn't a fellow lawmaker.

"Senator, its Sharon White," the voice on the other end responded.

"Sharon, how are you? Caught you on CNN being interviewed about yet another police shooting. Very impressive. Maybe I should get some lessons from you about dealing with the media." He was a skilled politician. She could not discern a hint of concern in his voice over Grafton's bill.

"Well, thank you, Senator," Sharon said with a laugh, "and I am sorry it has taken me so long to get back with you after our last discussion. But as you probably know, it is tough digging to get through Grafton's fortress"

"Preaching to Noah about the flood, Sharon."

She giggled again. She always smiled at his ability to disarm her. "Well, I know you could write a book about trying to navigate the Grafton River of Deceit," she said.

"Try a trilogy."

"But I've paddled upstream and have some information that you may find interesting. But first, let me ask you some questions so I know the information is reliable."

"Absolutely, Ms. White," Spring responded.

"Mind you, Senator, that I am somewhat out of the know when it comes to the politics of this state. You are correct...my professional obligations have diverted my attention from the inner workings of the statehouse."

"Well, Sharon that is what I do. You shouldn't apologize for that," Spring said.

"Actually, I should. I haven't been keeping my eye on the ball and that has cost you and now," Sharon paused, "maybe this state."

"How so?" Spring's tone changed from playful banner to that of a trial lawyer on cross-examination.

"Senator, what is the area outside of the T? Does that mean anything to you?" Sharon asked.

Spring chuckled. He coined the phrase. "Yes, of course it does. Those are the less affluent counties of this state."

"And the representatives from those counties, how well do you know them?" Sharon pressed on.

"Well, I thought very well. I helped many of them get elected and re-elected. But based on your questions, I am somehow doubting all of that."

"Do they have any particular allegiance to Hood?" she continued.

Spring laughed. "No. None. They're from different party lines. He only talks to them when he needs something, and they know that. Most of them won't even talk to him."

"Well, I think that has changed. Tell me about this anti-abortion bill. Grafton's bill."

"What's to tell? The bill states that if you have an abortion or perform an abortion then it is deemed a capital offense worthy of the death penalty." Spring paused. "But I think it goes even deeper."

"What do you mean by deeper?"

"I think this bill is tied to Grafton's future in politics. And I know you aren't a student of our political landscape, but there has been no mention of Hood running for the United States Senate. I think he has his eyes set elsewhere."

"Pennsylvania Avenue?"

"Perhaps?"

"I think you're correct. I talked with some politicos at CNN. There is mention of his name on a national stage. Have you heard anything like that?"

"Nothing concrete, but that doesn't surprise me," Spring replied. "Nothing surprises me with him.

"One more question—have you heard from any of the representatives from the T corridor about this bill?"

Spring paused. "Not a word. Do you know why that is?"

"Yes, I think I do. I received a phone call last night from a gentlemen named John Sessions."

"Yeah, Pepper's little henchman. We talked about him. You couldn't remember his last name," Spring replied.

"Well, I will remember it now. He informed me of a meeting between Grafton and these representatives. He told me that Hood promised them one billion in state funding if they passed his bill."

Over 40 years in state politics gave Spring a jaded view of a person's willingness to abandon notions of moral decency in exchange for political gain. There wasn't much that shocked him. But leave it to Grafton to surprise him to the point that he almost dropped the phone.

"How in the hell is he going to do that?!" Spring exclaimed.

"According to Sessions, he promised legislation to levy a tax on the sale of automobiles and boats and any other personal craft in this state," she replied.

"What?! He's going to introduce that legislation!" Spring shouted in the phone. His staff members could hear him through the office door. They looked at each other with their mouths open. They didn't even think he knew how to yell.

Sharon was shocked again by Spring's tone. He was the epitome of Southern class now reduced to yelling through the phone as if talking to a cable representative. All because of Grafton Hood.

"Senator, I..." she was interrupted by a rant by Spring.

"Unfucking believable." His office staff stood aghast behind the door. They didn't think he even knew how to swear. "I spent the past ten years trying to pass this same legislation to help their poor, backward-ass counties. And every time, Grafton defeats my bill. And what do they do to repay all that?"

"I don't really know," Sharon tried to slow his tirade.

"Those spineless hacks sell out their souls, their constituents, and this state to the very demon that they had me battle so vigilantly! No wonder their counties are trapped in the past. They are filled with people whose gene pool is dominated by stupidity and laziness!"

"Senator, I never thought I would have to say this to you, but you need to calm down," Sharon said in a stern voice. "As I learned from you, we need to deal with the situation at hand and not the emotions."

Spring regained his composure. He was embarrassed by his reaction. He had to face the facts. The enemy was now inside of the gate and his army let them in.

"I am sorry, Sharon. I am very sorry. I should be thanking you for the phone call rather than shooting the messenger." His long-time secretary opened the door to check on him. She had never heard such emotion from the man. He politely smiled and waved her out.

"How do you know all this? Other than a phone call?" he asked.

"I can show it to you."

"Show it?"

"Yes, Sessions videotaped some half-ass town hall meeting called by Grafton and these representatives that you are so fond of. It shows him promising them the tax legislation in exchange for his bill. And it shows him threatening a representative if he doesn't agree."

"Threatening? How did Sessions do that?" Spring asked.

"Micro videotape recorder inside the state emblem pin on his lapel," Sharon answered. "The footage is real."

"What are you going to do with it?" Spring asked.

"That's part of the reason I'm calling you. I could contact the U.S. Attorney's Office or commission my own investigation as to a possible ethic's violation, but..." Sharon could not finish her response.

"The backlash against this state would be tremendous. The nation already thinks our state is run on stereotypical notions of southern political corruption. Now, they will have documented proof transmitted through every news media known to mankind."

"Like I said Senator, I have not been keeping my eye on the ball and this is my state ,too. I owe all of my personal success to this state. And while an investigation of this magnitude would thrust my career into the next stratosphere, it would come at the expense of people to whom I owe a lot. People like you. So I am calling you to ask one simple question, what do we do?"

"Well, the more complex the situation, the more you need to focus on the small things," Spring replied. Spring now had his feelings in check. Now was the time for reason and logic.

"Like what?" Sharon asked.

"The video. This was just offered to you from a pawn of the Pepper's army. Did he say why he gave you the information?"

"Haven't talked to him. He just sent me this email with a note saying 'thought you would find this interesting. Hood in action'."

"And the video was attached?"

"Yes," Sharon replied. "It was sent from his personal email."

"Then I guess the first step is to find out what we can about our source," Spring said.

"John Sessions."

"Yes, we must discover who John Sessions is," Spring said.

* * *

"Grover Jasper on line one for you, Mr. Poe."

Ron was mentally and physically taxed since his meeting with Elad. He had lost 10 pounds of stress weight. And when his mind wasn't focused on the threats on his life and the lives of his children, he was consumed with images of his wife having sex with another man. He struggled to wear a face of normalcy while battling the emotional hurricane that brewed just beneath the surface. He strained not to cry every time he hugged his children. He fought the impulse to strangle his wife every time he brushed against her in bed—the marital bed that had been invaded by her infidelity. And now, he had to betray his closest friend in the world.

He had debated calling law enforcement but in his gut, he knew that Elad was capable of following through on every threat. This was his family and he could take no chances as to their safety. This was the only course of action.

"Miki? You okay?"

"Yes, I am better than I have been in years," Miki exclaimed. "I have a lot to share with you. I think I have found a way to reclaim my life!"

"Are you drunk? It's only 10:00 a.m.! How does someone even do that?" Ron asked.

"I am sober. I haven't had a drink in like two weeks," Miki responded.

"You're sober? Is this Miki Martin?" Ron jabbed. It was the most humor he experienced since meeting with Elad. Somehow Miki always calmed him and he would miss that.

"Real funny, asshole. Listen, we found this DVD made by Chandler. You remember Chandler Murray?" Miki asked. His words could not keep pace with his thoughts. "That doesn't matter. Anyway, we found this DVD and on it he describes…"

"Miki, stop talking and just listen," Ron interrupted as he stared at pictures of his children that adorned the walls of his office. "I don't want to know about any of that. Okay? I am your lawyer. You need to limit my knowledge. Remember?" He felt uneasy with the lie. Of course he wanted to hear Miki's news, but he knew a prolonged conversation would only test his resolve on what he had to do. This needed to be a quick and light interaction.

"You're right. You're my lawyer." Miki understood. It was far easier for Ron to represent him when he has all of the facts in his arsenal. Sometimes the complete truth is an unnecessary nuisance when trying to represent an innocent client. "I getcha...I understand."

"We don't have much time. I don't know who is listening to me or if anyone is listening to us." Ron said as he glanced through his office door window to see if anyone was looking at him. He was convinced that Elad contacted someone in his office.

"Listening to us? How can someone obtain authorization to wiretap a lawyer's phone?" Miki asked.

"Who said anything about them doing it legally? I am getting a lot of attention up here. People think I know where you are," Ron persisted.

"Attention? What kind of attention? I don't even know what that means? Attention?"

"That doesn't really matter for purposes of our discussion, which needs to be brief and you are somehow extending it. Just listen, okay?" Ron responded.

"I getcha. I getcha," Miki responded.

"You said that before, but I don't think you do. So just listen," Ron fired back.

"Now who is extending the conversation?" Miki quipped.

"Really, Miki." Ron sighed.

"Okay…okay…okay. I am listening," Miki said in a rushed tone.

"It's Friday," Ron replied.

"That's the information? I knew that before calling you," Miki grinned knowing that it would infuriate Ron.

"Miki! Are you serious?" Ron growled as he normally did when Miki tried to rile him. But it was actually a ruse. He wasn't used to playing Miki. Their relationship had been based on brutal honesty, sometimes too much. But Ron knew that he could not spook Miki for fear of risking his meeting with Elad. If Miki didn't show up to the meeting, then he assumed Elad's reaction would be swift and violent.

"I'm sorry. I'm sorry. I am sober and excited about life. I haven't been this way in years—eight, to be exact."

"Well, I am delighted that you are in a good place. In fact, I am overfucking joyed about it." Ron continued the ruse with the sarcastic reply. "But right now, you just need to listen to me. When we meet, you can tell me all about it." he responded.

"Meeting? When are we meeting? I can't come up there. Are you coming here?" Miki rushed.

"That's what I am trying to tell you," Ron said through his gritted teeth. "But you need to listen."

"Alright. When are we meeting?" Miki asked.

"I am heading down this afternoon and will probably stay in a hotel or something. I will come over tomorrow..."

"What time?"

"I don't know yet. I need to make sure that I am not being followed and make sure that everything is clear," Ron replied.

"Man, you are paranoid," Miki observed.

"Not really," Ron thought to himself. "So just be there tomorrow and I will be along as soon as I can. Okay?"

"We will be waiting with bated breath," Miki responded.

As their conversation was ending, Ron realized that this was probably the last time he would ever talk to his best friend. He was dumbfounded by his own actions. Miki was happier than he had been in literally eight years—just as he had said—and Ron was essentially going to kill him. He tempered his desire to warn and save Miki with his desire to save his children. At this point, his wife's demise would be welcomed.

"Um...Miki," Ron said in a low tone.

"Yeah, Saturday. You will be here. I understand," Miki said.

"I am really glad that you got back to a good spot," he paused as he fought off the tears. "I..." Ron stammered,

"I never told you that it pained me to see you suffer like you have. And I am glad that you dug your way out of that dark hole." A tear rolled down his eye as he hung up.

* * *

As soon as he hung up, his secretary buzzed him again. He assumed it was Miki wanting to respond to the abrupt end of the conversation, but it wasn't.

"Mr. Poe, line two is someone from the city police department. They say that someone broke into your car in the garage and they need you to meet with them to disable the alarm."

"My car? What the hell?" he said aloud. "Hello, this is Ron Poe."

"Ronnie," Elad responded. "Are you all packed up and ready for our big weekend getaway?"

Ron sat erect in his chair upon hearing his voice. He pressed the phone firmly to his ear. He didn't want to miss a word of instruction.

"How'd you get this number?" he asked.

"Ronnie…Ronnie…Ronnie. If I were there, I'd grab you by the back of the neck. We know everything. I am assuming you just got off the phone with the esteemed Mr. Martin," Elad replied in a light, upbeat tone.

Ron was stunned. He looked through glass walls of his office and into the office area of his staff. He scanned the cubicles to see if anyone was looking at him. There were no clear suspects. "Why would you think that?"

"Because his was the only number to come in as 'unidentified.' You're an insurance defense lawyer, not a criminal lawyer. All of your clients have numbers that can be identified. That number belonged to a burner phone. Do any of your insurance adjusters use burner phones to talk with their lawyer?" Elad responded.

Ron didn't know how to reply. He continued to scan the faces of his co-workers, hoping to catch the insider he was convinced was working with Elad. No one was looking up. The staff also had billable quotas and didn't want to lose one extra minute watching Poe.

"You're very quiet, Ronnie. Cat got your tongue?" Elad smirked. At this point, he was enjoying toying with his latest prey.

"I don't quite know what you want me to say," Ron replied.

"The truth. I just want the truth," Elad said. "In fact, let's play a little game of truth or dare, except I have kinda messed with the rules a little bit. Instead of me asking you 'truth or dare,' you ask me 'dare' and I'll tell you what you are daring me to do if you don't tell me the truth. Then I will ask you a question that requires a truthful answer. And if you don't answer it truthfully, then I will follow through on my dare. Did you follow those rules, Mr. Lawyer Man?"

"Sure," he responded in a monotone voice. Elad's voice was almost playful. Was this the same man in the garage? The same man that had kidnapped his son?

"Okay, then you go first," Elad said.

"You want me to say 'dare'?" Poe asked.

"What part of the fucking rules did you not understand?" Elad's voice went from pleasant to hateful.

Ron was caught offguard and thrown back into reality. This was indeed the same man. He responded without even thinking, "Dare."

Elad resumed his playful tone. "If you don't tell the truth, then you are daring me to cut your little boy's arms off at the elbow with a hacksaw and then beat them across your face as you watch him flaying in pain. I will have him wear the same Batman pajamas he wore last night. He will pray for the Dark Knight to save him but will only get the helpless sobs of his pathetic father," Elad paused. "Did you hear that dare?"

"Yes. Yes, I heard it," Ron replied as he closed his eyes, trying to get Elad's description out of his mind.

"So now for the truth! Did you talk with Mr. Martin?" Elad asked.

"Yes. I was talking with him just before you called," Ron answered.

"Great! Okay, now you're turn," Elad teased.

"Listen man, I don't need a dare. Just ask the questions and I will give you whatever answers you…"

"No Ronnie! No! This is my fucking game and my fucking rules. You will follow what I say or your world will end. So ask me to dare!" Elad barked in his low tone.

"Dare," he whispered.

"You have a daughter. She's about 27 and lives in the South Park area of Charlotte. She's a sous chef at an Asian restaurant located about two miles from her apartment. And man, she's hot as shit, like her mom. I wonder if she fucks as well." Elad snickered. "Every day she comes to work with her own set of Shun kitchen knives. One of those knives is an eight-inch Shun Classic Chef Knife. Can you guess the dare?"

Ron was silent.

"Okay, I guess not. So my dare to you is that if you don't tell the truth then I will use that knife to rape your daughter both anally and vaginally. And I will videotape the entire thing and make you watch it as I use that same knife to cut off your little boy's arms."

Ron leaned over and vomited in the wastebasket under his desk.

"Let me know when you're done throwing up and are ready for your question," Elad said in serious tone.

"I'm ready," Ron replied as he wiped his mouth clean.

"So, truth!" Elad exclaimed in an almost feminine pitch. "You've set up a meeting between the aforementioned Mr. Martin and myself?"

"Yes. I know where he will be tomorrow. He's expecting to see me."

"As am I, Ronnie. As am I," Elad replied. "Be in the garage at 7:00 tonight."

CHAPTER EIGHTEEN:
A MEETING AMONGST
SCOUNDRELS

It was just after 11:00 p.m. when Elad entered the office of Grafton's vacation home located off Wentworth Street in downtown Charleston. Pontet was seated in a lush leather chair at the front of Hood's desk. There was an empty chair next to him. It was for Elad. Grafton sat behind his 200-year-old oak desk—built by slaves for their owner just before the end of the Civil War. It was a gift Grafton secured in exchange for obtaining a Senate page position for the daughter of a political supporter. Grafton also received a sizeable contribution toward his "campaign debt retirement" fund—which was actually the down payment for the vacation home.

Grafton leaned back in a custom-crafted leather chair. It was an exact replica of the chair in Reagan's oval office. His eyes were closed as he awaited Elad's arrival. He knew the topic of tonight's meeting before Elad had asked for it. With the change in recent events, Grafton knew that he could no longer hide his past from Elad and Practical Solutions. While Practical Solutions could not undo the past, it was skilled in controlling the consequences. But it had to know the full landscape of the battle ahead. It was time for Grafton to reveal the demonic acts of his past.

Elad didn't say a word as he sat down next to Pontet. He ignored his Elite cohort and directed his attention to Grafton.

"I appreciate you seeing me on such short notice," Elad opened the meeting.

Pontet tried to interrupt before Grafton could reply.

Elad cut him off. "I wasn't talking to you." His yellow eyes glared at Pontet. "I was talking to the Governor," Elad said as he pointed in Grafton's direction.

"Allen, let him and me talk. There's Bombay at the bar over there. Why don't you make a drink and just digest this conversation rather than participate. Yes?" Grafton replied.

"Of course," Pontet said. He obliged the request and walked to the bar. Pontet worried that a full confession by Grafton would let Practical Solutions know that he had not been forthcoming with all information as was required. Pontet worried about the potential ramifications for his failure. But at this point, he could only subdue his concern with a strong gin martini—strong enough to power a small car.

Elad nodded in approval at Hood's dismissal of Pontet from the discussion. "Governor, I am not one to mince words or attempt to be politically savvy, if that's that a word, in these types of situations."

"I would expect not," Grafton replied. "You're a weapon. Not a politician."

"Well, sometimes that line is blurred," Elad said with a smile.

"Sometimes it is," Grafton said with a chuckle. "Allow me to also be blunt and cast aside diplomacy. What do you want to know, Mr. Patterson?"

Elad nodded again. He wasn't accustomed to this level of honesty without physical coercion. "Well, we have a real problem."

"Which is?" Grafton asked.

Elad left his chair and slowly walked to the bar occupied by Pontet. Pontet backed away, fearing he was about to get assaulted. Elad ignored him and poured two glasses of water. He returned to his chair and handed a glass of water to Grafton.

"What's wrong with your finger?" Grafton observed.

"Oh that," Elad looked at his finger, "nothing, I just slammed it in a car door. Let's focus on the situation before us. As you know, I work for an organization that gets paid a great deal of money to vet people like you for office. And when my employer taps someone as a viable candidate and then gets money for making such a selection," Elad paused he looked at Pontet, "well, they must be right."

"No one wants to pay millions of dollars to back a loser," Grafton replied as he took a sip of water.

"Exactly." Elad smiled. "And you see, my employer has thrown a great deal of support behind you as candidate on a national stage. And my employer only does that based in part on information provided by you and others." Elad shot another look at Pontet. "Information which has now proven to be incorrect," Elad finished.

"Again, what do you want to know?" Grafton said as he looked at Pontet.

"Well, my employer—and not me because I could give a fuck—wants to know about Athena Newton. How do you know this person?" Elad extended his index finger. "How you are connected to her death?" He extended his middle finger. "And how are you connected to the birth of her child?" Elad raised his ring finger.

Pontet coughed as a cue to signal Grafton not to respond to the question.

"Why don't you just make another, Juniper-boy? We will deal with you later," Elad fired. He paused to regain his composure. "Now, Governor Hood, if you please? Ms. Newton?"

Grafton leaned his chair forward and placed his elbows on the desktop and grasped his hands together under his chin. He then glanced at Pontet who continued to guzzle gin as he observed the interchange. He then stared at the yellow eyes of Elad.

"She and I worked in Charleston together—City Hall to be specific. Pontet got me the job," Grafton said.

Elad listened carefully. Pontet listened in fear.

"We started to flirt a little bit. It was harmless. I mean I hadn't engaged a woman in years. You know my past. Would you have the confidence to approach a woman?" Grafton said as he looked at Elad. "Well, I guess not."

"I am aware of what I look like. Please continue," Elad snapped.

"Anyway, I have weaknesses. Just like my dad. Sexual weaknesses," Grafton said as he stared into the table. "And those weaknesses are emboldened by the effects of alcohol. That's why I rarely drink. And so, I made a mistake."

"Governor, this may not be the time to have such an open discussion about all of that." Pontet interrupted.

"Shut up, Allen! We should have known of this a long time ago!" Elad shouted. He smiled at Grafton as he once again regained his composure. "I am sorry, you were saying. You made a mistake."

"So, Ms. Newton and I go out for a few drinks and I have a few too many," Grafton said, "and I decide that we needed to have sex." Grafton paused. "And I really didn't give her any say-so in the matter."

"You raped her?" Elad asked.

"Such an ugly term," Grafton replied.

"You had non-consensual sex? Does that seem more palatable Governor?"

"That is probably the term your employer's marketing department will use if it has to spin this story," Grafton said with a smile.

"Governor, I am the marketing department," Elad coldly replied.

"Ah, right," responded Grafton.

"And Ms. Newton gets pregnant as a result of this non-consensual act?" Elad asked.

Pontet continued to stare in amazement over the confession being offered by Grafton.

"Yes. Yes she does," replied Grafton. "I, of course, tried to deny that it was mine but she was adamant. She threatened to go to the cops and have me arrested if I did not accept responsibility."

"Did you have any reason to suspect that it wasn't yours? Was she a slut? Reputation for being loose?" Elad asked.

"Uh, no. In fact, the exact opposite. Based on the bleeding during sex, I am fairly certain that she was a virgin. So, I knew that she was pregnant with my child," Grafton continued.

"So, did you try to convince her to terminate the pregnancy?" Elad said.

"Yes, I actually used her father as an argument for the abortion."

"He was the cop who actually arrested Martin? How did you use him?" Elad asked.

"According to Athena, her father believed that God spoke directly to him through the Bible and that God told him that the white race was superior."

"Huh? Wasn't he black?" Elad asked.

"Yes," Grafton answered. "But he interpreted the Bible to say that it was God's will for the white race to procreate. That was the reason he took a Korean wife."

"But that's not white."

"No, but in his mind God would rather he marry a Korean than procreate with a black woman. Like I said, he was a different breed," Grafton said with a nod.

"So I assume, based on all that, Athena was raised in a fairly strict Christian household?" Elad asked.

"Oh yeah, a woman that attractive who abstained from pre-marital sex…absolutely."

"And so she's between a rock and a hard place. Dad doesn't want any more black babies per the Bible and she cannot have an abortion per the Bible," Elad concluded.

"Exactly," Grafton said.

"And you know all of this and tried to use it to your advantage?"

"Well, of course. I am not going to let a drunken mistake derail my political career. I leave drunken mistakes to my friend over there," Grafton said has he pointed to Pontet who continued to graze at the bar.

"And so?"

"I tell her that if she doesn't leave and have an abortion then I will tell her dad that the sex was consensual and then…" Grafton couldn't finish his sentence.

"She will have broken two of Dad's biblical laws versus just one. Correct?" Elad questioned.

"Exactly. And so she agrees, or at least, I thought she did," Grafton's voice trailed into a whisper.

"But that didn't happen and somehow your daughter spends her infancy being raised in a trailer park by a couple of white folks," Elad said.

"Well, I guess Athena's dad would have been happy with that arrangement," Grafton laughed.

"Wait, how did you know that?" Pontet asked Elad. He was barely able to stand but somehow had the presence of mind to ask the question.

Elad returned the question with a glare. Pontet pierced his lips in frustration about asking the question.

"It's a fair question. How did you know that?" Grafton asked.

Elad sighed. "Because I have seen Chandler Murray's 'Brown Recluse' folder. You remember that name, don't you?"

"Poor Chandler," Grafton remarked.

"Yes indeed, poor Chandler. And poor us, because Chandler's file details exactly what you tried to do in order to extricate Ms. Newton and your mistake from this world. And I recently met with the former foster parents of your daughter. They had just had a conversation with a couple that matched the descriptions of Martin and your daughter," Elad said emphatically.

"So now they know?" Grafton asked.

"They being?" Elad asked.

"Martin, the girl," Grafton answered.

"You mean your daughter," Elad could not help the dig.

"Yes, her. And the foster parents?" Grafton said.

"Oh well, it is a shame about the foster parents. Mobile homes can be real fire traps." Elad nodded at the television set that had been turned on but muted during their conversation. The local news was covering a fire at a local trailer park that claimed two lives. "That's how the marketing department of my employer handles these situations."

Grafton stared at the screen as he coldly asked, "You're certain Martin and the girl know all this?"

"Oh, yeah. I think they've known for quite some time. Martin is the personal representative of Chandler's estate. I assume that he found the original folder amongst Murray's affects and has been tracking down the clues ever since."

"Then if you knew all this, why ask me about it? What was the reason for the interrogation?"

"I needed to make sure that I knew the full story and any potential loose ends that I need to tie up."

"As far as I can tell, all the loose ends are in this room and currently trying to outrun the law for a murder charge. So what's the next step?" Grafton asked.

The answer to that question was the subject of much debate at Practical Solutions. Some didn't believe that the story could be contained. It would eventually leak out and Practical Solutions would suffer a tremendous public relations hit. They thought it would be a better idea to cut their losses—tie up all loose ends, including Grafton. But the prevailing sentiment was that if they could contain this story, then they would have almost total control over Grafton, even after he was elected.

Elad was instructed to clean up everything but not to touch Grafton. They were to press forward with the campaign. He didn't agree with the decision, but had his marching orders.

"The details aren't important. The less you know the better." He rose from his chair. "And at this point, I am late for an appointment and you probably need to get some rest." Elad glanced at Pontet who was swaying like a branch in the wind. "But I probably need to follow your campaign manager home. The last thing we need right now is a DUI," Elad said with a smile.

Grafton looked over at Pontet and shook his head at the sight of his drunken politico. He was as useful as a eunuch in a brothel tonight. The one bright spot of the evening was that he no longer had to go through Pontet to reach Practical Solutions. Elad was his new contact, but Grafton was unsure whether that was a good trade.

"Hey, Pontet. Last call! Let's get your ass in the car and head home," Elad commanded.

"Are we done?" Pontet slurred.

"Yeah, you're done," said Elad.

It was 1:00 a.m. and the Ravenel Bridge was practically deserted. The bridge crossed the Cooper River and connected Charleston to Mt. Pleasant and the neighboring barrier islands of Sullivan's Island and Isle of Palms. Pontet owned a home in the Old Village of Mt. Pleasant and Elad was headed toward Sullivan's. As part of the Sober or Slammer Campaign, there was a DUI crackdown at the base of the bridge heading into Mt. Pleasant. The crackdown had received a great deal of local press and, as a result, most of the downtown party-goers had either elected to stay downtown or left early.

Pontet was on a collision course toward the DUI checkpoint with Elad in tow. He was driving ten miles under the speed limit and was swerving from lane to lane like a slalom skier in the Olympics.

His phone rang. It was Elad.

"Hello," Pontet mustered as his car clipped the curb of the bridge sidewalk.

"Hey, Juniper boy, your tire is flat," Elad responded.

"Whaaatttt?" Pontet asked in a high-pitched tone.

"Your passenger side rear tire is flat. You're riding on the rim. That's why you're swerving so much," Elad answered.

"I thought it was because I was drunk," Pontet replied.

"Well, that's not helping things. But your tire is flat and there's a DUI checkpoint down there. No way you're passing the checkpoint with a flat. You need to stop before they see you."

"Checkpoint? Oh, shit!" Pontet exclaimed.

"Yes, checkpoint. Now, stop your car!" Elad screamed. "We need to fix it or leave the car and let me take you across."

"That's bullshit. You're bullshitting me!" Pontet countered.

"Ok, well, when you're in jail tomorrow morning and our governor is dealing with the PR mess on top of everything we discussed tonight, you tell me how much I am bullshitting you. Pull over. Now!" Elad commanded again.

Pontet looked in his rearview mirror and was blinded by Elad's headlights. He looked around the bridge. There was no other traffic and that caused him suspicion. Even at this hour, the bridge was normally packed. Maybe Elad was being truthful and everyone was scared away because of the checkpoint.

He stopped his car. Elad pulled directly behind him and turned off his lights. They were at the crest of the bridge and could barely see the checkpoint at the base.

"Turn your lights off!" Elad exclaimed as he climbed from his car. "We don't want for them to see us!" He pointed in the direction of the patrol cars.

"Right-oh!" Pontet heeded the command.

"Now, pop your trunk and let's see if we can get this thing changed. There's a little bit of light back here," Elad instructed.

Pontet pushed a button inside of the car and opened his trunk. He got out of the driver side door and staggered his way toward Elad, who was waiting for him at the trunk. The passenger side faced the sidewalk overlooking the Cooper River—about 190 feet below. Elad had a tire iron in hand as he examined the suspect tire.

Pontet stood next to him and looked at the rear tire. "I must be really drunk because that tire looks fine."

"Yes, you're really drunk and yes, that tire is fine." Elad slammed the brunt end of the tire iron into the left temple of Pontet's head. It severed Pontet's temporal artery. He was knocked unconscious but not yet dead.

Elad stared at the direction of the checkpoint. There was no movement. He then looked behind him and saw a pair of headlights approaching in the distance. He had about 30 seconds to get rid of Pontet's body.

With his adrenaline rushing, Elad mustered the strength to throw Pontet over the three-foot high concrete barricade that separated the road from the sidewalk. With Pontet's body hidden from sight of the approaching car, Elad quickly made his way to the trunk. As the car drove by, he gave them a polite wave and then pointed to the base of the bridge to alert the driver of the impending checkpoint. The driver returned the warning with a smile and wave. He never noticed Pontet's body only a few feet away.

Blood gushed from Pontet's nose. It was broken when his face slammed into the concrete after Elad threw him over the barricade. He was out cold but his body twitched from the facial and head trauma he endured. Elad climbed over the barricade and glanced at Pontet's limp body. He saw the blood pouring out.

"Shit! You were a mess when you were alive and you're an even bigger mess when I am killing you!" Elad exclaimed.

He took his coat off and wrapped it around Pontet's face. He didn't want any blood on his shirt. He then glanced at the checkpoint. The officers were busy with the car that had just passed. There was a five-foot high fence that separated the sidewalk from the drop. Elad stood Pontet's body against the fence and grabbed Pontet by the waist. With all of his strength gained from his Cross-Fit and P90-X training, Elad lifted Pontet until his feet were resting on Elad's shoulders. Pontet's head and shoulders were just above the fence.

With one last glance to the checkpoint below, Elad made a final push and thrust Pontet's body over the fence and into the murky water of the Cooper River.

"Bye, you drunken fuck!" Elad said as he wiped sweat from his brow.

Elad climbed into his car and used a hand towel to wipe away any traces of sweat and blood from his hands and face. He resumed his journey toward the checkpoint. He had a fake license and the car was a rental in the name of Allen Pontet. Still, he was worried about the encounter…"taking out police officers was always so messy," he thought to himself. But just as he was approaching the two patrol cars, another vehicle raced around him and tried to outrun the checkpoint.

Both patrol cars left the checkpoint in pursuit, allowing Elad to drive away without interruption. Elad was onto his next appointment on Sullivan's Island. Ron Poe was still waiting for him.

CHAPTER NINETEEN:
CONSEQUENCES OF FRIENDSHIP

Ron Poe opened his eyes as he regained consciousness. He didn't know where he was. He was groggy. He had felt this same way only once before after knee surgery about 12 years ago, except this time he wasn't lying in a recovery room and had no memory of how he got here.

The first thing he noticed was a coffered ceiling. It reminded him of the ceiling in his living room. This would be the most benign discovery he would make in his effort to ascertain what happened to him.

He looked to his right. He was lying on a hardwood floor. He scanned the room. It was empty. He didn't see any windows. He noticed that the drywall had yet to be painted. He had the sense that he was alone and decided to test that theory. He closed his eyes and held his breath. It was complete silence. In his foggy mind, he theorized that if someone else were in the room then he would have heard them breathing. He was convinced he was alone.

He lifted his head to look toward his feet to make his first in a series of disturbing discoveries. His feet were in the air and he was in a metal chair lying on the floor. He decided to look to his left but that decision was with a sting of pain unlike he had ever felt. He quickly moved his head back to the right. He breathed hard as he waited for the pain to subside. Then another discovery…his breathing sounded different. It sounded like he was enduring a dental procedure with a spit vacuum in his mouth. He tried to open his mouth. It was painful but not as bad as looking to his left. He felt that his jaw was crooked. When he closed his mouth, his top and bottom teeth were not meeting evenly.

"Hello?" Ron asked. He was shocked by his voice. The first thought that came to his mind was highly politically incorrect, "I sound like a mentally-challenged person."

He knew that there was something very wrong with his left jaw.

But he was not yet panicked. His brain was in a state of shock from the concussion that he didn't realize he sustained. Ron knew he was on the floor and he knew that he probably had a broken jaw. But he felt like he was dreaming—the reality of the situation had not yet taken root. Ron then decided to get off the floor. And yet another unexpected result—he couldn't get up.

His arms were restrained behind him and he felt cold metal against his wrists. He moved his fingers across a metal chain extending from each hand. Ron thought to himself, "Are those handcuffs? Am I handcuffed to a chair?"

While the fear slowly started to creep in, Ron was convinced he was dreaming. He remembered an article that stated your brain doesn't allow you move in your sleep in order to avoid injuries. This is the reason why people sometimes cannot fight back when being attacked in a dream. Too bad he couldn't recall reading articles about concussions. Ron opened and closed his eyes several times to make sure that he was awake. And then another discovery—he was lying in something wet. It was on the left side of his face. He now knew he was definitely awake and the fear was running over him.

He tried to find the source of the moisture by slowly moving his head to the left. He grimaced in pain and then screamed as he discovered the source. It was his own blood. The left side of his white, button-down Oxford was now crimson. He then made another unwanted discovery—the foul stench of urine and feces. He looked down and realized that it belonged to him. He had urinated and defecated in his pants.

Now, the fear overcame the effects of his concussion. His chest convulsed as breathing became heavier. He was deafened by the slurping sound of trying to pass air through his cracked jaw. Each breath enhanced his anxiety. He violently shook his arms trying to free himself from the chair. In his spastic effort to free himself, he didn't notice that he was rocking the chair back and forth until it was too late. And then everything went black again. Ron shook the chair so hard that he swung it to the left side. His broken jaw landed directly on the hardwood floor. He passed out from the pain.

When he awoke, the pain was there to greet him. Poe let out a perverse scream from his mangled jaw. "Ow-www! Owwww!" He was panicked. "Help! Someone please help me!", Ron cried as he heard the deformed voice emanating from his mouth.

For the most part, Ron's life was devoid of any real speed bumps. Until recently, his issues were more akin to a midlife crisis rather than soul-altering events. But over the last month, he encountered the ugly parts of life he assumed he was immune to. But at this moment, he was experiencing sheer terror, and he could not ever recall feeling such despair. And then it hit him. He had experienced this feeling once before when he thought someone had taken his son at the ballpark. He then realized that there was one person who had and could make him feel this this way—Elad. The concussion could no longer ward off his memory. He recalled in vivid detail everything that happened to him, causing him to make one last discovery—he was in real danger.

* * *

Ron had met Elad a few hours ago in the parking garage. Elad then instructed Poe to follow him. They were headed toward Charleston on I-26 when Elad exited the highway about halfway there. They pulled into an abandoned gas station about a mile from the interstate. Poe was forced at gunpoint to climb into the trunk of Elad's car. From there, they continued their trek to Charleston via the backroads. The ultimate destination was Sullivan's Island and a beach house owned by Practical Solutions. Elad released Poe from the trunk and at gunpoint led him to an unfinished room above the three-port garage.

There were no windows in the room. He placed Poe into a metal chair more befitting a workshop than a house. He handcuffed Ron's hands to the steel back of the chair. Ron winced in pain as the handcuffs were tightened across his wrists. Elad smiled at his reaction.

"Those cuffs a little tight there, R Dog?" Elad asked. Ron didn't respond. Elad cocked his right hand to his left shoulder and then backhanded Ron across the left cheek. The hit was hard enough to slightly fracture his nose. Ron gasped in pain. He did not know violence, but Elad was a virtuoso in the area.

"Now, Ronnie, when I ask a question, then you give me an answer. Just like our other little game, I make the fucking rules. And the rules are that no answer or an untruthful answer will result in physical and mental discomfort for you. So that slap was just a warning because you were not fully acquainted with my rules. But you are now, aren't you?"

Ron did not immediately respond. He was still shocked by the previous hit. He had not been physically assaulted since he was in elementary school—and it was a girl. Elad once again cocked his right hand and backhanded him. This time Elad's knuckles connected with

Ron's forehead. The force of the hit fractured one of Elad's fingers but he ignored the pain. The blow nearly knocked him unconscious and blood erupted from his head. Ron had always heard that a head injury bleeds profusely and he now had personal knowledge of that fact.

"Again, are you familiar with my rules?!" Elad screamed.

"Yes, yes. I am familiar with the rules," Ron stammered. He was dazed from the two headshots but could only hope that someone heard Elad's scream and the police were being called. Sullivan's Island was a quaint town whose rich inhabitants did not tolerate anything that would disrupt their affluent lifestyle.

"OK, let's get this out of the way because I can see by your eyes that you think there will be some sort of rescue. Well, get that fairfetched dream out of your head. You have a better chance of the Easter bunny walking through that door before any police rescue," Elad said.

Ron stared into Elad's yellow tinted eyes. "Was there a question in that?"R on asked for fear of receiving another hit.

"Ah, you are a smart lawyer aren't you? Already learning the rules. And no, there wasn't a question in that statement," Elad said with a smile. "But just to alleviate any doubts that I am your only salvation from this hell, let me tell you a couple of things. Okay?"

"Okay," Ron quickly answered.

"Good job, Ronnie. Playing by the rules. Just like Simon says," Elad responded. "Let's start with your car. It's gone. The gas station where we dropped it is a notorious hot spot for folks that actually want their car stolen. Little fun fact that law enforcement doesn't advertise. People who for whatever reason don't want their car...well, they drop it there and it's gone. They report it to their insurance company whatever they want as to where the car was stolen. That spot is the Bermuda Triangle for vehicles. Your BMW is probably half way to Alabama by now. So you know what that means?"

"That no one will find my car and suspect that something has happened to me," Ron answered.

"Following the rules and giving good answers!" Elad exclaimed. "Now you're getting in the spirit of this!"

Ron looked around the room and tried to wipe blood from his face with his left shoulder.

"I notice that you're observing the somewhat drab confines of this room. You see Ronnie, this is my room," Elad said proudly and held out both arms to showcase his masterpiece. He directed his attention back to his prey. "You don't seem impressed. And that's normal because most people aren't but they should be. You are sitting in a true anechoic chamber. Do you know what that means?"

"No," he quickly answered.

"Playing the game so well! Quick and honest answers!" Elad shouted. He then walked to Ron and leaned into his face. "It means that this room is soundproof. And not just any kind of soundproof—this is like soundproof on steroids. Behind that drywall are three-foot thick, acoustic wedges with double walls of insulated steel and a foot-thick concrete. This very garage has been structurally reinforced to support this little room. Now, aren't you impressed?" Elad concluded.

"Um, yes," Ron timidly answered.

"You wanna try it out? You can scream at the top of your lungs and no one will hear," Elad asked.

"Uh, no."

"Well, maybe you will later. Let's see where the evening takes us," Elad said.

Elad took off his jacket and loosened his tie. He retrieved his revolver from the inside vest pocket before tossing his coat to the ground. "Only one problem with the room, no furniture. Got to put everything on the floor. Speaking of which, these floors are stain resistant." Elad pointed to the ground.

Ron looked at the floor and then looked back Elad.

"Hopefully, we won't need to test that feature of the room. But that will be up to you." Elad walked directly behind Ron and emptied the chamber of his gun. Ron nervously listened as the bullets fell to the hardwood floor. Elad reached down and picked up one bullet. He placed it in the chamber, spun the cylinder and then slammed it shut. Ron listened intently. "Do you know what I just did?" Elad asked in an eerily calm tone.

"Well, I can't see you so I don't know exactly what you have done," Ron replied.

"That's good Ronnie...very good. You keep playing like this and we won't have to test the functionality of this room." Elad walked in front of him. He showed him the gun. "This is a Ruger LCR .357 revolver. I know it looks kinda small but believe me, one shot at point blank range and the bullet, as well as your brains, will be on the backside of that wall. Do you believe that?"

"Yes," he said as he glared at the gun. Ron's mind and stomach were spinning out of control. He was suppressing every urge to vomit in anticipation over the next exercise in torture that Elad crafted for him. At the same time, he struggled to focus enough mental energy to intelligibly respond to Elad's series of questions. One misstep and he could only imagine the physical pain he would endure.

"And can you guess how many bullets are in the gun?"

"Yes...one."

"So, as pleasant as our interchange has been, I am afraid that we need to get down to business. We're gonna do a little Q and A. Where I will do the Q and you will do the A. So, let me start with the Q and if you answer this question honestly, then you will get to leave this room without any more unpleasantness," Elad said as he gently wiped blood from Ron's eye. "Where is Miki Martin?"

"I don't know." While he was resigned to his decision to set up a meeting with Miki, Ron's response was more of an instinct to protect his friend rather than a calculated answer.

Without hesitation, Elad pressed the barrel of the gun to Ron's head and pulled the trigger. Click. Ron could not comprehend his near-death experience. He began to hyperventilate and a steady stream of urine flowed down the pants leg of his thousand dollar suit.

"Did you just piss yourself?" Elad said as he recoiled to avoid the stream. "Ronnie…Ronnie…Ronnie, do you not fully understand your circumstances?"

He didn't respond. He couldn't. His mind was too focused on his breathing that was now strained and out of control. Elad took his left hand and punched Ron in the groin. His breathing became more labored as he tried to absorb the blow. His eyes widened as he sat in a pool of his own urine, gasping for air.

"The rules, Ronnie! The rules! I ask a question and you give an answer. Nod, if you understand."

Ron nodded emphatically. He felt like his testicles were now lodged in his stomach.

"Why don't you calm down a little and let me educate you as to your present set of circumstances. You need to process this before answering my next question," Elad said as he wiped his brow from the sweat. The last punch exerted a tremendous amount of energy.

"You're in a place where no one even knows to look for you nor will they start looking for you for several few days or however long you told your wife would be gone. And that's assuming that she even notices that you're gone in between her fuck sessions with tennis boy. And you're in a room where no one can hear you and you have to get past me in order to get through that door. Like

I said before, I am your only salvation right now and it wouldn't be in your best interests to piss me off."

Ron closed his eyes. He had to concentrate and not blurt out any more instinctive answers. He envisioned his family. He thought of the faces of his youngest son and oldest daughter. While he didn't know if he would survive this encounter, he had to protect them from Elad. But he couldn't do that as a pool of waste. He needed to start with his breathing. He had to control his breathing so that his mind could focus. With his mind filled of images of his children, Ron was able to breath normally again.

Elad stood back and observed him. "There you go, big boy. There you go. Slow that breathing down." Ron opened his eyes and looked directly at Elad. "You look a little angry and more focused. You ready to resume our Q and A? And that was a question by the way," Elad said.

Ron nodded.

"Great. Let's fire this up one more time. Where is Miki Martin?" Elad asked pressing the barrel of the gun against Poe's temple.

Ron hesitated before his answer. He sighed hard and responded. "I know and will tell you after you let me out of this room. I have to have assurances that my family and I will be left alone. And only then can I give you Martin."

"You damn lawyers, always find a way to manipulate the rules. Because technically speaking, you gave me an answer, and a truthful one. Only problem for you is that I make the rules and can change them whenever I want. So new rule, I must like the answer as well."

Elad instantly pulled the trigger. Click. Ron tried to contain his physical reaction but couldn't. He started to hyperventilate again. This time the smell of feces filled the room. He felt the warm liquid flow down his leg and onto the floor. He was intoxicated in fear and his mind debated whether death would be a better alternative to enduring more Elad's interrogation. But once again, the thoughts of his children and the repercussions that they would suffer prevailed over this physical reaction to the fear. He focused on his breathing. Control the breathing and he could still control his mind. He had to save them, and pissing and defecating would not aid in that quest.

"Goddamn, Ronnie, you literally smell like shit. It seems that your body has a better grasp of this encounter than your mind. Don't you get it?" Ron didn't respond. Elad slapped him across the face with his left hand. The right hand had a firm grip on the gun.

"One of two things will happen here. This bullet will leave the gun and blow off your skull. Or, you will give me an honest answer. It's only a matter of which one comes first. That's why there is only one bullet. I am prepared for the consequences of either one. Save your life and the lives of your children and just give me the fucking answer."

"If you get Martin, then you won't need me. If I am dead, then I will have no way to protect my family," Ron retorted. His mind was overcoming the body and Elad was shocked. Resiliency was not a character trait he attributed to his victim. "So I will stay alive until you get him. I know this. It is the reason you didn't let me see you load the gun. It's empty. I am your only hope, and based on the money that went into this room, I would say you're under an immense amount of pressure to get me to talk. So now we just have to work the circumstances under which I will give you Martin."

Elad grinned with his almost unperceivable lips. He showed the gun to Poe and opened the chamber. Poe's eyes widened in disbelief as he saw a single bullet in one chamber. It would have been the next shot. Elad spun the cylinder and slammed it shut.

"Guess that theory is out the window." Elad smirked. "So, let's begin our Q and A anew." Elad pressed the barrel of the gun against Poe's forehead. "Where is Miki…"

Elad's cell phone rang. Elad fumed as he looked at the incoming number. He had to answer.

"Yes," Elad answered. He listened to the voice on the other end and grimaced. "Of course, I will be there. I just wasn't expecting it to be this soon." He listened to the response. "I understand and agree that the situation must be addressed." He looked at Ron. "I am on my way."

Elad pulled the gun from his head. He then walked behind Ron and retrieved the bullets from the floor. He slowly placed each bullet into the chambers and then slammed the cylinder shut in Ron's ear.

"Well, Ronnie, looks like you get a temporary reprieve. And while I would love to leave you here to test the acoustics of this room and that deadbolt on that door, I am not." Elad took his right hand with a firm grip on the gun and cocked it across his left shoulder. He then slammed the butt of the gun against Ron's left jaw, cracking it in one place. The blow knocked Ron unconscious and his chair went backwards slamming the back of his head against the floor. For the first time in his life, Poe had sustained a concussion.

With Ron out cold and lying on his back in the chair, Elad kicked his left jaw two more times before exiting the room, breaking his jaw in a new spot with each kick. He had to meet Grafton downtown.

* * *

Elad pulled his car into the garage and lowered the door behind him. He had not been followed from his rendezvous with Pontet. Elad was exhausted from the day's events. Between kidnapping, torture and murder, even a hired gun has his physical limits. He had lost all patience with Ron and purchased an item at a late night convenience store that he knew would force him to talk.

He returned to his little room of horrors to find Ron lying on his left side of the floor. He was slurping for breath through his offset jaw. Elad walked over and lifted Ron upright and off the floor.

"Damn, Ronnie, I don't think your Armani suit is built to withstand the rigors of blood, shit and piss. You're a mess of a man right now, aren't you?"

Poe immediately nodded. Even with a concussion and broken jaw, he remembered the rules of the game.

Elad stared at Ron's hands and then glared back at him. "Your nails, are they manicured?"

Ron nodded.

Elad gave another lipless, evil grin. "Wow, man who gets his nails professionally manicured. That says something. I mean I can understand a movie star or some sort of celebrity doing that, but you're just a regular guy. You know what that tells me?"

Ron shook his head.

"It tells me that you are man from a pampered lifestyle. Someone who pays to have his nails professionally sculpted is not someone with the fortitude to truly withstand being chained to a chair and beaten. It tells me that the physical damage inflicted upon you probably pales in comparison to the psychological carnage that you have endured. That is the damage that will not heal as quickly."

Ron slurped harder for air as his anxiety grew over Elad's next move. He wasn't a religious man, but at that moment his was expending all of his mental energy in a prayer that Elad not pull out the gun.

"You see, Ronnie, our little Q and A session will haunt you forever. You will never be the same. You will never experience happiness as you once could. The horrors of tonight will eternally skew your view of the world. The slightest downturn in your life will result in immeasurable anxiety as you have now discovered how cruel life can be. Your fear of the world will far exceed any optimism toward life that you once possessed. But your pristine nails tell me even more. Can you guess?"

Ron shook his head.

"Well, most fathers want to protect their children, especially their daughters. They have a relentless desire to make sure that their daughters have an almost sheltered life. So when I see a father and his lifestyle, then generally, I can assume that his daughter leads an even more privileged life."

"Leave my daughter alone," Ron mumbled through his distorted jaw.

"I don't think you're in a position to make any demands." Elad said with a laugh. "But you have some control to see that your little girl doesn't experience all that you have tonight. And based on how soft you are, I shutter to imagine her reactions to a little Q and A with me."

Then Elad retrieved from his jacket the item that he knew would crack Ron. It was a hand-held mirror. He shoved it in his face and made him stare at the reflection.

Ron sobbed at the sight of his face ravaged by his time with Elad. His jaw was offset by an inch. The left side of his face was caked in blood and his left eye was swollen to the size of a golf ball. Blood filled it like air in a balloon.

Ron tried to look away but Elad grabbed his face, making him look in the mirror. Ron let out a garbled scream of pain. He sobbed uncontrollably as he was forced to stare at his image.

"This is how well you have fared tonight. Imagine what she will look like. I cannot even imagine how beautiful her nails are. But I will find out as I pull every single nail out of her perfect little hands that are probably soft and smooth, as she has never known a day of physical labor."

Elad released his face and Ron immediately stared at the floor away from the mirror. He was a 'mess of a man,' as Elad had described. He felt utter shame. He was not the father that his daughter needed. He had failed her. He endangered her life all because of his friendship with Miki. He should have immediately contacted law enforcement when Miki called. His daughter would now have to face the ramifications of Miki's mistakes

As Elad predicted, Ron's mind was far more damaged than his body. The item had worked. Elad then retrieved the revolver and pressed the barrel under his chin. Ron barely acknowledged cold steel against his skin.

"All of the chambers are full this time," Elad said. "So the only mystery is which comes out first, Martin's whereabouts or the bullet? One last time, where is Martin located?"

"1977 Carolina Blvd., Isle of Palms. There is a key in my right pocket."

Elad removed the gun from under Ron's chin. He reached into his pocket and retrieved the key. It had a small piece of tape across the top which read "1977" in faded ink.

"Thank you, Ronnie," Elad said in an almost giddy tone. "I am a pretty good read of people. I feel confident that you have told me the truth. So that means good news and some bad news."

"What's that?" Ron said in an exhausted tone.

"Good news is that your daughter will never meet me," Elad replied.

"And the bad news?"

"You will never see her." Elad drew his weapon and fired a single shot between Ron Poe's eyes. His lifeless body slumped in the chair. For Ron, it was a merciful ending to a life that would have been forever wrecked because of the night's events. Elad was correct. He would have never recovered. He was actually thankful when he saw Elad draw the weapon.

"Well Ronnie, I gotta say that I am just a little tired," Elad said to Ron's corpse. "I am gonna get some shut eye, meet your friend Martin in the morning and take care of all the bodies at one time. Does that sound like a plan?"

Elad stared as if expecting a response. He then slapped the corpse across the face.

"Rules, Ronnie, the rules," Elad said as he left the room.

CHAPTER TWENTY:
NO ALTERNATIVE

Saturday morning and Poe was almost an hour late. Miki looked out from the front door window every five minutes. He knew it was a risk to be in plain sight, but his nervous energy prevented him from sitting still. While Miki was anxious about Ron's tardiness, Gabbie was in far worse shape. She was terrified.

She spent the past several days fixated on the information they had learned. She was the illegitimate daughter of the state's sitting governor. Her father extorted a police officer in a scheme to kill her mother and anyone connected to that murder. Her father had to know of her existence from the Chandler Murray file. She could only imagine the number of people Murray approached with that information in a quest to clear his name. Her father sent the men to kill her. And while that attempt failed, it had flushed Miki and her out. They had no one but each other as they tried to avoid a statewide law enforcement manhunt. But she now knew that their adversary was no longer just the police. It was something far sinister—her father.

Then she saw the local news, and it fueled her terror. The broadcast showed footage of a fire at a mobile home park claiming the lives of two people. The news identified the victims—her foster parents. Her father's presence was now in this area. He was closing in. She was convinced that her father orchestrated this meeting with Ron Poe.

"Miki, did you see this?" She pointed to the television screen.

Miki quickly glanced in her direction and then returned his gaze to outside the window. "Yeah, it's a TV. You watch stuff on it." Miki chuckled to himself. He needed a moment of brevity to calm his nerves.

"The Beckwiths…those charming inbreeds that helped raise me…they're dead."

"What?" Miki turned and walked toward her. He caught the tail end of the story before it went to commercial.

"They died in a fire. It's still under investigation," she said. Miki's stomach sank. He knew that this wasn't a fire caused by a combination of alcohol and cigarettes. They were killed simply because of an attachment to Gabbie's lineage.

"Let's just keep waiting on Ron. He is probably just being cautious." He tried to remain calm. He knew that a panicked decision would only be a careless one.

"Or maybe, he has met up with my dear old dad and they made a deal that will lead him to us—more specifically, to me," Gabbie replied in an angry tone.

"That's not like him. Hood couldn't buckle him. Ron's got his own political pull."

"Miki, wake up. This ain't about political bullying. This is about killing anyone remotely connected to my very existence in this world. So when I say they made a deal, it wasn't an arrangement granting Ron personal gain. It was a deal to save his life in exchange for ours."

"His father-in-law is this state's eldest senator. You don't just threaten a guy like that without consequences. It isn't like burning a mobile home or extorting an alcoholic cop."

"Oh, because he's a lawyer with some good family connections? You've seen everything that Hood can, and will, do. Do you really think he will stop because of that?"

Miki quietly processed the question.

"Or, let me ask it this way, are you willing to bet your life on the assumption that your friend is somehow untouchable?" Gabbie pressed. "Does your friend have a wife and children?"

"Yes," Miki whispered.

"Well, accidents happen all the time," Gabbie pointed to the television set that had broadcast the news of the fire.

She was making sense and wearing through Miki's armor of optimism. While he believed Ron was the key to resetting his life, Gabbie was bringing him back to reality.

Gabbie grabbed him by the shoulders and looked into his eyes.

"Miki, I am not willing to risk my life on a bet that your friend is somehow immune to Grafton. I don't even know if someone like that exists. But if that person exists, it ain't Ron Poe."

Miki's eyes watered at the thought that he put his friend in danger. He knew it wasn't a selfish decision but one dictated by circumstance. But it was a circumstance that he created. He shouldn't have been in a strip club parking lot in the early hours of the morning. He should have used that courtroom victory as a springboard to resurrecting his practice but, instead, he used it to fuel his lifestyle of happy hours and late night trysts. And that decision now impacted his only true friend.

"I shouldn't have gotten him involved. That was a mistake." Miki was on the verge of crying but contained it.

"Listen, that's one thing we have in common—an ability to make tremendous mistakes. But we don't have time for that shit. Grafton won't wait until we are done moping about bad decisions. And if we stay here, it is going to be a bad decision that we won't regret. Because you can't regret anything when you are dead."

Miki shook his head to clear the images of Ron suffering at Grafton's command. "Listen! He will show up! I don't want to give up hope just yet. He's only an hour late."

"Ok," Gabbie fumed, "well, we're in this together so we both have a say. I say run and you say stay. So, let's compromise. They're building a house across the street. I say we take the motorcycle and park it behind the house.

We gather our stuff and watch from that house. If he comes, then that's great. But if he doesn't, then we get the hell outta here."

"Fine."

They relocated to across the street to the plush vacation home being constructed. They watched from an unfinished room on the third floor. About a minute into their surveillance, Miki noticed a car pass. Twenty seconds later, the same car passed again, heading in the opposite direction. Another 20 seconds later, the same car returned and parked in the driveway of their former refuge.

Miki's stomach sank as he noticed a red-headed man exit the driver side door. Miki had never seen him before. They continued to watch as the man walked up the stairs and used a key to cautiously unlock the door. His entry into the home was deliberate, as if he was trying not to make a sound.

Gabbie and Miki looked at each.

"We gotta go," they said in unison. They raced down the stairs and jumped on the back of the motorcycle. Miki sped down the street as Elad began his search of the empty house. They slipped away without catching his attention.

Miki drove the motorcycle toward Mt. Pleasant, a town that separated Charleston from the barrier islands of Sullivan's Island and Isle of Palms. It was a tense ride. Miki's head spun wildly as he tried to spot anyone with red hair driving a car. Gabbie chose to keep her head down, pressed against Miki's back. She was too scared to look.

The growth of Charleston had spurned a building frenzy in what was once a small town. Mt. Pleasant was now larger than Charleston. Highway 17, a six-lane road, was the main thoroughfare for the town. The town planted Palmetto trees on both sides but still couldn't hide the commercial nature of the area. On either side was an endless maze of tract-built neighborhoods and strip malls anchored by high-end grocery stores. There were numerous hotels for the tourists wanting to enjoy the spoils of downtown Charleston and the beaches of its barrier islands.

Miki located a hotel near the base of the Ravenel Bridge—the site of Pontet's demise. But he needed to make sure they weren't followed before checking in. He drove into and out of three different neighborhoods. Each seemed to have the same pattern of development—vinyl-sided homes near the highway and large brick homes located deep inside.

They passed families playing in the front yard or simply taking a lazy Saturday stroll. The families barely noticed the fugitives cruising through their area of the world. Miki longed to be part of their normalcy. After an hour, Miki was satisfied that they weren't being followed. It was time to get off the road before that changed. He and Gabbie checked into the hotel.

He felt safe, or at least safer. The effects of his adrenaline subsided and his mind quieted. While he was relieved that they escaped, his thoughts turned back to Poe. The red-headed man had a key to the house that he probably got from Poe. Miki knew Poe didn't willingly give up that key, or Miki for that matter. And more importantly, that meant Grafton knew Poe was a link in the chain leading to Gabbie and, like the other links, Ron Poe had been broken. Miki's feelings of guilt and remorse overwhelmed him.

He sat on the edge of the queen size bed and sobbed like a baby. Gabbie tried to comfort him but she could not quell his emotions. He simply needed to cry it out. He tightly hugged her and soaked her shoulder in his tears. Gabbie welcomed the embrace and shed tears of her own. Her father essentially buried her alive at birth and she had been climbing her way out of the grave ever since. And now, he was trying to bury her again.

While they had been intimate many times, this was their most intimate. It wasn't sex at the end of a drunken evening or to stay active as they remained sober. This time they were providing emotional support for the other's tortured soul. Neither had found this level of comfort in another person. It wasn't love because that wasn't needed at this time. It was more valuable. It was an attraction to another person who could actually relate to your pain—because no one person could soothe it. For the first time, neither felt alone.

Miki and Gabbie finally corralled their emotions and started to process the new information. They came to the same conclusion—Grafton would not stop. The also realized another important fact. Despite his best efforts, he had still not found them. They were emboldened by their ability to continue to elude him. Miki knew their next move would be the most critical.

"Maybe its time that we talk to the police? Show them what we have," Gabbie suggested.

"Thought we went over this. We have paper clippings and a video from a dead, disbarred attorney. Nothing has changed."

"Ron. If you're right, then he is missing. They would have to investigate that," Gabbie replied.

"Yeah, we would probably be their prime suspects. They'll still just lock us up and then Grafton will know exactly where we are." Miki smirked.

"Then we leave the country. We cross over the Mexican border. Hell, people do that shit all the time. It should be easier for us because we're actually trying to get in," Gabbie replied.

"And then what? Lead a miserable existence as fugitives in Mexico? Always looking over our shoulders? Leading the lives of fugitives in Mexico City?"

"How about Cancun? Blue seas and white sand beaches! That's not a bad place to live. We get some fake backgrounds. Hell, you could probably be a lawyer down there."

"Gabbie, that sounds grand but it takes one thing which we don't have—money. I don't know how to get a fake background but I am pretty sure that it ain't free. And I know that law school isn't free. And even if it were, I am not going to reinvent my life to become a lawyer again. That really didn't work out well for me the first time."

"Alright, smart guy, what is your grand plan? Because right now, you're just offering problems and we have plenty of those. In fact, I would say we're all stocked up." Gabbie gave him a gentle pat to the cheek.

Miki grabbed her hand and turned the pat into a gentle caress. "Well, this idea hit me when we were riding around. I saw a Hood Campaign Headquarters building about a mile away."

"Campaign headquarters? I thought he was done being our governor?"

"Who knows what your father is up to?"

"I prefer the term sperm donor."

"Right." Miki grinned. "Anyway, it had a Hood Rally sign. It reminded me of something I saw on the news a few days ago. He's coming here for some sort of rally to support his anti-abortion legislation."

"So?"

"We meet him," Miki answered. He looked her dead in the eyes so that she knew he wasn't joking.

"What? Meet the man who is trying to kill us? That's your solution?"

"Think about it. Maybe we need to turn the fight to him. I don't think he is accustomed to that."

"No, I think he probably is," Gabbie said confidently. "But it was a cute idea." She gave him another pat to the cheek but not as soft this time.

"Just listen. We can't approach anyone else because we have nothing to corroborate our story. He is the only one that will believe us because he's the only living soul that knows the actual truth. And he knows we have the one thing that can back up our story."

"What's that, Big Guy?" Gabbie quipped and patted his cheek again as if addressing a toddler.

Miki grabbed her wrist and pointed at her veins. "You."

Gabbie paused as she soaked in the suggestion. "So we somehow meet him and tell him everything we know?"

"Yep." Miki nodded. "We show him the Murray video and tell him that we have documents to support everything. We then threaten him with your DNA. We threaten all this unless we are paid to go away." Miki smiled and gently patted her cheek. "What do you think of that?"

"So threaten him directly because none of his middle men will believe us?"

"Exactly."

"But what about…"

Miki interrupted. "Gabbie, Poe's dead. And with that death, so are our resources. We have no money and no place to go."

"What about your parents?"

"My mother is as much a ghost as yours and my father is more apt to turn me in for reward money than loan me anything. This is our only option."

She knew Miki was correct. They could not continue to outrun Grafton. He had the ability to eternally track them down. As perverse as it sounded, Miki's plan was their only option.

"Well, how do have this meeting with him?" She shrugged her shoulders. "Do we just call him up? Hey Dad, it's your baby girl. When can we meet?" Gabbie mocked as if she had a phone to her ear.

"Very helpful," Miki said with an irritated tone. "We're going to spend the last of our bucks to buy you some..." Miki smiled, "well, let's just say outfits that showcase your figure."

"Ah, great idea. Say, let's just invite him to the strip club so we can chat while I dry hump the pole," Gabbie practically hissed. For Gabbie, her escape from Grafton was an escape from a life where her body was her only asset. And now, Miki was asking that she lapse back. She recoiled at the notion.

"That's not what I am saying." Miki knew he offended her. "We need to get you into that headquarters as a volunteer. We need you to catch the eye of the manager. Perhaps invite him for a drink or something? And while he's away, then I can see what I can find out about Grafton's itinerary."

"And what if it's a woman?"

"Then I guess I need some clothing that showcases *my* figure," Miki fired back.

"Don't flatter yourself."

On the following Monday, Miki and Gabbie went to Grafton's campaign headquarters to volunteer for the rally. Gabbie was dressed in a white, thigh-high dress. Her top two buttons were undone, showcasing her cleavage and the fact that she didn't need a bra for support. Noticeably, there were no panty lines. Miki was dressed in a tight black Polo shirt with a pair of slim fit J-Crew jeans—just in case.

Miki gave her a wink when they were introduced to the campaign manager. He was 38 years old and the low man on the campaign totem pole. He was recently fired as a manager of a local chain restaurant after being accused of making inappropriate comments to the underage hostesses. It was something he had done his entire career, but no one ever called him on it. This time was different. The hostess was the daughter of the treating doctor for the regional manager of the chain. Black-balled in his industry, he was forced to earn a living organizing a rally for Grafton. It was a six-week gig and he didn't know what he would do afterwards. He jumped at the drink invitation from Gabbie. It was a distraction from his present woes.

Gabbie heard his entire story (except for the reason he was fired) and thought to herself, "once again I am using my body to cheer up depressed men." She blamed

Miki for all of it. Miki smiled as he gathered information on Grafton's itinerary. He knew the verbal tongue lashing was in his future.

CHAPTER TWENTY-ONE:
LUNCH, EPISODE II

Grafton was alone in the backseat of his state-issued black SUV as it headed to downtown Charleston. The vehicle was quiet except for the occasional voices mumbling through the radio transmitters of his security detail. Normally, the car would have been filled with the sounds of Pontet's voice espousing theories of political attacks on would-be opponents. Elad had silenced that voice, and Grafton enjoyed the peace. He needed to think. He stared out the window at the Charleston Harbor as his mind churned to comprehend the events of the last few days.

This should have been a moment to savor. Like his daughter, he was buried alive years ago. He was shoved into an unmarked grave amongst other nearly successful politicians. It was a graveyard of living ghosts lying in state and consumed by thoughts of what might have been. But Grafton scratched and clawed his way from the grave, and ran from the cemetery.

His bill had a third reading before the Senate, with the vote scheduled for this afternoon. The legislation would hit his desk tomorrow morning. With one signature, it would become law and Grafton would have fulfilled his deal with Practical Solutions. The rally scheduled for this afternoon was supposed to be a dual event—announce the passage of his legislation and then announce his candidacy for the Republican nomination for President of the United States. His escape from the casket should have been officially complete. But the consequences of his past stared at him like a mirror—no matter how many times he looked away, the image was still there.

Elad reported that Martin and the girl were still free. He told Grafton that until the threat was quelled—Elad's term for dead—then PS wouldn't back his candidacy and Grafton should wait before announcing it.

To compound matters, Spring wanted another lunch meeting. At this point, Grafton viewed the meeting as useless. The legislation was certain to pass. There was nothing that Spring could offer. He thought that perhaps the meeting was Spring's effort to curry favor with him as the next president. Grafton thought to himself, "Who knows, maybe the old man wants an ambassadorship." He took the meeting more as a diversion from his present concerns about Miki and Gabbie. It would be a nice escape—a lunch meeting where he could gloat over a once formidable opponent.

Grafton picked a restaurant tucked away on Queen Street. It was once the toast of the Charleston cuisine. But after the influx of tourists and culinary experts from the entire eastern seaboard, only locals provided a customer base for the restaurant. Spring was seated at a two-top in the back. He was dressed in a blue Seersucker suit with a lime green bow tie. With his glass of sweet tea adorned by two lemons in hand, Spring was glancing over the menu. He looked up as Grafton took his seat. Grafton sat down before Spring could stand to greet him. In the world of politics, that was code for "let me sit down and hurry with the meal, because I don't have time for you."

"Governor, how are you this morning?" Spring put down his tea and extended his hand.

Grafton shook his hand and flashed him a huge grin. "I am doing very well." He wasn't about to give Spring a hint as to his present issues. This was a lunch to turn the dagger of victory into Spring's back. "And you?" Grafton placed the linen dining cloth on his lap.

"I am good. Guess I am licking my wounds a little bit over the success of your pending legislation," Spring replied with a chuckle.

"You mean law, don't you?" Grafton turned the dagger.

"I guess so," Spring replied.

"Not much guess work in it," Grafton laughed. "Third reading and then onto my desk for a signature. Did you want one of the pens that I will use to sign it?"

"No, sir. I am sure plenty of other folks would love a crack at that pen. But I am not one of them," Spring replied.

"Then to what do I owe this lunch? This was about a two-hour drive for you."

"Well, in a nutshell, I wanted to talk about roads," Spring answered. The comment took Grafton by surprise but he refrained from showing it. His mind was flooded with images of his meeting with the legislators from outside the T. He knew exactly where Spring was headed and Grafton searched his mind for the person who may have informed Spring about the meeting.

The waiter interrupted.

"Gentlemen, care to hear the specials?"

"Not really. Senator, do you?" Grafton replied.

"No. I know exactly what I want," Spring said with a grin. "I'll take the shrimp and grits."

"And I'll have a bowl of she crab and side salad," Grafton replied as he handed his menu to the waiter without even looking at him. He was focused on Spring.

Grafton impatiently waited for the waiter to gather Spring's menu, refill his tea and leave.

"What about roads? My administration is almost done and the legislative session is practically done for the year." Grafton tried to play it off.

"Oh, I am keenly aware that your term is almost up. What has sparked my interest is a bill that was recently introduced to increase the allowable sales tax on personal property, specifically boats and cars. It basically earmarks almost one billion in tax revenue to construction and repairs of roads in some of our…" Spring paused, "well, less affluent counties."

"Senator, I must profess ignorance as to the legislation. I have been focused on my anti-abortion bill." Grafton knew exactly what Spring was talking about. He helped to draft it behind the scene, per his promise.

Spring took a sip of his tea. "Well, Governor, I have known you for a long time both in the legislature and as governor. I have seen you involved in legislation pertaining to the manner in which the state euthanizes stray dogs and cats."

"Well, that had to do with lowering the cost of killing strays to save the taxpayers' money," Grafton replied.

"Be that as it may," Sping took another sip of tea, "my point being that I have never seen *any* legislation to which you profess ignorance—especially a billion dollar tax hike."

"Senator, what are you saying? That I have somehow sponsored a bill that I am unaware of?"

"No, your name is nowhere to be found on it. But what I do know is that this bill is flowing—unimpeded—through legislative channels that you normally use to ground such legislation to a halt. I understand that it is approaching a first reading on the House floor."

"Well, I appreciate you bringing this matter to my attention. Although, I am somewhat surprised."

"How so?"

"Because you have attempted to pass similar legislation. It seems that you would have liked for me to stay asleep at the helm."

The arrival of their food was like the bell at the end of a round of boxing. Both fighters retreated to their corners.

Each ingested their meal as they planned their next series of punches upon the sound to return to battle.

Ding! Ding!

Spring put his elbows on the table and folded his hands over his dish. He rested his chin on his fingers and stared at Grafton. "I guess if I was a keen student of politics, then I would assume that you brokered a deal."

Grafton stopped eating and laughed. He wiped his lips with his napkin and placed it back in his lap. "You're not a student of politics...you're a professor. In fact, I think you actually teach a graduate class at the university. And so, professor," Grafton sarcastically said, "I think you know there's nothing wrong with the exchange of votes between representatives based on the particular needs of their constituents. That idea is as old as democracy itself."

"Perhaps."

"Senator, I can't help it if certain representatives of this state are more concerned about jobs for their counties rather than a woman's right to choose. They had a need and I met it. I had a need and they met it. That's politics. Democracy in action," Grafton said as he waved his hands in the air.

"Governor, I get how politics work. But it isn't whether you stroke deals with individual representatives, it is how you do it. Don't you agree?"

"What do you mean?"

"Well, we all know that a lobbyist cannot outright buy votes."

"Of course not. Ethics and campaign finance reform have created a minefield to cross in order to buy votes. One wrong step and…boom!"

"So you agree that a lobbyist could not gather together a group of representatives and promise them a lucrative amount of state funding if they agreed to vote a certain way?"

Grafton had two choices—abandon the lunch or answer the question. While his political instincts screamed for him to run, he was dealing with PS. He needed to know exactly what Spring knew and who else knew it. If there was a threat to the legislation, Elad would need detail in order to quell it.

"I agree with that notion," Grafton replied.

Spring leaned across the table, staring Grafton in the eyes without batting an eyelash. And in a tone just above a whisper, he said "Then why did you think you could do it?"

"What?" It was the worst thing he could say. He had met an accusatory question with another question. It was the second closest thing to a confession.

Spring removed the dagger from his back and now had it firmly placed in the small of Grafton's back. After years of political bullying, Spring was exacting years of frustration and humiliation. His human nature took over. He dropped the façade of elder statesman. There would be no more politico speak. He would address Grafton man-to-man.

"Your meeting with the representatives from outside of the T...folks that I have spent decades trying to help," Spring pointed his finger as if lecturing a child. "You brought them in and made them an outright promise of tax money if they supported that abomination of human rights that you call a bill. You narcissistic son-of-a-bitch, you brought all of the hapless gazelles of this state into the lion's den and you devoured them. Do you have any idea of the firestorm that will be unleashed if the press gets a hold of the video?"

"Video?" It was another question with a question. Grafton was on the ropes and there was no bell in his future. This fight would only end by knockout.

"Yes, Grafton, a video."

"From whom?" Grafton acted incensed by the accusation.

"Sharon White," Spring causally replied. Grafton could not contain his surprise. "You know, the chief law enforcement officer for this state? She is seated five tables behind you in case you want to say 'Hi'." Spring pointed in her direction.

Grafton slowly turned around and caught her eye. She gave him a huge smile and waved. He turned back around and returned his focus to Spring. He had to regain his confidence and mount an attack to Spring's onslaught. But the dagger was buried too deep.

"The video even has you actually threatening a representative who questioned your so-called deal."

Grafton recalled in exact detail his exchange with the freshman House member. He sighed and then spoke in a low whisper. "Julius, do you really want the people of this state to endure a brutal media campaign that will only embarrass and belittle them?"

"Don't even try that shit, Grafton. The United States survived Nixon and his tapes. It survived Clinton and his cigars. I think this state can survive you. It will be a few bad months for us, but a lifetime of pain for you." Spring wiped his mouth. "And while I never fully discovered from under what rock you crawled, when this tape hits the airways, I can assure you that the media underbelly will. It will be a feeding frenzy of epic proportions."

"Well, if you're so confident of that, then why not release the tape now? Share it with everyone," Grafton retorted.

"Because by holding onto the tape, I can save the state any further embarrassment. I will destroy the tape if you agree to withdraw your bill and never try to occupy any office that has the term 'public' affixed to it. Ever."

"Well, if you think I am going to withdraw my bill…" Grafton tried to reply.

Spring interrupted. "It is not what I think, it is what I know. Because if you don't, then Sharon over there," Spring pointed in her direction, "will send an email with the video attached to three major news networks and a producer with 60 Minutes."

Grafton looked at her again. This time she replied by holding her cell phone in the air and waving it back and forth. She still had the same grin.

Ding! Ding! The waiter approached.

"Gentlemen, are we finished?"

"Oh, absolutely," Spring cheerfully replied as the waiter cleaned the table. "Please don't let our full plates fool you. It was delicious."

Grafton sat silent. His mind hummed from the fury of thoughts racing through it. It was a complete knockout. The waiter continued to clean the table. If it had been a boxing canvas, it would have been soaked in red in Grafton's blood.

"And my associate over there will be picking up the check," Spring informed the waiter as he pointed to Sharon.

"Yes sir, she already has it taken care of. Y'all enjoy the rest of your day."

"I will," Spring bubbled as he turned his attention back to Grafton. "Grafton...Grafton," Spring said as he snapped his finger.

"What, Julius?" Grafton muttered.

"I think you have some phone calls to make. I will give you an hour to withdraw your bill," Spring pointed to his watch, "so tick...tick...tick. Just like the beginning of 60 minutes."

Spring got up from the table. He didn't even attempt a handshake, but instead, gave Grafton a hard slap on the shoulder. It was the closest he would come to a physical retaliation for the last lunch when Grafton threatened Spring's daughter and grandchildren.

Sharon met him halfway through the restaurant and they were escorted away by two plain clothed officers with her division.

"How'd it go?" Sharon asked.

"As expected," Spring answered. "He has an hour to withdraw the legislation or we send the email. You have it ready?"

"I do." She smiled. "Any mention of John Sessions?"

"He didn't ask and I didn't volunteer. He'll figure out the connection soon enough but that has no bearing on us."

"Exactly," Sharon replied as they entered the backseat of her state-issued SUV.

"Any word on my son-in-law?"

"None since his car turned up in a chop shop in Arkansas."

As soon as Spring left, Hood made his first phone call. Tybee Peppers answered. After enduring a 30-second profanity-filled tirade, Tybee was able to utter his first words in the conversation since saying "Hello."

"Slow down, slow down. You're going too fast for me," Tybee said.

"A parked car is going too fast for you, Tybee. There was someone videotaping my entire meeting with the representatives. Who was it?"

"How should I know? It could have been any one of those people," Tybee replied.

"Tybee, try to exercise that useless organ which inhabits your skull and think about that theory. Those folks had no idea what we were going to discuss before their meeting with me. Plus, Spring knows about my private exchange with a freshman House member. There was no one close enough to have heard that conversation except your detail. So, who was there?"

"It was small security detail—John and a couple of other folks." John Sessions sat across Tybee's desk and listened intently to the conversation. "Only my most trusted people."

"John who?"

"John Sessions. I don't know if you have actually met him but he's been with me since your first term. He was one of my first hires. He's rock solid." Tybee glanced over at Sessions, covered the receiver of the phone and whispered, "He's gone paranoid. Something about a video tape. Did you see anyone taping in there?"

Sessions looked perplexed as he shook his head.

Grafton got up from the table and made his way to the exit. His security detail followed.

"Well, something is not adding up. The only people who had a clue as to the agenda of that meeting were me, Pontet, you and your folks. I know we sure as hell didn't video... Hold on, Peppers." A young lady interrupted Grafton as she approached for an autograph.

"Governor Hood! Governor Hood! Could you please sign this campaign poster? It would mean so much to my mother."

His security detail tried to intervene, but Grafton waved them off. Her beautiful appearance helped dismiss any thought that she posed a threat. Also, the restaurant was filled with patrons and he didn't want a report circulating that he dismissed a supporter. He thought to himself, "Who knows who is videotaping me right now?"

He positioned the cell phone between his cheek and shoulder. "Well, hello young lady. I appreciate the support today and in the future. To whom should I make this out to?" Grafton replied as he took the pen to sign.

"To my mom, she loves you!"

"And what's her name, sweetheart?"

"Newton. Athena Newton," Gabbie replied with a huge smile.

Grafton's neck straightened as he stared Gabbie in the eyes. His phone fell to the ground and shattered. His security detail tried to intervene again, but he waved them off again.

"Leave us alone," he said laying eyes on his daughter for the first time.

"Governor…Governor," Tybee said and then hung up his office phone. "I guess I lost him," Tybee said to Sessions.

"What was that all about?" Sessions asked.

"I don't know. I think he's starting to lose it. He claims that someone videotaped his meeting with those representatives."

"Videotaped him? Huh? What makes him say that?"

"Well, it was kinda hard to understand with him dropping the f-bomb between each word. But it sounds like Sharon White says that she has a video of the meeting. Have you talked with her recently?"

"It's been a while. She said she was doing some background research as to security folks for the Governor. She told me it was routine and she had a couple of questions about my background."

"Like what?" Tybee asked.

"She was curious about my aliases," Sessions calmly replied.

"What aliases?" Tybee answered.

"I will tell you later," Sessions said he retrieved the Glock 23 from his shoulder holster concealed by his jacket.

Tybee instinctively put his hands in the air. "John, what the fuck are you doing?"

"Executing a plan that has been years in the making. And you're going to help me finish it or I am going to tell everyone that you told me to make that video. And if I do that, you will be banished to the political hinterlands of this state. Doesn't matter whether you are a Republican or Democrat, no one likes a snitch."

"I...I don't understand," Tybee stammered.

"And you don't have to. Just do as I say and you will get out of this mess without a scrape."

CHAPTER TWENTY-TWO:
REUNION FROM HELL

"I said 'leave us'," Grafton shouted at his security detail. They were hesitant to abide by his initial command. This time they acquiesced and climbed into the SUV. Grafton turned his attention to Gabbie.

"How do you know that name?" he asked.

"I already told you. She was my mother until you blackmailed a cop into having her killed her in order to save health insurance benefits for his mother."

For one of the rare moments in his life, Grafton was speechless. He couldn't tell whether he was more surprised by her knowledge or her brazenness to confront him directly.

"Cat got your tongue, Dad?" Gabbie grinned. "This is a burner phone."

"I know what it is," Grafton hissed.

"Good. Now, listen to me very carefully. Take this phone, get in your car and wait for my call."

"Tell me why I shouldn't have you arrested on the spot. You're a wanted fugitive along with that Martin fellow. Aren't you?"

"Well, *Dad*," Gabbie sarcastically said, "I got your attention with one simple sentence. Imagine how much attention I will get when I really start talking. Take the phone, get in the car and I will call you."

Grafton snatched the phone from her.

"Tell your driver to take a right at the stop light just ahead and head down King Street. I will call in exactly one minute."

Grafton opened the door and began to climb inside.

"And, Pop." Grafton stopped and peered over his left shoulder at her. "If you try to circle around to find me, I will call the cops myself."

Grafton slammed the door and the vehicle proceeded in the direction instructed by Gabbie.

As soon as the car was out of sight, Gabbie sprinted across the street into a parking garage. She raced up the stairs to the rooftop floor where Miki awaited on the motorcycle. It was a beautiful, cloudless day and the sunlight temporarily blinded her as she left the darkness of the stairwell.

"Well, how'd it go?" Miki asked.

"Oh, he was simply overjoyed to see me," Gabbie replied.

Miki chuckled. "Yeah, I bet the embrace was priceless."

Gabbie dialed Grafton's number. He picked it up in the middle of the first ring.

"Yeah," Grafton answered.

"Tell me exactly what you see out of your window on the right-hand side."

Grafton looked. "A bunch of stores."

"Name one quickly, or I hang up."

"Um," Grafton fumbled for answer, "M. Dumas."

Gabbie covered the receiver and mouthed the answer to Miki.

"That's right," Miki nodded.

"So far, so good. Stay on that course because there will be another question at the end of the conversation."

"Can't wait," Grafton whispered to himself.

"I will make this short and sweet. We recovered the Murray file entitled Brown Recluse. I assume that is you. Correct?"

Grafton didn't respond.

"Listen, Daddy-O, you need to answer my questions if you want to make it out of all this with your political hide intact. Brown Recluse is you, correct?"

"Yes, I was tagged with it during my first term in the legislature."

"Somehow, I don't think it was a term of endearment," Gabbie said with a sneer. She was relishing in tormenting the man who had both created and destroyed her. He had followed her every command so far and she could tell that he was intently listening to each word from her mouth. She was experiencing something that was until now devoid in her life—a sense of empowerment.

While he hated to interrupt her moment, Miki rolled his hands as if to command her to move on with the conversation. If all went according to plan, she would have plenty of time to malign him.

Gabbie nodded at Miki's request. "Like I told you, we know about my mother's death. We met my now-deceased foster parents. We know that you had a hand in the death of Ron Poe. And I feel confident that we can trace you back to the attempt on our lives. Simply put, we know it all."

Grafton was silent on the other end as he gazed out of his window. He watched the tourists and locals as they walked along King Street and its array of shops and restaurants. A few hours ago, he would not have traded places with any of them. But at this moment, he wished he were in their shoes.

"Did you hear me?" Gabbie pressed.

"Yes, I heard you," he responded.

"And you're still on the line. I will take that as an admission to these accusations," Gabbie said, barely able to contain the excitement in her voice.

"What exactly do you want?"

"Well, given everything that you have done to rid this world of me, I don't think we can foster some sort of daddy-daughter relationship. But what you can give me is money and anonymity. So that is what I want."

"I am not sure how I can do that."

"Oh Dad, c'mon now! Where's that 'can-do' spirit you employed when you eradicated my mother? I am a chip off the ole block and I will not take 'no' for an answer."

"I bet you won't," Grafton replied.

"What's out of your window now?" Gabbie asked.

"We're approaching Huger Street."

She covered the phone and mouthed Miki the answer. He nodded.

"Well done!" Gabbie exclaimed. Miki smiled and shook his head. They were both nervous as hell over the plan but Gabbie was playing a beautiful poker face. "Maybe she was a chip off the ole block after all," Miki thought to himself.

"Now, keep this phone handy and I will call you later to give you the time and place where we will meet. Okay?" Gabbie instructed.

"I understand," Grafton coldly replied.

"Nice connecting with you, Pop. Can't wait to spend some more quality time together."

Grafton hung up and instructed the driver to take him to his hotel where he knew Elad was waiting. This would be yet another conversation he wouldn't enjoy.

"He hung up on me," Gabbie said with a smirk.

"Shocking," Miki replied.

"Should we go?"

"Not yet. Let's give it a few minutes to make sure that he doesn't send someone looking for us. If he does, then we know a meeting is too dangerous."

"And if he doesn't?"

"Then we know we have him," Miki replied.

* * *

Elad sat in Grafton's $500 a night hotel room located in the heart of downtown Charleston. He silently watched as Grafton dismantled his legislation and announcement for presidential election with a series of phone calls. Grafton explained to each caller that he recently learned of the tax legislation for roadwork. He claimed there was an Internet article being circulated linking passage of this anti-abortion bill to this roadwork/tax bill. He told his supporters he was doing it for them. Elad listened to over a dozen phone calls spewing the same political rhetoric.

"Listen, I know we worked hard. Don't you think I hate this? But this is my last term. If my bill passes along with this tax bill, then y'all have to deal with the repercussions next election cycle. Our party controls the legislature and I want to see another Republican as governor. That will never happen if our constituents lose faith in our willingness to cut taxes. It will tear us apart between those who want abortion control no matter what it costs and those who only care about tax breaks. I think a much wiser Republican once said that a house divided cannot stand," Grafton concluded with each phone call.

After the dust settled from the phone calls, Grafton plopped into the king-size bed and looked over at Elad seated on the hotel sofa. Grafton took off his Salvatore Ferragamo tie and threw it to the floor. He unbuttoned the top two buttons of his white Stefano Ricci dress shirt. His gray Brioni dress slacks were wrinkled from the day's activities. It was an outfit meticulously picked for a man announcing his candidacy for presidency, but now worn by a man simply trying to survive.

Elad broke the silence.

"What time is she supposed to call?"

"Soon, I guess."

"And she didn't tell you where?" Elad asked.

"No."

"Well, I think it goes without saying that my folks are very disappointed. And disappointment is not something that they handle well," Elad replied. He had been texting them while Grafton made his calls.

Grafton closed his eyes. He had time to absorb the meeting with Spring and conversation with Gabbie. As he had done in the past, Grafton formulated a way out of a dire situation. And while he wanted to shut off his mind and simply rest, he needed to forge ahead. He needed to deal with Elad.

"You gonna kill me, Elad?" Grafton asked with his eyes still closed.

Elad stared at his injured finger as he twirled it around his thumb. "That's a pretty bold question. Your officers are just outside of that door. I say yes and this becomes a real shit show as they come to arrest me. But if we are going to talk candidly…"

"Yes, let's," Hood said in an exacerbated tone.

"I think you know that is an option which we may exercise. And of course, you won't know when that will happen. I guess we need to see how things play out with the girl."

"We meaning when *you* and I meet with her?"

"Well, of course. You didn't think I'd have you meet with her alone?"

"That's why I asked the question. She's a loose end and I see how you take care of loose ends. And assuming that she meets the same fate as Pontet, then that leaves only me as a loose end."

"I guess it does, Grafton."

"And naturally, I will want to meet with her alone. None of my security in sight…right?" Grafton opened his eyes and stared at Elad.

"Yep." Elad nodded and stared back at Grafton.

"So, it will be just you and me at that point. And I will be the only person alive who actually knows how badly PS fucked up this vetting," Grafton said as he pointed to himself. "And that is not good for your business."

"No. No, it most certainly is not."

Grafton sat up and swung his legs across. He put his feet on the floor and sat at the corner of the bed. "And you see, I knew all that going into it. I never make a move without analyzing the risks and rewards. And I am excellent at maximizing the rewards and minimizing the risks."

"Oh, regardless of what happens, Grafton, we're all very impressed."

"Then, you'll love this. I took a cue from Chandler Murray," Grafton said with a closed mouth grin.

"Huh?" Elad asked.

"I have created a video and a folder. It details my brief but intimate interlude with PS. It shows account numbers where the money flowed. It talks about our arrangement. It gives a history as to Pontet and his role with your organization. It gives my theory as to his death. I was even able to narrow down your house on Sullivan's Island. God knows what happened there. My folks tell me that Spring's son-in-law is now missing. According to Pontet, he was Miki Martin's friend. Maybe we can ask Martin tonight? I am sure he will be there with her."

Elad tried to remain unfazed. It wasn't the first PS relationship that turned sour. He had dealt with these threats before, but Grafton was different. He survived adversity that would have crushed most politicians. Grafton outmaneuvered an entire legislative body to pass a bill that only served his political goals. Elad was faced with an adversary willing to kill his only child if she posed a threat to his survival. Elad knew that this wasn't a bluff, but he had to remain calm.

"Well, if you are taking a cue from Chandler, then this folder...assuming it exists...is in some safety deposit box," Elad responded. "You've spent time with me. I think you know that I will find a way to that box."

"Assuming you can find them."

"Them?"

"You didn't think I would leave it in just one box. And I hope you didn't assume that all the boxes would be located in this state."

Elad was silent.

"Elad, you've spent time with me. I think you know I have in place the means necessary to disseminate this information to the public in the event of my unfortunate demise."

Grafton's burner rang.

"Ah, that must be her. Hold on a second. Barry!" Grafton shouted. One of his armed security officers entered the room.

"Yes, sir. Everything okay in here?"

"Oh yes, Barry. We're fine. I need you to get Tybee on the phone." Grafton's burner continued to ring. "I need to talk with him in a second. Stay here."

Grafton answered the phone. Gabbie was on the other end. He listened as she relayed the instructions.

"I understand. I will be there at 7:30 sharp." He hung up the burner and turned his attention to Barry. "Is Tybee on the phone?"

"Yes sir," he said as he handed the phone to Grafton.

"Peppers, you there? Great. Listen, it has been a day. I need some alone time. I am taking my boat out tonight. I am going up the Intracostal Waterway just outside Isle of Palms. Gonna do some night fishing in Copahee Sound. It's just off Deewees. I am taking Mr. Patterson with me so I won't need any detail. Should be back by 10:30 at the latest. Okay?"

"Yes, sir," Tybee responded as he stared at the barrel of Session's gun pointed at him.

Grafton hung up. "That will be all, Barry," Grafton said as he motioned for him to leave.

He turned his attention back to Elad. "This is what we're going to do. You're coming with me to meet with the girl…"

"Your daughter," Elad interrupted.

"And her friend." Grafton ignored Elad's jab. "And then you're going to do what you do best—kill them. And then I will drive you back here and you will catch the first plane going anywhere that is not here. And I will never hear from you or the PS again. And if I do, you will see me on every major news network and the *New York Times* bestsellers' list. The whole world will learn of your employer."

"You're going to commit political suicide?"

"Yes, if it means saving myself from a homicide," Grafton fired back. "But there is still a win-win for us in all of this."

"How so?" Elad was intrigued. How could Grafton possibly find a way to salvage this?

"As you know, there are two U.S. Senators for every state. Our eldest U.S. Senator is just that…elder. I have enough contacts in this party that could…well…sway him to retire. If he does that in mid-term, then the Governor of this state appoints a replacement."

"Assuming it is a Republican?"

"Please. This state bleeds red. And even though my bill wasn't passed, it has given hope to the powerful mass of Christian Conservatives that such a bill could pass. Plus, I have fallen on my sword to defeat a tax increase tied to my bill to protect the rights of unborn children. And I will blame the liberal Democrats for all of it."

Elad silently listened.

"I will become a deity in the Republican Party for this state."

"And Spring's threat to go viral with the video in your attempt for a run at office?"

"He's got his victory. He doesn't want to drag this state through the mud. Plus, he's old and if I can get some spin as to Poe and his connection with Martin..." Grafton grinned, "well, the old man won't have the fortitude to endure a messy re-election bid. Plus, he will want to shield his daughter from the press reporting her adulterous ways. I am sure I can find a way to leak that. Just gotta reach out to her boyfriend."

"What about Sharon White? She doesn't scare so easy," Elad questioned.

"Sharon White has greater aspirations than this state. She's on everyone's short list to be the next head of the FBI. You think she wants this scandal attached to her nam? She would be crucified because she didn't release the tape as a political favor for Spring."

"Because he's a politician mired in a scandal about his daughter and the mysterious circumstances surrounding his missing son-in-law," Elad added.

"Very good. Perhaps, we will make a political advisor of you yet. There's less blood."

"Not really."

"And then, after I have been in the Senate for a while," Grafton paused, "because you know I will win re-election…"

"Republican deity and all that," Elad chimed.

"Perhaps then, PS and I can revisit what we tried to do. But this time, we will know that all loose ends have been tied up."

Elad digested Grafton's plan. He had been given the discretion to clean up the situation as he deemed fit. The paramount concern was to protect the organization. At this point, killing Grafton was no longer an option. Grafton would leak everything. The only way to eliminate that threat was a commonality of interest—again assist in Grafton's rise in power.

"Where's your boat?" Elad calmly asked.

CHAPTER TWENTY-THREE:
THE END

It came to Miki as he looked at the key chain for Poe's beach house—the key to his boat. When the Athena Newton scandal was at its zenith, Miki liquidated all assets to raise cash for a good criminal lawyer. He sold everything except his car and boat. Miki assumed he would triumph in court, exonerate his name and resume his once lucrative legal career.

For the first year, he clung to these items as motivation to persevere. But as life continued to knock him down, the car simply became a means of transportation and the boat was sold to Poe for an exorbitant price. Miki refused a loan from Poe, but offered the boat. Poe reluctantly agreed on the condition that Miki could buy it back at a fraction of the price.

While he was invited many times to spend a weekend at the beach for a guy's fishing trip, Miki refused. The boat became a painful memory of what he had lost. He had not seen it in over six years. He even resorted to unfollowing Poe on Facebook upon seeing posts showing Poe beaming with a bountiful catch made on Miki's boat. As Gabbie and he drove to the marina at the north end of

Isle of Palms, Miki's stomach was fluttering like a butter-fly in a box. It was nervous anticipation over the execution of his plan and the potential rewards, if it was successful.

It was an unseasonably warm May evening. The cloudless sky would soon yield to a star-filled night. The smell of salt air became stronger as they approached the marina located at the end of 41st Avenue. The marina was perfectly situated at the watery intersection of the In-traoastal Waterway and Morgan Creek. The calm water of the creek made it easier to launch. As they rode toward the launch area, Miki surveyed the line of boats parked in dry storage. He cracked a smile knowing that his boat wasn't on a trailer but in a slip. In his day of wealth, Miki often referred to the drive to get your boat from dry stor-age as the "drive of shame." He characterized the ring of salt water staining the hull of a boat in a slip as the "ring of honor."

He parked the motorcycle. Gabbie and he made their way across the wooden walkway of the multi-slip floating docks. His heart sank as soon as he saw it—a symbol of what he once was and perhaps his vehicle to get back there. Spring and Poe had kept it in beautiful condition. It was a 26-foot Regulator with a hard top center console and sporting twin 250 Yamahas. The hull was baby blue with a white interior. It was designed more for the ocean than the inland waterways. During his first summer with it, Miki crossed from Daytona Beach to Marsh Harbour off the Abaco Islands. Miki continued to admire his boat as his mind wandered to the details of the trip.

"Liberty Truckin'," Gabbie read aloud the name of the boat painted on the port side of the boat. "That's cute."

"Yeah, most folks think it is a play on words. You know, the supposed freedom you feel cruising on the water."

"It's not?"

"No," Miki said as he climbed into the boat and cranked the engines. They fired right up. "God, I miss that sound."

"Then what's it mean?"

"It's the name of the trucking company we sued that resulted in my first big payday and the purchase of this bad-ass vessel," Miki answered with a grin. Gabbie had never seen him this happy. He exuded a carefree attitude that shocked her.

"You act like someone going on a midnight cruise rather than heading to blackmail the governor of this state," Gabbie observed with a laugh.

"Oh Gabbie, the fun we would have on this boat with a full tank of gas and a bottle of Patron."

"Bottle? Have you met you? More like two," she chuckled.

Miki smirked as he nodded at the statement. "Can you unhook the bow line and I will get the stern?" Gabbie stood on the dock starring at him as if he spoke in tongues. "Unhook the front line and I will get the back," Miki translated.

"Oh you are one of those," Gabbie said.

"One of what?" Miki asked.

"One of those guys who gets near a boat and all of the sudden they are a *captain*," Gabbie threw in an air quote, "and not just a dude with a boat."

"Well, technically speaking, this is a pleasure craft," Miki corrected her.

"Well, technically you're broke and this pleasure craft doesn't even belong to you," Gabbie retorted.

"Just get in the damn boat."

"Aye, aye Captain Shithead," Gabbie said with a salute.

"Did you bring it?"

Gabbie reached inside her jeans pocket and retrieved three Q-Tips in a Zip-lock bag. "I'm going to swab his mouth, get a DNA sample and confirm what we already know. But what if he resists?"

"Then I'll use this to pry his mouth open like a tiger shark." Miki retrieved a hand-held gaffing hook stowed near the fishing rods.

"Kinda hoping he doesn't cooperate." Gabbie smiled and then gazed at the marina and waterway. "Where are we headed again?"

Miki backed out of the slip. "We are going to take the waterway north, head toward Dewees Island. I think it is still there. Poe told me he saw it last time they were out."

"A floating house? Is that what you said it was?"

"Kinda, it's more like a floating party room. A buddy of mine built it a few years ago. He took a pontoon boat and stripped off the top and engine. He turned it into a floating deck. He then anchored it in the Copahee Sound with two Chevy truck engine blocks. Then he built this shed-like structure on top. In the hotter months, he would bring out a generator and window AC unit to keep it cool."

"It's got a window?"

"Yeah," Miki laughed. "It has cleats for docking. During the fall, he would bring out a TV so we could watch football. I would have a blast out there."

"Well, this experience may be a little different," said Gabbie.

Miki ignored the comment and embraced the moment of being on the water. He breathed slowly to allow the salt air to fill his lungs. He often referred to it as tonic for his soul. His ears were enveloped with the low hum of the engines mixed with the splashing waves against the hull. He could feel the slight but perceivable vibrations from the Yamahas. His heart raced as he approached the end of the no-wake zone. He patiently waited until the boat was a few yards beyond the buoy, signifying that he could throttle up.

"Hold on," he instructed. Within a few seconds, they were cruising at 40 miles per hour down the Intracoastal.

As Gabbie and Miki raced down the Intracoastal, Grafton and Elad were heading across the Charleston Harbor toward the ocean. Grafton commanded his Sea Ray 470 from the leather seat at the cockpit of the sunroom. While Miki had a boat, Grafton boasted a 47-foot yacht complete with master bedroom and bathroom in the lower cabin.

Technically, a prominent real estate developer in the Charleston area owned the yacht, but in reality, there was no mistaking that it belonged to Grafton—the name *Brown Recluse* was painted on the stern. Elad was in the couch positioned to the portside of the cockpit. There was an outside seating area and diving platform adjacent to the sunroom toward the stern side.

The sun was in its final dissent over the Holy City but Grafton ignored the soft orange glow over the ocean. He was focused on orchestrating what he hoped was the last meeting with his daughter. With the doors open, the salt air filled the sunroom. Unlike Miki, there wasn't enough salt in the entire Atlantic to provide the tonic necessary for Grafton's tortured soul. Grafton was not soothed by the sound of the yacht's hull cutting through the waves. He might as well have been driving a car on the interstate. He did not care about the journey…he just wanted to get to his destination.

Elad looked out his window on the port side as the yacht passed by Sullivan's Island and then, the Isle of Palms. To the starboard side, there was nothing but the ocean quietly succumbing to the dark of the approaching night. There were a few large tanker ships anchored in the distance for the evening. Elad tried to focus on the ships rather than the motion of the yacht. But this did little to ward off the nausea of his motion sickness.

He had no problems with air travel or vehicles. But he never conquered seasickness. He attributed it to his lifestyle. He was not afforded many opportunities to ride in a boat. Not many people desired to see him in nothing but a bathing suit. And while traveling in Grafton's yacht was akin to riding on a bus, Elad was close to adorning the fine woodwork of this vessel with every ounce of fluid in his stomach. He could feel the cold sweat dripping from his body. His dizziness prevented him from even attempting to stand. To compound matters, Elad knew it would take at least a half an hour after they got off the boat before he would feel normal. The fury of the day's activities caused him to forget to take medicine for the trip. He was now enduring the consequences of that error. He could only hope that Miki and Gabbie would be close enough for him to shoot and not miss.

"How much longer?" Elad immediately cupped his mouth to force down the vomit.

"That is the north end of Isle of Palms." Grafton pointed. "And that's Dewees Island. We're going between the two. So not much longer."

Elad acknowledged the answer with a simple nod. He continued to focus on the ships in the distance.

Grafton was so focused on navigating that he failed to notice Elad's appearance. He looked even worse than normal. His face was dripping wet and his left leg was nervously shaking. "Are you alright?"

"Fine," Elad tersely responded.

"That's the exact opposite of how you look right now," Grafton said with a furrowed brow.

"Just fucking get us there," Elad hissed through his gritted teeth.

Grafton shook his head. "Are you seasick?"

Elad didn't respond.

"You're riding in a yacht, not some 14-foot Boston Whaler in the open ocean. How does that even happen?"

"I will be fine."

"Don't say 'you're fine' again because clearly you aren't. You can't even stand up. Can you?"

"I will once the boat stops."

"Well, this is great. My ruthless trained killer is reduced to an invalid because the waves got a little bumpy."

"You got no one to blame but yourself for all this," Elad retorted.

The remark incensed Grafton. "Well, my advice is for you to start firing early and often," Grafton paused as he turned the yacht port, "because if they get an inkling as to your condition, then we're both going to be nauseated."

Miki stood on the floating party barge watching as a large yacht made its turn from the ocean and headed toward him. The sunset was almost complete and his anchoring light provided the only source of illumination. The brief reprieve from life provided by rediscovering his boat vanished as soon as he saw the yacht approach. Miki secretly wished that it would make a hard turn, signifying that it wasn't Grafton. He didn't know if he was ready.

But it did not veer course. Miki knew this was it. There was no more running. No more turning back. In a few minutes, his life would irreparably change—the only mystery was how.

Many life-altering events occur unexpectedly and instantaneously. This is a blessing because it would be a hideous torture to make someone wait for the moment they know everything will change. It would be like telling someone the day that they will die and then telling them to wait for it. Miki was enduring such a torture as he haplessly watched the yacht inch toward him.

Gabbie stood next to him and intently stared as Grafton approached. The lighthearted excitement at the dock had given way to reality. Her mind was not nearly as busy as Miki's. One thought consumed her—my father has come here to kill me.

She rubbed the Q-Tip swab in her jeans pocket. Gabbie knew Grafton was nothing more than a biological donor in her creation. This meant his genes flowed in her. He was a survivor, just like her. She read Chandler Murray's file cover to cover, including his theory about Grafton's parents. Just like her, Grafton should have been dead and buried long ago—killed by the transgressions of the father. But here he was…in a million dollar yacht. And so she drew on that DNA and thought, "What would I do if I were him? What would I do to survive this situation?" And the answer was simple, "I would kill them."

Miki continued to watch as the yacht slowed from inches to what now appeared to be millimeters. He was backing the stern to dock. With the flick of a switch, the stern lights flashed on with the intensity of a spotlight. Miki and Gabbie were momentarily blinded.

Normally, Elad would have used that moment to walk from the sunroom onto the deck and kill them both before the boat ever stopped. Instead, his motion sickness tethered him to his seat—just like he had done to Poe. He was waiting for the yacht to completely stop before mustering the courage to stand.

With his eyes adjusted to the light, Miki continued to watch as Grafton gently nestled the diving platform to the dock. Hood flicked another switch to drop the Windlass anchor from the bow. They were docked.

"You ready?" Grafton said without a trace of fear or excitement.

Elad sighed. It was just as he feared. The effects had not worn off. "Just give me a second."

Grafton climbed from his chair and headed toward the stern. "Time is now. Let's go."

"Wait. What's the plan?"

"What's the plan? Isn't that your area of expertise? I guess I assumed you would simply do that thing you do where you kill people. Kinda thought that would have happened when I hit the flood lights."

"Okay. Okay. You just go out there and distract them a little. I will follow and take care of it from the boat."

"You in any condition to shoot from the boat? Should I lure them inside?" Grafton asked.

Elad stood with the confidence of a toddler. He grasped onto his seat to stop his swaying. He could feel the vomit start to creep up his throat. He paused for a moment to force the liquid back down. "No. That will be much too messy. And this isn't really your boat. Just go. It will be fine."

Grafton grimaced at hearing the word "fine" again.

Grafton opened the doors and walked about halfway onto the deck. He showed no emotion at the sight of Martin or Gabbie. Rather, he looked at them like rodents needing to be exterminated.

"Hey, Pops," Gabbie greeted him with a childish grin.

"Yeah. Right." He looked at Miki. "So you must be Mr. Martin. For such a lackluster lawyer, you sure do display an amazing amount of tenacity, and bravado for that matter."

"Well, maybe when all this is done, you can use your political might to secure me a position in the White House. That is where you want to end up, correct?"

"I don't think we came here to discuss my political ambitions. What do you want?"

"Why don't you come over here, give your baby girl a hug and we can talk all about it?" Gabbie chimed in.

"Why don't y'all come over here and let's discuss it inside? I think my accommodations are a bit more plush than your floating Hoover shack."

With a drunk-like gait, Elad made his way to join Grafton. He opened the door and gingerly stepped toward Grafton. As soon as he walked on the deck, he could feel the waves gently bumping against the hull. For Elad, it felt like he was floating on a raft in a hurricane. His stomach was churning again and Elad knew that throwing up on Grafton would hardly invoke a sense of fear in his adversaries.

"Whoa! Who the fuck is that?!" Miki exclaimed upon seeing Elad. He reached down for the gaffing hook at his feet.

"He's just my associate. I didn't know what y'all were planning. And based on the hook in your hand, I am glad he came."

"Is he drunk?" Gabbie asked.

"No," Grafton casually responded as looked over at Elad. "Just a little seasick."

Elad focused on his right hand and slowly rubbed it up and down his leg. He pressed his left arm against his shoulder holster concealed by his coat. All he needed to do was focus his energy to perform a move he had done countless times. He would quickly draw the weapon and discharge it before his victims even knew they were shot. He practiced the move to perfection but timing was key. He actually began pressing the trigger just as the gun cleared his coat. It looked like he was going throw the gun at the victim. But between the nausea and dizziness, he was worried that he would possibly shot Hood or even himself. So he continued to rub his leg until he felt the confidence to execute the move.

"Why the fuck is he rubbing his leg?" Miki barked.

The door from the sunroom opened again. John Sessions appeared.

Elad's fear of getting seasick clouded his mind and he forgot to check the yacht before it left. By the time he thought of it, they were already on the water and he was no position to check. Sessions was stowed away in the bathroom of the lower cabin. He forced Peppers to disclose the location of the hidden key for the yacht.

"What the hell are you doing...," Elad never finished his sentence. Sessions fired a shot from his state-issued Smith & Wesson Bodyguard .38 Revolver. It entered Elad's right eye and exited the back of his skull missing Miki by a few feet and shattering the window of the party barge.

Miki dropped the gaffing hook and instinctively raised his hands. Gabbie followed suit. Their eyes locked onto each other. This was most certainly not part of the plan. They then turned their attention back to the shooter. He was still behind the glow of the floodlights. Miki could not see his face.

"Sessions. What the fuck was that about? And what the hell are you doing? I told you no detail," Grafton commanded.

The shooter stepped from the dark and into the light. Miki immediately recognized the face and he turned to Gabbie. She returned the look.

"What?" she whispered.

Miki didn't respond. He glanced back over at the shooter to make sure he was correct and then looked back at her.

"Do you know him?" Gabbie asked.

Miki nodded.

"Who is it?"

"It's your grandfather," Miki replied.

"Sessions! Did you hear me?" Hood moved toward him but stopped in his tracks as soon as he saw the .38 was now pointed at his head.

"Yes, Grafton, I heard you. But you can take Mr. Patterson's death as my official resignation from your security detail. And my name is Frank Newton." With the gun firmly aimed at Hood, he looked over at Miki. "Martin! You can put your hands down!"

He then looked at Gabbie. For the first time, Frank Newton saw his granddaughter. Athena was his only daughter. He and his wife didn't have other children or grandchildren to ease the agony felt over her death. Their marriage could not survive the ordeal. They divorced two years later and his wife returned to her family in Korea.

In the years that followed, Frank often dreamed of what it would have been like to be a grandfather. He knew he was a stern father but always felt that he would the kindest and softest granddad a kid could hope for. But he abandoned that dream with Athena's death until learning of Gabbie's existence. And since that time, he was haunted by nightly dreams of his daughter holding an infant. Athena's face was masked in blood as she tried to give the child to him. Every time she would say the same thing, "You couldn't save me, but maybe you can save her."

As Frank gazed upon his granddaughter, his eyes welled in tears. She was more beautiful than her mother. She took his breath away, just like Athena did when she was first born. He was speechless as he studied every curve and contour of her face. After a solid minute of staring at her, Frank finally summoned the courage to speak his first words to her.

"Gabriele, are you okay, baby?"

She stared back at him with the same intensity. A single tear rolled down her left cheek. In this tense moment, she felt exhilaration over the discovery of grandfather and the fact that he was here to save her.

"Yes, sir, I am fine," her voice quivered from emotion. They continued to look upon one another in silent admiration.

But a slight movement from Grafton interrupted their moment. Frank quickly wiped his eyes dry with his left hand and focused his attention on Grafton.

"Don't move again," he said in a deliberate tone that shook Grafton to the core.

"I won't, I won't. But can you please lower your weapon. I am not going anywhere, Mr. Newton," Grafton nervously replied.

"You think you're telling me something I don't already know?" Frank questioned. He then paused to collect his thoughts before addressing Grafton. He had rehearsed the speech a thousand times, but as soon as he saw Gabbie, he forgot every word.

"Frank, I don't know what you're thinking, but we have enough information to end him. You don't need to do this," Miki interjected.

Frank laughed in response. "The only thing that can end him is in my right hand. I learned that long ago," he shouted. "Grafton, does the name Aisha Watson ring a bell?"

Hood shook his head.

"Didn't think it would. She was the mother of the cop you blackmailed into killing my daughter. She was part of my mother's small section in church. When she died, I took my mother to her funeral. That's where I met Ms. Watson's son, Christopher."

Hood swallowed hard as he continued to stare at the barrel of the gun.

"So he and I meet one night and he confesses everything. Tells me of his guilt and remorse. He had no idea who my daughter was. That his life was a living hell because all he does is obsess about her death. You know, all of the normal emotions that most humans would experience after performing such a heinous act. Well, perhaps you don't."

There was no response.

"We left the bar that night and he assured me that he would go on the record. He could not live with the shame anymore. But the next morning, I couldn't get in touch with him. He died in a one-car collision in the early morning hours. The last remaining link to my daughter's death wiped clean by a bite from the brown recluse."

The ghostly image of Athena holding her infant filled his head. Frank inhaled deeply and exhaled to wipe his mind clean.

"So, that day I vowed to prove the truth of what you had done. And to do that, I needed to get as close to you as possible. Enter Tybee Peppers. I heard through the grapevine that he was recruiting for an elite security detail for the governor."

Grafton was paralyzed in fear. His life's transgressions were facing him from both sides.

"Well, I immediately met with him and used a fake name. I quickly gleaned what everyone else had told me. Tybee was an imbecile. I was his first hire and he was in charge of vetting my history. And all I needed to do was give him my same records with a new name and a few fake references. After that, I was in charge of background for all security detail. And no one ever questioned the background of John Sessions. Tybee Pepper's right-hand man."

"Tybee," Grafton fumed under his breath.

"So as his right-hand man, I became intimately involved in the investigation and pursuit of my granddaughter. I learned all about the Chandler Murray file and your illustrious background. But I had nothing to do with that twisted fuck's operation." Frank pointed to Elad's body. "You hear that, Miki, I had nothing to do with Poe's death!"

"I believe you, Frank," Miki replied. "And as much as I would like to see Grafton's brains sprayed into the waterway, it won't get us anywhere. Just put the gun down."

"Yeah, Granddad, we have proof of all of it. The only thing we need from him is a swab of saliva to confirm he's my father. That and your conversation with the cop will be enough. You don't need to do this," Gabbie pleaded. "I lost my mom. I don't want to lose you."

The tears began to stroll down his cheek upon hearing her voice. "Oh baby, if it was only that simple. Tell her Miki, is the conversation with the dead cop even admissible in court?"

Gabbie looked at him for the answer.

Miki reluctantly responded. "No. It's hearsay." He paused. "It doesn't fall into the exceptions of the dead man statute. You could never prove that the statement had anything to do with his death."

"You see sweetie, Murray's file makes for great copy but it isn't anything that will stick against this one," Frank pointed at Grafton. "He will find his way out of it. He has the will and ability to make it all go away. He proved that with my daughter and almost did it again with you."

"Frank, what do you want? A confession?" Grafton calmly asked.

His demeanor incensed him. A gun pointed at his head and yet, Grafton approached it like negotiations over a piece of legislation. "I think that I...no," he pointed to Gabbie and Miki, "we have earned that at least that," Frank barked.

"Then fine, Frank. Fine." Grafton fumed. "You're correct about everything you have said. I had your daughter killed. I had everyone associated with her death killed. I came here to kill your granddaughter."

"Your daughter!"

"Yes, Frank! Yes! My fucking daughter! You're right about all of it." Grafton took a second to regain his composure. "But that's history and this is the present. I cannot redefine my past but I can define my future."

"Why don't you save that shit for Pinterest?" Frank barked.

Grafton ignored the comment. "No Frank, it is the truth. And you know that. I cannot bring back your daughter but if you will listen to them," Hood pointed to Miki and Gabbie, "and yourself, then you will realize that I can figure a way out of all of this. We *can* make a deal that will save everyone in this situation."

"There is only way to make a deal with you."

"No!" Miki and Gabbie exclaimed in unison.

And Grafton Hood experienced something he had not felt since Atlanta—fear. It was his last thought as the bullet left Frank's gun and tore into Grafton's forehead. His lifeless body fell on top of Elad's corpse.

Miki and Gabbie's shoulders slumped in unison at the sight of the shot. Grafton had won again, even in death. First, he killed Athena and now, he doomed her father to the gas chamber. Gabbie began to sob uncontrollably.

Frank also cried, hearing the pain of his granddaughter, but he methodically holstered his weapon as he walked toward Grafton's body. His foot shoved it off Elad and Grafton's corpse was on its back. Frank grabbed his smart phone and clicked a picture. He then clicked a picture of Elad's body.

"Hey, put your hands up again."

"Huh?" Miki asked.

"Just do it," Frank commanded. They obliged and Frank snapped a picture. He spent a few seconds with his phone and then turned his attention back to them. "Gabrielle…sweet heart….please stop crying." He paused to wipe away the tears streaming down his face. He hated to hear her cry. "You got something to swab his mouth."

"Yes sir," she mumbled.

"Please bring it to me, angel," Frank instructed.

She walked over to the boat and embraced him in a hug tight enough to squeeze sap from a tree. He soaked it in for a moment and then took the swab and Z-lock from her.

"Gonna be plenty of time for that honey," he replied as he knelt and retrieved his sample. After placing it in the bag, he pushed the play button on his smart phone. Grafton's voice filled the air starting from the beginning of their encounter.

Gabbie instantly stopped crying and looked at Frank. Miki approached the boat toward her. She spun around and looked him. Miki could see the optimism in her eyes but didn't share it.

"Frank, that's great but I don't know how it will help you," he coldly observed.

Gabbie spun back around and looked at her grandfather.

"It wasn't designed to help me. It was designed to help y'all."

"I don't understand," Gabbie stuttered, but Miki understood completely. He nodded and shot Frank a smile of gratitude. "What's he talking about?" she asked Miki.

"That little playlist of Grafton's greatest hits was emailed to Sharon White," Frank replied.

"Who's Sharon White?" Gabbie asked.

"Head of the state's law enforcement agency," Miki answered.

"You will meet her soon enough, baby girl. She'll be calling any second now because I sent her a text picture of our esteemed governor, his Dahmer-like colleague, and you two. You know the governor is technically an employee of the state."

"And the state is liable for the actions of its employees," Miki responded.

"Which means what?" Gabbie asked.

"The state is deemed responsible for Grafton's actions. We can sue the state for everything he has done. We can probably use the lawsuit as leverage to drop the charges against us and get an ass of money to repay us for the shit that this son-of-a-bitch caused." Miki pointed at Grafton. "It means we just got a do-over, Gabbie."

Gabbie turned to Frank. "So does that mean you won't go to jail?"

Frank yielded the question to Miki.

"Probably not, I mean he did kill our state's highest elected official," Miki paused, "but I am pretty confident that we can get the charges reduced to involuntary manslaughter."

"So, what's that mean?" Gabbie asked in an excited tone.

"A few years sweetie, a few short years. And just think, we've already done that," Frank said with a grin that spanned from ear to ear. He tossed Miki the phone. "When White calls, tell her that you're my hostage and that I have demanded that only she and one other officer come here to get me."

"I'm on it," Miki fired back as he grabbed the phone from the air.

Frank turned to Gabbie. "Now my little angel, why don't you climb onboard and I will tell you all about your mom and you will tell me all about you."

"Okay," she sobbed.

Frank grabbed his granddaughter and drew her into his chest. He turned around and shouted to Miki. "Hey! We're going to need a good lawyer. You know anyone?"

Miki smiled as he looked at the ringing phone. "I've got the perfect woman in mind."

EPILOGUE

At 5'6 and weighing about 175 pounds, Avie Rittenburg's nickname was the fire hydrant. But it had nothing to do with his physical stature; it was based on his reputation as an attorney. Like a fire hydrant, he was not imposing but everyone knew his ability to defuse any raging inferno of litigation. Over his 40 years of practice, Avie secured some of the state's largest verdicts for the injured, but also represented corporations trying to minimize damage created by missteps of its employees. In his mind, Constitutional rights applied to everyone.

He earned enough money to retire many years ago but still came to work each day at his modest office located on Broad Street in Charleston. Avie simply enjoyed the practice of law and often told people he was blessed to have made so much money doing a job he loved. But he was also raised to know that all services came at a price. He had a few, select clients because most people cannot afford $750 an hour. He secured a financial legacy for his children and now worked for his grandchildren's future. His newest clients were the State of South Carolina and Practical Solutions, each facing a potential lawsuit by Miki and Gabbie.

Avie brokered a meeting with Miki and his lawyer, Katherine Murray. She also represented Gabbie. Frank Newton was presently represented by a public defender, but there were a dozen high profile criminal defense attorneys itching to represent him pro bono. They deemed the publicity priceless. Avie called Katherine a week after Newton was arrested and suggested that any civil action filed on behalf of Miki and Gabbie would have more settlement value prior to filing suit.

The details had not been fully leaked. Sharon and Spring used their resources to contain the story. The official press release stated that the governor had passed away from natural causes. Grafton had no family and Pontet represented the closest thing to a friend. But the press pigs were digging through the trough and it was only a matter of time before the truth was rooted out. Avie's clients desperately wanted to avoid that, which meant paying to keep Miki and Gabbie silent.

Everyone agreed to meet at Avie's office.

Katherine was dressed like a model for a *Vogue* article entitled "Business Fashion." Miki was dressed in a tweed blazer, white Oxford and blue jeans. He sat at Avie's modest six-chair conference room table with a view of Broad Street. Miki looked at the table and thought of the countless multi-million dollar decisions made at the table. Perhaps he would be another notch in the table's belt. He gazed at the tourists wandering the Holy City in search of the next historical attraction they could visit in a quest to brag to friends about their eloquent vacation.

Dressed in a pair of dark pants, a baby blue dress shirt and white bow tie, Avie entered the room. Few men can actually wear pants' braces without seeming pretentious—for Avie, it seemed natural.

"Ms. Murray. Mr. Martin. It is a pleasure to meet you both," Avie said in his high-pitched voice drenched in a Charleston-raised Geechee tone. He went to shake Miki's hand first.

Miki gave him a firm handshake and stared him in the eyes. "Well, I don't know how much of a pleasure it actually is, given the situation," Miki responded with a smirk. Katherine shot him a hard glare. They had agreed that he would not speak.

Avie chuckled at the comment. "Well, I won't allow the difficulty of the circumstances to diminish my actual pleasure in meeting you. I have done my research. You should be commended. You've made a hell of a comeback." Avie then fired his first weapon—his smile. It naturally put others at ease, like receiving a warm grin from your grandfather. Miki realized he was not immune to it and quickly glanced away. This was the most important meeting of his life and he had to focus.

Katherine ignored the smile and Avie's attempt at pleasant conversation. She begrudgingly shook Avie's hand and hissed, "Where is everyone else? Where are the decision makers?"

"Why don't we all sit down and discuss that?" Avie calmly responded.

"Why sit down if the money folks aren't even here?" Katherine was incensed. She wanted to simply file suit but Miki was her client and he demanded that they meet first. Miki fired his own hard glare at her. She ignored it and continued on her rant.

"We came to see if we can get paid, not sit around your table chat about the case. If we wanted to chat about the case then I would have scheduled some depositions. My first being to depose Sharon White, your state's law enforcement guru, to see how much she knew and what she concealed. That half-ass J. Edgar Hoover loves to speak to the media; let's see how she will handle me."

Avie ignored the tirade and systematically continued on his quest to have her sit down. Miki was already seated and staring at Katherine in the hopes of compelling her to do the same.

"Ms. Murray, I have no doubt that Ms. White would rather be interviewed by the toughest media bully than face a deposition with you. I mean, who wouldn't? Now, please sit down and let's see if we can reach a compromise without my clients being grilled by you."

Katherine was actually disarmed by the back-handed compliment and slowly slid into the seat next to Miki. She could feel Miki's eyes transfixed on her and did not look in his direction.

Avie watched her sit down and shot another smile in Miki's direction. Miki quickly looked down at the table. "What kind of wood is this?"

"Walnut, I think," Avie responded.

"Now that we have the chemical composition of the table established, can we get started?" Katherine chimed.

"Yes, of course, Ms. Murray. Again, thank you for accepting my invitation to see if we can get this matter resolved in an amicable fashion because that is what will best for everyone involved in this nastiness."

"Nastiness. That is an eloquent way of describing it, but I prefer to be more blunt." Miki looked at Avie as if to say, "shocking, right?" "I prefer the term shit storm. This is a shit storm created by your clients that they never fathomed that anyone could weather. And they certainly didn't think that a broken down drunk of a trial lawyer and ex-stripper would escape it."

Miki glanced at her and thought, "And I am paying a third of my settlement for you to represent me?"

Katherine continued. "But I didn't come here to listen to you pontificate about the law or this case. I came here to see if your clients can cut a check big enough to persuade us to make this 'nastiness'"—Katherine slung air quotes at Avie—"all go away."

"Ms. Murray, please calm down," Avie softy replied.

"Oh, I am calm. If I weren't calm, you'd be watching my tight ass walk the fuck out of this conference room and across the street to file my lawsuit."

Miki interrupted. "That's enough, Katherine." She turned around and looked at Miki in awe.

"Miki, I thought we agreed you wouldn't say anything," she seethed.

"Well, I wasn't until you took ten minutes to sit down and now, you're been ratting on about storms created from feces and the firmness of your ass cheeks." Miki shook his head.

"Should I leave the room and give you some privacy?" Avie asked.

"Yes," Katherine replied.

"No!" Miki commanded. "We're all good here. Please excuse our little exchange of ideas as to how this meeting should flow."

"It's all fine. This is all very informal. Just a meeting between lawyers." Avie's physical mannerisms downplayed the disagreement between his adversaries, but his mind was furiously trying to process it and how to manipulate it to his advantage.

"But it does bring up a good question. Where are the folks with monetary authority?"

"You're looking at him." Avie brushed the few remaining grey locks on his nearly baldhead. "I have full authority. I have the number we are willing to pay to make it all go away."

"Great, what is it? Give us the number, leave the room and we will let you know if it is enough."

"Ms. Murray, you know that's not how it works. We are here to negotiate. I am not going to start the negotiation process by giving you my client's top number and then negotiate upward from that. Typically, the plaintiffs make the opening offer."

"Oh, you want an opening demand. Let's start with 60."

"Million?" Avie asked with a trace of emotion.

"No, pennies," she sarcastically replied.

"Katherine, that's not what we talked about," Miki whispered.

"Goddamn it, Miki! Who is the lawyer in this case? You're not even licensed to file these pleadings!"

"Again, I am happy to leave the room if you need some time to talk," Avie interrupted.

"That's not necessary. We're fine." Miki fumed. "She's right. She's the lawyer. I guess I will let ya'll do the talking…just keep piped down over here."

Avie assessed the situation before responding. Katherine clearly saw this case as more valuable if it went to trial. First, the publicity would be astronomical. She would become a household legal name. Second, she didn't have great client control with Miki at this time. But as litigation ensued, that control may actually tighten, especially if Miki's name was dragged through the mud as would be a major component to the defense. Miki would probably become angry with the other side because he would have to relive his past indiscretions and Katherine would most certainly fuel that anger.

"Alright, he's piped down over here. What's your counter? And it better not be anything south of 10."

"I am thinking, Ms. Murray."

"Should we leave the room and give you some privacy?"

"No," Avie laughed, "you're not distracting me."

Avie then assessed the potential settlement figure if he allowed Miki and Katherine to leave the room. Practical Solutions relied on anonymity and once this suit was filed, it would become a hot topic discussion on every major news network. He also knew that the case would probably only increase in value with each deposition taken by Katherine. He shuttered at the testimony to be offered by the person responsible for hiring Elad Patterson.

But on the other hand, if he offered too much and they rejected it, then if settlement negotiations resumed, today's top offer would become the bottom number in the range of negotiations. His clients were staking millions of dollars based on Avie's opinion. He made his decision. Katherine was too much of a wild card and Miki probably had more control over this case today than he would in the future.

"What about 20?"

Miki replied before Katherine could even muster a thought. "If you have 20, then you have 30?"

"Damn it, Miki!" Katherine screamed.

"Just simmer, Katherine. This is my life and my case," Miki commanded.

"And Gabbie?"

"I think it's safe to say that she will follow my lead on this. We've been through a little bit together. Think I have earned her trust."

"Fine." Katherine relented. "Evidently, 30 is the figure for today. Do you have it?"

Avie scratched his chin as he contemplated his response. Based on Miki's response, he was convinced his opinion was correct. This was the day to settle this case. After today, he would have to deal with Katherine.

"Let me make a phone call," Avie replied.

"Thought you were Mr. Authority?" Katherine jabbed.

Avie grinned at the jab and quietly made his way from the room and into his office.

After he was sure the door was closed, Miki turned to Katherine and smiled. "I told you it would work."

"The ole good cop, bad cop routine," Katherine quipped. Miki just kept grinning. "I was prepared to go to trial on this—I think they would have paid a bunch more."

"Listen, once Practical Solutions becomes a household name, which they will once suit is filed, then it is finished. Kaput! They won't have any money to pay anything. Then that would leave us with the state to sue. And per law, we can only get $600,000 at the most from it."

"I guess you're right."

"I am right coming out of your mouth. That must be like sipping on hot vinegar." Katherine simply shook her head. "We both know this isn't exactly a lawsuit that gets tried overnight. There will be all sorts of legal posturing and motions to stop you from deposing a host of people. Invocation of 5th amendment rights, trade secrets, everything you can think of to stall this lawsuit. This case wouldn't be tried for another three years, not to mention what it does for Frank Newton."

"I know that was Gabbie's largest concern."

"Yep. She told me 'I have known nothing but poor, so the money is no big deal. But I have also known nothing but being along, so having family is a big deal. Whatever the deal, Frank needs to walk'." Miki smiled as he thought of her face.

"And this way, he will. The suit will have a confidentiality provision which means you cannot talk about any of it, including the death of Hood." Katherine continued to beam.

"The only witnesses to the crime cannot talk."

Katherine heard Avie's footsteps approaching the door. "Okay, get your game face back on."

Avie entered. "We are settled at 30."

"I'll bet. Fucking dumb-ass," she fired at Miki.

"This case is bigger than just you, Katherine."

"Ms. Murray, if it is alright with you, I am going to bring in one of my associates to help draft this agreement. It may take a bit. We will have to word this confidentiality agreement very strongly. Perhaps, you and your client can grab some lunch while we draft it and come back in an hour."

"I'm not eating with this village idiot. I couldn't keep my lunch down at the sight of him."

"Laying it on a little thick, Katherine," Miki thought to himself.

"Well, I am sure Mr. Martin will be disappointed at losing the pleasure of your company at lunch," Avie remarked as he shot a smile toward Miki—who didn't look away this time.

"Whatever." Katherine waved off the comment. "I'll get the wiring instructions for my account. I want the money in there within five days."

"That shouldn't be a problem," Avie replied.

Miki stood up and shook Avie's hand as he left the room. "I'll grab Gabbie and be back here in an hour to sign everything."

"You're about to become a very rich man, Mr. Martin," Avie said.

"Should have never been made a poor man, Mr. Rittenburg." As Miki strolled out of the office and into downtown Charleston, he felt something he had not felt in years—a sense of pride in who he was.